JIMMY AND FAY

JIMMY AND FAY

A SUSPENSE NOVEL

MICHAEL MAYO

MYSTERIOUSPRESS.COM

OPEN ROAD

INTEGRATED MEDIA

NEW YORK

Cover art by Mauricio Díaz

978-1-5040-3607-8

Published in 2016 by MysteriousPress.com/Open Road Integrated Media, Inc.
180 Maiden Lane
New York, NY 10038
www.mysteriouspress.com
www.openroadmedia.com

For Marcia

JIMMY AND FAY

CHAPTER ONE

I want to say that it started when Fay Wray walked into my speak, but that's not right. It was two years before—September 1931—the day we killed Maranzano.

It was the middle of a hellishly hot Thursday afternoon. The weather was so bad people were fainting and having heart attacks on the street. It wasn't much cooler inside the Grand Central Building but I can't say that I noticed. Even if you're not going to be the one who pulls the trigger or plies the blade, you pay attention to the important things and block out everything else. You just don't want to screw up in front of the other guys.

I went up the west stairwell to the ninth floor, just like I'd done the day before, and walked down the hall past the offices of the Eagle Building Corporation. I carried two straw boaters in a brown paper bag, and had a .38 in the pocket of my suit jacket. I gimped along on my stick and timed it so I was outside the door when a guy opened it to go in. About half a dozen men and a secretary were in the outer office. The door to Maranzano's office was closed, but I knew he was in there. He ran some of the biggest rackets in the city and had proclaimed himself to be the king of the Italian mob. He thought that having a new office at a swanky address like that, a couple blocks up Park Avenue from Grand Central Terminal, gave him some kind of respectability. Other parties didn't see it that way. I'll get to the reasons for what we were doing by and by.

I went back down by the east stairwell and out to Forty-Sixth Street. Red Levine was on the other side of the street. Even at that distance, I could see his freckles. He was in charge of the actual killing. I'd been told there were four others involved, but I didn't know all of them. I gave Red a quick high sign. He nodded to the two guys with the Chicago hats and they stepped smartly toward another door. I went back up the east stairway to the ninth-floor landing and eased the door open so I could hear when things got interesting. It didn't take long.

Red and the other guys were in Maranzano's office by then. They had phony IRS credentials to get past the secretary. My job was to make sure they had a clear way out and to keep an eye out for another individual who was rumored to be involved, that individual being Vincent "Mad Dog" Coll. Word was about that Maranzano had hired Coll to kill Charlie Luciano. Meyer Lansky, who was Charlie's friend and mine, wanted to make sure that didn't happen, but I'm getting ahead of myself again and, besides, all these damn names are confusing.

You see, it was like this. Maranzano knew that IRS agents were looking into his affairs. The tax guys were doing that because Lansky's brother, Jake, had set them on Maranzano and made sure that Maranzano knew about it. So Maranzano ordered his guys not to bring their guns to the office. Wouldn't look so good, a law-abiding businessman having a bunch of armed thugs on the premises when the accountants showed up. Even though he made his money on illegal booze, dope, whores, extortion, loan sharking, and all the other things that make life worth living, he wanted to look like he belonged there with the bankers and railroads and do-good societies in the Grand Central Building.

Standing in the ninth-floor stairwell, I heard footsteps scuffing up from below. I let the door ease shut and had my .38 out when that son of a bitch Coll came into view. He stopped when he heard me cock the pistol. Even though the light was dim, he recognized me and knew what was up. Without a moment's pause, he spun around and threw himself back down, two steps at a time by the sound of it. As it happened, that was the last time I saw Coll until the night he got himself shot, but it's a story that I've told before. Then I heard something else in the stairwell, a hesitation in his step and the clatter of something hard hitting the concrete.

I followed and found the pistol that Coll had dropped, a .38 like my own, on the sixth-floor landing. I didn't touch it. Then from above came two muffled shots. I turned to go back up but stopped when the door opened right in front of me and I saw a man and a woman staring at me.

The guy had a black Vandyke beard. He wore a dark suit, a red vest, and a fez. I knew the woman. She was a well-built blonde in a classy peach-colored suit with a big floppy bow at her throat.

Surprised, she said, "Hello, Jimmy."

I said, "Hi, Daphne. Take the elevator."

They stepped away, closing the door, and I went back up to the ninth as fast as I could.

Right as I got there, Red came through the door. He was moving fast but not hurrying. Behind him were two guys I didn't know. Bareheaded. I gave them the straw boaters and followed them down the stairs. With my stick, I was a lot slower, so they were gone by the time I got outside. I ambled back outside and found a place to have a cup of coffee while I waited for the sound of sirens.

Here's what happened.

Back when Prohibition got started, the Italians had a leg up on everybody else in the bootlegging business. Families in the tenements always had operated these alky cookers in their kitchens and basements where they made little batches of dago red. Some of it was all right, but most of the tarantula juice I tasted would gag a rat. But what do I know? They loved the stuff, and when alcohol became illegal, other people wanted it. The neighborhood bosses started buying the swill, and they leaned on the guys to make more. The most important boss was Joe Masseria. He'd been in charge of things with the Italians for as long as I could remember. Lots of people wanted to take over from him. I saw one of the first times a couple of guys shot up a dress store trying to kill him. Salvatore Maranzano came over some time in the twenties and set up an operation that put a crimp in Masseria's business. They hated each other.

Truth is, the nasty homebrew was fine for their little part of the world, but the big money was to be made selling good hooch at much higher prices to a larger well-heeled clientele. Arnold Rothstein figured that out. He brought Meyer Lansky and Charlie Luciano into the business. I helped.

Working with Benny Siegel and Frank Costello and some other guys, Meyer and Charlie built the biggest, richest booze business in the city. Masseria and Maranzano both wanted it. You've got to understand that they were old-fashioned Mustache Petes who didn't think that Italians should work with anybody else. No yids, no micks, no spics. Hell, as I heard it, they didn't even trust other wops unless they were from the same neighborhood of the same little village back in the old country. Charlie got his start working for Masseria but had been on his own for the most part. He tried to stay out of the way while the old bastards fought it out. Each of them had a couple hundred younger guys he could count on for dirty work, and for the past year or so they'd been killing each other one or two at a time. That was fine until they put the pressure on Charlie to pick a side.

I was in their office in the Barbizon Plaza Hotel one afternoon when Lansky decided to end it. Everybody else was gone. It was just Meyer, Charlie, and me. I was there because I'd made a round of payoffs to Tammany and had picked up some messages for them at the same time. Charlie looked glum. Meyer was serious. He told me to pour a drink and sit down. Then he asked me how much I knew about the business with Masseria and Maranzano and told me how they were putting the screws to Charlie.

Of course what the old guys didn't understand was that you didn't get Charlie without Meyer. Sure, they were friends, but there was a lot more to it. As far as I could tell, Meyer was closer to Charlie than he was to his own brother. Charlie was the smooth talker and glad-hander that everybody wanted to be around, but Meyer was the brains. He handled the organization and the details. Charlie never made an important decision without talking it through with the Little Man, as some people called him, and they said it with respect. Yeah, Charlie had the reputation as a tough guy who was quick with his mitts and a gun, but Meyer was always looking out for him.

When Charlie started talking that evening, I realized that he'd had a few. He said that Joe the Boss had been around since he was a kid and now this guy Maranzano wanted to be "the boss of all the goddamn greaseball dago bosses." He waved his drink around when he said it and I could tell that he was mad, too. "That's just fucking nuts. Even if he could get the rest of those fucking guys in line, they'd never stand for it for long. Boss of bosses, my ass."

"That's right," Meyer said. "There's only one way to get out of it." He paused and stared at Charlie until he was sure that Charlie was listening to him. "We've gotta get both of them."

Charlie shook his head.

Meyer went on, "If you agree to work with either one of those fucking assholes, he'll kill you. That's the truth of it. They want your business. They want *our* business. They'll tell you they just want a little slice of it, for you to show respect, but they'll try to take it all. You know that."

Charlie nodded.

"Here's how we'll do it," Meyer said. "You tell that crazy

Maranzano you'll kill Masseria for him. After we do it, things settle down. Then we'll kill Maranzano."

He turned to me. "Do you want some extra work?"

"What do you have in mind?"

Meyer said that because they'd been killing each other for so long, the Italians were deeply suspicious of other Italians. They knew that Charlie hung around with Lansky, but they didn't think much of him. And they didn't pay any attention to the guys like Benny and Red and me that worked with them. The hard part to killing the bosses was working out a place where they'd let down their guard.

With Masseria, it was pretty easy. Charlie arranged to go to a joint where the old guy liked to eat out on Coney Island. Since I didn't know the area, I just followed along in a backup car, trailing a big sedan with Benny and Vito Genovese and Albert Anastasia and Joe Adonis. We pulled up outside the place. They went in. I heard shots. The doors swung open a few seconds later. They came out with Charlie, tossed their guns into a valise I had on my lap, and we drove away. I dropped the valise in the East River that night.

Five months later, we did Maranzano. That was tougher. Since we were working in Midtown and wanted to keep everything on the QT, Meyer and Red thought to do it with knives. But that was too risky even with four guys, and when you set out to kill a big boss like Maranzano, you make damn sure you kill him. So they had guns along with the knives. I looked the place over while Red kept track of the old guy. We weren't in a hurry until we learned that Coll was in the picture. Meyer knew Maranzano would attract more attention than Masseria—that's why he came up with the business about the hats. He got his hands on a couple of quality hats that were made in Chicago and said as much right there on the haberdasher's label, then told Red to have his guys wear them going in and to make sure to leave them in Maranzano's office. I had the boaters so nobody would remember two guys without hats leaving the building.

It was a Lansky touch. Simple and smart, and it worked. Straight off, the DA sent cops to Chicago. It didn't hurt that the legitimate business Maranzano conducted in the office had to do with getting alien immigrants into the country, and the cops decided that was why he'd been topped.

But sitting there with my coffee that afternoon, I couldn't stop thinking about the couple on the sixth floor. I couldn't get anywhere with the guy. All I could focus on was the beard and the fez. But Daphne, she was another story. Daphne was one of Polly Adler's most popular and expensive girls. I knew she was a favorite of Charlie's, and I thought she was a sweet kid. So what was she doing dressed like a secretary in Midtown in the middle of the day when she usually wore nothing at all and did her best work late at night? I figured the guy in the fez must have some exceptionally peculiar requirements in the sack. As it turned out, that was true, just not in the way I was thinking.

I didn't figure it out until somebody put the touch on Miss Wray.

CHAPTER TWO

It was Thursday, the second of March, 1933, about 7:00 in the evening when Fay Wray came into my speak. She had another woman with her. They were both wearing overcoats and they stayed close together as they handed them over at the cloakroom and looked for someone in the crowd. Being about my height, that was tough for them, but I could tell they were worried.

I got up from my table at the back and made my way toward them through a happy bunch of Roosevelt supporters. Connie reached the two women first. Her eyes opened wide, and she stammered for a moment before she said, "Oh, my gosh, are you . . . Yes, of course you are. I can't believe this!"

It was the happiest I'd seen her in a week.

Miss Wray brightened and smiled right back at her. She leaned in, touching Connie's arm, and spoke so softly I couldn't hear what she said. Connie nodded, looked around, and waved me over. Nobody else in the joint recognized her. I thought it was pretty damn neat that she was there, but I didn't let that show.

Connie said, "This is Mr. Quinn."

"Miss Darrow . . . I mean Miss Wray. It's an honor."

She gave a slow cool look, not letting anything show. I didn't know what to make of it. Finally, she said, "You're not what I expected."

Neither Connie nor the woman who came in with Miss Wray—an alert, pretty brunette—looked like they knew what she was talking about. I sure as hell didn't.

Before I could answer, she said, "Detective William Ellis asked that I meet him here. I believe some gentlemen from the studio will be joining us, too. We need to talk privately."

Ellis? What the hell? I asked Connie to bring a bottle of the good champagne and led the two women up the stairs in back to my office.

Now, the truth is that Miss Wray was not the first celebrity or even the first movie star who'd dipped a beak at Jimmy Quinn's. Mayor Jimmy Walker stopped in from time to time before they threw him out, and when Longy Zwillman was squiring Jean Harlow around, he brought her in. And there had been others, but it just wasn't the kind of place where anybody rushed to the phone to call Walter Winchell when a famous so-and-so showed up. Winchell dropped by from time to time, but to drink, not to find material.

And on that day, Miss Wray was not really famous. A month later she wouldn't be able to set foot on the sidewalk without somebody asking for an autograph, but not yet. You see, the movie *King Kong* had opened at Radio City Music Hall that morning, the world premiere. Connie and I were right at the front of the line. We sat with Freddie Hall, who wrote about movies for the *Times*. The three of us loved it. I thought it was maybe the best moving picture I'd ever seen, and I thought it was pretty amazing that one of the stars was in my place. Her being there somehow didn't seem to be real. But like I said, I tried to act like it happened every day.

Up in my office, the women sat next to each other on the

leather divan. I cleared the newspapers from the table and sat behind my desk. Miss Wray was carefully examining every-thing—the bookcase, the little bar, the leaded glass lamp, the rug, the armchair. And me. There was something about the way she studied me that I did not understand. She was wearing a tweed dress and a belted jacket, the same outfit she'd had on that morn-ing when she introduced the picture. It might have been the same clothes she was wearing in her first scene in the movie where she tried to steal the apple. She sure looked about the same as she did on-screen. Wide forehead, huge eyes, tight little mouth, but when she spoke, she didn't have that fruity, half-British accent that most people in the movies seemed to have. She sounded more normal in person. She introduced the woman with her as Hazel. Hazel still looked worried and maybe a little scared, like she was not used to being in a speak, even a respectable classy speak like mine.

Connie came in with the Dom and four glasses. I uncorked, poured, and offered a toast, "To your absent costar, the Eighth Wonder of the World."

Miss Wray looked at Connie and asked, "Is he serious?"

"And how. He's been talking about nothing else for a week. Dragged me to the first show."

The door banged open. Detective William Ellis shouldered through and the room seemed smaller. "Quinn," he said, "I gotta talk to you." Then he noticed the women and said to Hazel, "You must be the actress."

Miss Wray, unruffled, said, "Try again."

Ellis shrugged and said to her, "So you're the one they've got the dirty pictures of?"

Hazel shot to her feet and got in Ellis's face, "Absolutely not! She had nothing to do with that filth."

They had my attention.

I told Connie to fetch Ellis a gin once she'd finished her cham-pagne. She knocked it back and stopped to whisper something to Miss Wray on her way out.

Ellis settled into the armchair and said to Connie, "There'll be two lawyers from RKO here soon. Send 'em back here."

She looked at me. I nodded.

Thinking he was in charge, Ellis held out a hand and snapped his fingers. "Let's see the pictures."

Miss Wray ignored him. She leaned back on the divan, crossed her legs glamorously, and said, "Perhaps when the gentlemen from the studio are here."

Connie showed them in a few minutes later, when she brought Ellis his gin.

Their names were Grossner and Sleave and they were both balding, slightly paunchy men who looked like they didn't laugh much. They wore black three-piece suits fully buttoned, and dark ties, I don't remember which color. Sleave wore the kind of glasses that pinch the bridge of your nose. Grossner was taller and wore regular glasses.

He looked around the room and said, "Given the sensitive nature of our business, I think it should be kept as quiet as possible. Miss Wray's assistant and the bar girl can wait downstairs."

Miss Wray said, "Absolutely not. Hazel is part of this."

I leaned back in my chair and said, "There's no reason for Connie to leave," but she shook her head and slipped out.

After the door clicked shut, Sleave said, "We have spent the afternoon speaking with the studio in California."

Grossner muttered, "The long-distance charges alone are going to be astronomical. Twenty-five dollars just to connect."

Sleave paid no attention and said to Miss Wray, "We have come to a decision. If indeed the situation is as you describe it, we will *not* comply with this extortion. But we will, of course, provide you a bodyguard. He should be at the hotel when you return from the reception."

"What do you mean?" Her voice was cold.

Sleave tugged at his vest and cleared his throat. "We have spoken to several senior executives in both the legal and production departments, and if these pictures are indeed *not* of you, then the studio has no real reason to accede to these demands. Of course, since you choose not to share the contents of these pictures, we cannot be certain. In fact, we have only your word that they exist—"

"Hazel has seen them, too. She saw them first."

Hazel's head bobbed up and down. "Yes, they're horrible."

Sleave didn't sound like he believed her. "So you say, but unless we can examine the material, paying six thousand dollars is simply out of the question."

Miss Wray stared at him for a long time before she opened her purse and took out a small leather address book. She looked at me and asked if she could use the phone. "It will be long distance," she said, looking at Grossner. "I'll take care of the twenty-five dollars."

"Of course," I said. The lady had brass.

She picked up the handset and said to me, "This is the private number of Merian Cooper. He directed the picture. But that was two years ago. Since then he has been promoted. Yes, Mr. Selznick was in charge of the studio while we were making the picture, but he recently resigned and now Mr. Cooper runs things at RKO."

She looked at the book and dialed "O." Beads of sweat popped out on Grossner's forehead.

"Operator, connect me with Los Angeles, California."

Grossner held out a hand, pleading. "Please. We really think it best if we do *not* involve Mr. Cooper's office. That is what we have been trying to do all afternoon. I am sure we can accommodate anything you desire."

She put down the phone. "I want this to be settled right away without so much as a whisper from Louella Parsons. I have been through this before and it will not happen again."

Things had started that morning while she was at the premiere. Hazel was at the hotel where the studio had put them up—

the Pierre. Hazel had been her stand-in on *King Kong*. They'd become friends and the studio brought her along so Miss Wray would have some company while she was promoting the picture. As nice as it was to stay at a tony joint like the Pierre, Hazel and the production manager of *King Kong* had fallen for each other, and she really wanted to go back to California to see him. She stayed at the hotel that morning accepting flowers and congratulatory telegrams and the like. She opened all the messages and kept them together in order of importance so they'd know who needed a telephone call that day or a personal letter or a signed eight-by-ten glossy.

The little package that they delivered to the room was with a bunch of telegrams. It was a thick sealed envelope. "Fay Wray—Personal" was written on the outside.

Hazel opened it and found a small book or booklet. When she opened that, a handwritten note fell out. It read: "$6,000 or we send copies to every newspaper, fan magazine, and gossip column in the city. Have the money ready in 24 hours."

Miss Wray said, "Show it to them."

Hazel opened her purse and took out the note. Sleave snatched it out of her hand. He quickly passed it to Grossner, who gave it to Ellis. Sleave said, "Let's see the book."

Hazel looked at Miss Wray. She nodded and said, "It's all right. It has nothing to do with us."

Hazel reached into her bag again and produced a thin book. She held it with her fingertips like it was white hot. As she passed it to Sleave, I could see that the cover was thick, flexible paper and *Kong* was printed on it in blue lettering.

The two lawyers did a poor job of hiding their intense interest in the book. They may have steamed up their glasses.

After they'd had their look, the taller one cleared his throat and said, "This is absolutely outrageous. Scandalous."

The shorter one said, "It is a blatant violation of our copyrighted material, our sets and costumes."

"No," Miss Wray interrupted. "That's not me and those are

not our sets. We didn't shoot anything in New York. It was all on the Culver City lot."

They didn't shoot anything in New York? That surprised me. Freddie Hall had explained how they used movable models and shot one frame of film at a time, but I can't say I really understood it. I knew it must have been some kind of trick photography for the city stuff because I'd have heard about it if they'd really wrecked an El train, or if there'd been a giant ape on the Empire State Building. But I didn't think about any of that while I was watching the picture. It was only when she said it that I thought about how they did it. While I was in the theater, all of it—Skull Island, the big wall, the dinosaurs—they were real, real enough, anyway. I didn't want to think about the reality behind them. I enjoyed being fooled.

Ellis demanded the book and flipped through it quickly. Whatever it was, he'd seen worse. Or better. He went to hand it back to the lawyers, but Hazel grabbed it and jammed it into her bag.

The detective took a slug of his gin and said, "All that funny stuff there in the book has something to do with this movie, right? *King Kong*? Don't know anything about that but it's easy enough to see that it's not you in the pictures. Still"—he turned to the lawyers—"if you want to do this the easy way, pay 'em. Six thousand dollars isn't even chicken feed. My captain told me that the studio wants this handled without any official police involvement, is that right?"

"It's publicity, bad publicity, that we're worried about," said the shorter one. "But we'd like you to be available if the situation were to become uncomfortable."

Ellis nodded in agreement. "Of course we can handle that, but it's been my experience, in matters like this, that the people on the other end won't have anything to do with a cop, even if I'm helping you unofficially."

The lawyers looked at each other and nodded.

"That's why I suggested we meet here. Quinn has a lot of

experience handling cash without calling attention to himself."
Ellis's smile had a nasty edge.

I said, "Sure. We can call Detective Ellis's precinct and talk
to some of the officers he works with if you'd like more details
on my bona fides. They know exactly what I do. Firsthand, you
might say."

Ellis's nasty smile disappeared and before I could name
names, he jumped in. "I'm just saying that where the law is concerned, Quinn works both sides of the street. Hell, he runs a
speakeasy. He has dealings every day with guys who are not one
hundred percent legit. They trust him, and I can promise you
that he won't run off with your money. That's about all you can
ask for in a go-between."

There was some more back and forth with the lawyers, and
they agreed that when the guys with the dirty picture book called
again, they would stipulate—that was their word, *stipulate*—that
I was to be their representative. And for the six grand, they
wanted every copy of the book. That's when Miss Wray piped up
again and said she'd be happy if she could get assurances that all
the books had been destroyed. The lawyers seemed disappointed.

After that, they started to get pissy about my fee. I cut it off.
"No discussion. It's ten percent, no matter how it turns out. You
make a deal for me to drop the money, I get six hundred bucks
whether it goes through or not."

They didn't argue the point.

Finally, I said, "One more thing. Do you have any suspicions
as to who's behind this?"

The lawyers shook their heads. So did Hazel and Miss Wray,
though they cut their eyes at each other like they were thinking
something else.

"So you don't think it could be somebody who's got a grudge
against the studio or Miss Wray? Somebody who just got fired?"

More head shaking from the four of them.

"All right, then. I'll ask around to see if any of the guys I know
are involved. I haven't heard of anybody who's working a racket

like this, but maybe somebody knows somebody who does. That's assuming you'd like to know who you're dealing with."

Miss Wray spoke up first. "I just want to be sure nobody else ever sees those pictures. That's all I care about."

She wanted them destroyed. The lawyers and the studio just wanted to be sure nothing put a dent in their ticket sales.

Hazel whispered something to Miss Wray, and they had a quick quiet conversation before they stood up. She said, "Give him the book, Hazel. He's got to know what he's dealing with."

Then she turned to the lawyers. "We're going now. We're late for a reception. You must understand how important this is to me. I will not hesitate to call Mr. Cooper at any time. Please remember that. Your positions may depend on it."

She said that with the sweetest smile you ever saw, and for the second time, at the mention of Cooper's name, I saw them sweat.

On their way out, Hazel handed me the little book and said softly, "If you learn anything at all about who's doing this, come to the Pierre immediately and contact Fay before you talk to them."

CHAPTER THREE

After the RKO gents left, Ellis sat there working on his gin. He was wearing a well-cut navy suit with a boldly patterned tie. His striped shirt had a tight white collar and a silver collar pin. A little overdressed, and he didn't look as good as I did. I had a lightweight double-breasted charcoal worsted that fit unusually well, a white shirt that didn't pinch my neck, and a wine-red tie. Never bothered with collar pins myself.

"Didn't mean for them to drop in on you cold, like that," he said. "I was gonna call, but we had a floater. Young girl, possible suicide. Chewed up by a propeller. I hate to see that."

"What's your part in all this?" I asked.

"Not much. This is so much crap. Some guy made some dirty pictures that look like some other broad and he figures maybe he can pry loose a little scratch from the movie studio. I can't see why the hell they're even giving him the time of day, but what do I know? They got in touch with Boatwright, my captain, said they wanted somebody on hand who would be discreet while they decided what to do. For now they want police advice, not involvement, so here we are."

He was the guy they'd call for something like that. Ellis had a reputation for knowing which rules to bend, not talking to anybody he shouldn't be talking to, and never embarrassing the department. His tight-ass captain found him useful and had learned not to ask too many questions.

"I had another reason to see you, too. Talked to a guy from the Sanitation Department. He's gonna come by, look you over, tell you what you gotta do for your licenses. Walk you through it."

"How much?"

"With him, couple of drinks and a fin. For starters."

"That's better than the bastard from the Fire Department. He's an asshole. Wanted fifty to walk in the front door. We gotta find somebody else."

Ellis said, "He's supposed to be the best, but he's not the only one who can help us."

You see, I was facing a terrible turn of events right then. Franklin Goddamn Delano Roosevelt had been elected. He was going to be inaugurated on Saturday, and he had promised that the first thing he was going to do once he was in office was end Prohibition. So, within a year or so, I'd have to go legit if I wanted to continue selling alcohol. And other than delivering the occasional bribe, dealing hooch was all I knew how to do. Now, dammit, I was going to have to do it legally, and I had no idea how to go about that. Ellis was helping me get to the right people to lubricate the system and make my legalization go as smooth as possible. That meant paying off the right guys, and not paying off the wrong ones. Until then, my payoffs and deliveries went mostly to men near the top, not the grunts I'd be dealing with day to day when I went legit.

But back to the matter at hand. Ellis said, "The sanitation guy can wait. For now, let's figure that whoever has these pictures is going to get in touch with the broads tonight or tomorrow. When the studio men get the money and have the details, call me. I'll tag along to keep the captain happy. If it goes down right, maybe these studio guys will call me again when there might be real money involved."

I didn't say anything. Hell, $600 was real money to me.

"Call me when you know something," he said and left.

I poured a short brandy and took out the book.

It was about five inches by seven inches, bound on the short side with a couple of heavy staples that looked to be made out of copper. The covers were soft thick textured paper. Inside was a mix of words, drawings, and photographs. The first page read: "Kong is the Beast. She is the Beauty."

There were two pictures on the facing page. The first was a pencil or crayon drawing of a snarling gorilla's head that looked a lot like the real King Kong but not exactly. The second was a full-length photograph of a blonde on the observation deck of the Empire State Building. She could have been Miss Wray in that first scene, with the same tweed jacket and a dress almost to her ankles. But unlike Miss Wray, this blonde's dress was slit open to midthigh, and her jacket and blouse were unbuttoned, displaying a lacy bra that was being tested to its limits. The blond hair looked almost exactly like Miss Wray's under the cloche hat. The face was sort of like hers. If I'd only seen the ads in the papers, I might think it was her, but anybody who saw the picture would know this wasn't the real thing. Must have been pretty tricky getting her to open up her clothes like that without attracting a lot of attention on the observation deck.

In the next shot, she was in a little fruit stand and reaching for an apple. It looked like the photograph could have been taken on the streets of New York. It didn't have that clean, no trash, no horse manure look of a city street in a movie. The caption read: "Destitute, she is reduced to stealing food."

The next photo was of the girl in a diner. It looked like another real place. Blouse still unbuttoned, she was sitting across a table from a guy whose face you couldn't see, just slicked-down dark hair. The caption was: "Salvation! A job with a moving picture company, and a voyage to a far distant land. . . ."

The next photo was of the girl in a shower stall. The billowing steam covered the key body parts like little clouds. It didn't need a caption.

The next was the only one that looked at first like it could have come from the picture. It was captioned: "The producer wants to see if she can express fright and tells her to imagine the Beast!"

The blonde was wearing what looked to me to be the same filmy fairy-tale dress that Miss Wray wore in that scene on the ship. Long, dangling sleeves, wide neckline that didn't cover her shoulders, a shiny woven belt that crossed under her breasts and then came down in a Y at her crotch. But where Miss Wray looked like she was really terrified, this girl looked like she just broke a nail. Not that most guys would have noticed. She didn't have anything on under the dress, north or south.

The next was another drawing, this one of the ship at anchor by the island. The caption was: "At last! She arrives at the lair of the Beast!"

Then there was another photograph of the blonde being taken from the ship, I guess. She was still in the fairy-tale dress with her arms spread wide, gripped at the wrists by the hands of a couple of colored guys. I think she was supposed to look like she was afraid and screaming again, but it still didn't wash.

The caption was: "Led to the altar to be a Sacrifice to the Beast!"

The stone altar in the next photo looked an awful lot like the one in the real movie. There was a lot of smoke and stone steps going up to two stone pillars about six feet tall with leopard skins piled around and human skulls on the pillars with weird symbols carved into them. The blonde was tied between the pillars with thick, scratchy-looking ropes. She was supposed to be screaming in terror at the next picture, a guy in a gorilla suit surrounded by fake trees no taller than he. It was a good gorilla suit with a really nasty face that looked a lot like the one in the first drawing. But it was still a gorilla suit, a gorilla suit with a hole in the crotch. Inside the gorilla suit was either a black guy or a white guy who'd smeared his Johnson with shiny black greasepaint—a different kind of blackface, I guess.

In the next photo, her dress had been ripped, revealing that she really did have a great set of knockers, though you couldn't see them clearly through the smoke. You could see that she wasn't a natural blonde.

The last picture surprised me. In that one, the dress had been torn open and she was spread-eagled on a big black furry hand. It didn't have the threadbare look of the props in the other photos, and the girl had been carefully posed and lit. She just looked great. I mean, it was one of those images that stays with you for a long time.

Twelve pictures. The ship and the first Kong shot looked to me like they'd come from the real moving picture. But I knew I could be remembering it wrong. The shots on the observation deck and the fruit stand didn't have anything to do with what I'd seen on the screen that morning. The real city was spread out behind her in the photo on the observation deck, and the deck didn't look anything like that narrow little ledge that the real Kong put her down on, and it didn't have the round thing at the top where he hung on while the bastards in the planes shot him down.

But what was really unusual about the little book was how clear and carefully detailed the drawings and photos were. Most of the dirty picture books you saw weren't much better than those cheap little Tijuana bibles, crude quick sketches that some guy had knocked off in a few seconds and then printed on the cheapest pulp paper he could find. This was quality workmanship. Somebody spent a lot of time and money re-creating the stuff from the moving picture, and he'd taken a hell of a lot of care to get exactly what he wanted in each image. In one close-up of the blonde, you see the elaborately elongated eyebrows and you could count her lashes.

Even the lettering of the captions was crisp and sharp at the edges, and the words were framed by an elaborate angled design at the corners. When I looked at that part more closely, I noticed the letters *AOS* were repeated in the design, the kind you used to see in silent movie intertitle cards. Remember, talking pictures had only been around for a few years then. For me, they were still almost a novelty because I'd been going to nickelodeons ever since I was tall enough to put a coin on the counter or could sneak in the back.

Yeah, moving pictures caught me when I was a kid and they never let go.

And sitting at my desk, it came to me that some of the photos in the book could have been lobby cards for real Hollywood pictures. Lobby cards weren't nearly as sexy, but the quality was the same.

It figured that the first thing to do was to ask the guys I knew to see if any of them had a hand in it. I knew where to start.

I was getting ready to go out when Connie came in. She told me that Frenchy was running short on beer. "He's tapping a new keg now but wants to know if we should order more for the weekend. He's counting on a big crowd Saturday afternoon because he's been telling everyone that we'll have the inauguration on the radio."

"Yeah, we should be ready," I said and then explained about the blackmail attempt, if that's what you called it, on Miss Wray and what the studio lawyers wanted to do about it. At first, she was interested, but it didn't take long for her to cross her arms across her chest and give me the cold look I'd been seeing so much lately.

I thought she'd snapped out of it when I took her to the moving picture, but that was just about the only time she was like her normal self and it didn't last. The rest of the time lately she tried to act like there was nothing but business between us. "Yes, sir," she'd say. "No, sir," she'd say. "Where do we store these new glasses?" she'd say.

Sure, Connie worked for me, but there was a lot more to it than that. We'd been keeping each other company for some time. She considered herself to be a "good girl" and we'd had several long discussions about that and I thought we were getting a lot friendlier. You see, a few months earlier, six months to be exact, I got caught up in some dicey business involving a girl I used to know, a bunch of Nazi bastards and four crates full of money. Before all that, Connie lived in a nice hotel for women that Marie Therese had arranged. But one morning as this business was warming up, Connie happened to be waiting for me in my room at the Chelsea when some guys broke in and three of them got themselves killed. In the confusion of the moment, and to keep her out of it, I got Connie another room in the hotel. It was supposed to be for a few hours until the cops left. But then, somehow, without anybody saying anything or making a decision about it, she wound up living there. A few at a time, her clothes and things found their way to the fifth floor of the Chelsea. The hotel was closer to the speak than the women's place, and it just felt better for her to be there upstairs. And, yes, I was footing the bill.

For a while, it was pretty terrific. Even though neither one of us ever spent the whole night in the other's room, we got more comfortable with each other. Not as comfortable as I might have liked, but I can honestly say that I wasn't in a hurry and tried not to pressure her. Things were warming up nicely until about a week ago when she slammed the door, so to speak.

That night in my office, I got fed up and asked her straight out. "What is it?" I said. "Why are you acting this way?"

"I don't know what you could be talking about," she said and turned for the door.

"No, Connie, come on, I'm serious. What's going on?"

Then she cocked her head and gave me that big-eyed look that said I should know what was going on without her having to tell me.

We stared at each other until I said, "All right. I give up. I guess you'll tell me when you're ready. I'm going out now. I may

be able to get a line on this business for Miss Wray. If you or
Frenchy need me for anything, you can reach me at Polly Adler's
place at the Majestic. Frenchy's got the number."

At the mention of Polly's name, Connie's eyes narrowed and I
swear I saw a little steam rising from her ears. She swore, "Goddammit, Jimmy Quinn—"

"Wait a minute," I said, cutting her off. "It's not *that*. If it was
that, do you think I'd be telling you about it? No, this is for Miss
Wray."

Polly's place was such a high-toned establishment that
nobody even called it a bordello, let alone a whorehouse. It was
just Polly's.

Then I had another idea and said, "Do you think I'm two-
timing you? Is that's what's been bothering you?"

Her eyebrows popped up and she raised her hands like she
was asking for guidance in dealing with such an ignoramus. I'd
seen Marie Therese do exactly the same thing with Frenchy a
hundred times.

On her way out, she said, "I'm sure I don't care who you spend
your time with."

I checked my money roll and my knucks and slipped the picture book back into my breast pocket with my notebook. I didn't
even think about getting the .38 out of the safe.

Frenchy and Arch Malloy were working behind the bar. I told
them I'd be back in a couple of hours.

CHAPTER FOUR

I caught a cab and told him to take me to the Majestic Towers on West Seventy-Fifth Street. It was around 9:00. I thought this was going to be one of those two-bird situations. Polly Adler had a huge apartment at the Majestic Towers. That time on a Thursday night, there was a fair chance you'd find Charlie there. If anybody local was peddling the pictures, Charlie probably knew who he was. Or Polly. Like I said, the book wasn't anything like the cheap junk they sold out of the back rooms of the peep shows and burlesque joints. It was meant for the carriage trade, and that was Polly's clientele.

The cabbie let me out at the corner on Broadway near the apartment building and the awning over the sidewalk. The doorman was a guy name of Orlendorfer. He wore a gray topper and a bright red coat with gold buttons. Considering the getups that a lot of doormen had to wear, his wasn't bad and it looked warm.

"Hello, Jimmy," he said as I approached. "I'll bet you're here to see Polly. Guess you hadn't heard."

"She moved again," I said.

"About three months ago to the East Side. I got her cards. Just a second," he said and went inside.

I buttoned my topcoat against the cold, and by the time Olly got back, I wished that I'd thought to bring gloves. He gave me a card with a phone number and a picture of a red parrot.

"She's at Madison and Fifty-Fifth," he said. "Dropped by a couple of weeks ago and gave me some cards to give to the guys and girls who hadn't got the word. Said she was just about ready to open up again."

He sidled a half step closer and lowered his voice. "If you're heading her way, you might want something to give you a boost," he said and produced a little glassine envelope of cocaine from his coat pocket.

I said no thanks and slipped him a buck. He asked if I wanted him to hail a cab and I said no again. I had another stop to make before I saw Polly and headed east toward the park.

Meyer Lansky lived a few blocks away on West Seventy-Second and Central Park West. His place was called the Majestic. Yeah, I was walking from the Majestic Towers to the Majestic. It could be confusing. Lansky lived in the Majestic when he was in town. His son Buddy was three years old, and he had cerebral palsy. Getting the right medical help for the kid had pretty much taken over Lansky's life. Since the business with Masseria and Maranzano, he and his wife had been going from one specialist to another. The best man they found was in Boston, and Lansky bought an apartment there close to the hospital. But if he was in the city, I wanted to ask him about the dirty pictures. Now, don't get me wrong. I never heard of him being involved with any business like that. Booze and gambling took up all of his time, and lately the gambling was more important. Still, he liked to know what was going on. He didn't move to the Upper West Side by being ignorant.

The guy working the desk in the lobby of the Majestic called Lansky's apartment and told me to go on up to the third floor. The place was classy and really big with lots of rooms. I'd been there before and knew that in the sitting room in the daylight, you looked right down into the trees in the park. I guess it was the biggest and fanciest part of the place, and that's where Lansky met me, but he spent most of his time in the library. I envied that room and he knew it.

That night, his tie was loose, his vest was unbuttoned, and his cuffs were turned up. I tossed my overcoat on the back of the sofa and we went into his library. It had beautiful wooden bookshelves on most of the walls, all crammed full, and I knew he'd read most of the books. He also had a fireplace, a big desk, a couple of comfortable armchairs, and a good floor lamp. I told myself that if I was ever able to move up from the Chelsea, I'd have a library like that.

I saw three stacks of paper on his desk, and I could tell by the letterheads that it was correspondence with doctors in California, Chicago, and Austria. Without asking, Lansky poured a couple of good brandies, the same Delamain that he sold to me, and we toasted nothing in particular. We sat and I apologized for interrupting his evening.

"You're not interrupting anything," he said, sounding tired. "I'm just trying to make sure that I'm doing the right thing. It's damn difficult when the doctors disagree with each other. You trust the ones who seem to make the most sense, but what do you know? Anna and Paul are in Boston with Buddy. I'm going back tomorrow." Paul was his younger son. "What brings you up here?"

I didn't know exactly how to explain what I was doing so I asked him if he knew anything about *King Kong*. He shook his head and smiled like he thought the words were funny. I guess they were.

"Well," I said, "it's a moving picture, a really expensive moving picture about this giant ape who falls for this blonde and they come to New York—"

"Wait a minute, what're you talking? A giant ape falls for a blonde? That's nuts."

"I know but while you're watching it, it makes sense, and here's the important part. The actress who plays the blonde is this girl named Fay Wray. Picture opened this morning at Radio City Music Hall and she was there to introduce it. When she gets back to her hotel, she finds that somebody has put together a dirty book that looks like it was based on the movie with pictures, photographs of a blonde that looks just like her, but she's mostly naked. Guys who sent the book say they want six Gs from the studio or they'll give copies to the newspapers and gossip columnists."

"But it's not this girl?" he asked.

"No, but it'll embarrass her, so she wants the studio to keep it quiet, even if they have to pay up."

He frowned. "That still doesn't make any sense. Have you seen the book?"

I passed it across to him. Still frowning, he thumbed quickly through the pages and handed it back.

"I still don't get it. What has it got to do with you?"

I said, "Some big cheese at the studio got in touch with some big cheese at the police department and asked for help from a cop, somebody who'd keep this mum and look out for their interests. They got Ellis, the detective, you know who I mean, big guy, dresses sharp. That guy. He set up a meeting at my place and said I should be the go-between because of my vast experience in delivering money."

Lansky nodded. He saw the sense in that.

"But before I do anything," I said, "I want to know if Charlie or Ben or any of your guys are in on this. If they are, we can settle this tonight. I'll tell the studio guys to pony up and they will."

Lansky thought and shook his head. "Not that I know of. Nobody in our outfit has said anything, but Charlie might know something I don't."

"Where would I find him?" I asked, knowing the answer.

"Polly's, this time of night. You know she moved, right?"

I nodded.

"I haven't seen much of Charlie lately. He's talking about cutting himself in on the hookers and whorehouses once Prohibition is over. It's a stupid idea. . . . Like, say, the numbers, too much work with too many people getting a piece for not enough money. He oughta find something else."

"What are you doing?"

"Casinos and carpet joints. The profits aren't as good as booze, but they're steadier, and if you run a good efficient operation, you can't lose. We do fine at the Piping Rock in Sarasota Springs. We can do the same in other places. Simply a matter of finding the right locations and the right men in office. I've got some things in mind. When you're ready to leave the city, let me know. There's always room for you."

I said thanks and I'd think about it, but the truth was that the idea of leaving New York scared the hell out of me. Still does, really.

He went on, "Right now, with the bills for Buddy's treatment, I can't afford to spend time on something that isn't likely to pay off any time soon. Casinos are steady."

Lansky was right. It brought me up short when I realized that I was worrying over dirty pictures involving a guy in a gorilla suit while he was figuring out how to help an ailing son. If I'd thought about that more seriously, it would have put things in perspective. He settled back in the chair and sipped the good cognac. "It's not like it was. The easy money days are past us. Do you remember that night with A. R. in the Park Central when he talked about what Prohibition was going to be? Hell, you were just a little kid then."

"I may have been a kid, but I remember it. I thought he'd gone nuts. Close down the saloons? Crazy."

Lansky said, "I knew he was right in what he was saying, but I didn't know how easy it was going to be. All you needed was to get your guys in the right places at the right times and shoot the hell out of any guys who got in your way. You just needed cars and trucks and guns."

"No," I said. "There were a lot of guys with cars and trucks and guns. We were smarter."

He shrugged it off.

I went on. "Smart enough to buy off the right people."

He nodded and maybe even smiled a little. "But it was a young man's game then, and besides, it's over. Once they got rid of the mayor, the jig was up." He shook his head. "Fucking greedy vice cops."

He was talking about Jimmy Walker, who'd been cashiered six months before. That was Roosevelt's doing when he was governor of the state. I guess you could say that it went back to the Committee of Fourteen and the Society for the Prevention of Vice and the Wilcox Foundation for Wayward Girls and finally the Seabury Commission. All of them were outfits that tried to reform New York. They got started back when I was a kid and sex was for sale just about everywhere you turned in my neighborhood. These guys did their damnedest to get rid of it. That was impossible as long as the Tammany boys were in charge of the Magistrate's Court and the vice cops. You see, being a vice cop wasn't like being a real cop. Vice was a patronage job, one of the best.

Between the court and the cops, those guys had a hell of a racket. Being a vice cop gave you all the quiff you could handle, and a license to steal. Say a vice cop busted a hooker or a madam and her girls. First thing, he sent them down to the Magistrate's Court at the Jefferson Street Market where every one of the judges, lawyers, bail bondsmen, and jailers were in on the deal. Most of the women knew how the system worked. They spent a few hours down in that grim pile of Victorian brick and paid their money to everybody who had a hand out. If they'd shelled out enough, they were declared not guilty and went back to work a few hours later.

But the goddamn vice cops got greedy and started framing women who weren't in the business. They went after single women—landladies and nurses mostly—whose work put them in situations where they were alone with men. The cops and their stoolies would say that they were propositioned, and then they hauled the gals down to the Magistrate's.

I guess most New Yorkers didn't get too upset when the bulls were shaking down fallen women. But once word got out about how they were screwing over widows and Florence Nightingale, people took it seriously. And that's exactly what the Seabury Commission did. For months, it was all you saw in the papers. Then the Commission Report really stuck it to the mayor, and the governor made it clear that if he didn't resign, he'd be kicked out.

Mayor Walker and his girlfriend decided it was a good time to visit Europe. The rest of the Tammany mob shut up and kept their heads down.

Truth is, I got along well enough with most cops, but that was easy for me to say. I mean, as long as I was running a respectable speak, they were happy enough to leave me to my business and to accept a free drink from time to time. I made sure that the patrolmen who worked my block got a little something extra every week. If there was an honest upright police officer who believed in enforcing every letter of every law, well, I never met him. Sure, there was the occasional cop who'd take your money and turn on you as soon as it suited him. Those you had to deal with.

But I had no respect for the goddamn vice cops, and I didn't know anybody who did, and that included their brother officers.

Lansky said, "You know with this book, you ought to check it with Al Marinelli."

"Why?" I asked. Al Marinelli was what you might call the accountant for Tammany. If you were paying off any of their guys, the money went through Al. He and I had been associates for a long time.

"Look, chances are that whoever put this book together is also working with the dirty books you find in Times Square," Lansky said. "So somebody's making sure the cops leave them alone, and it's not coming cheap, considering how the monsignor gets so tight-assed about 'art magazines.' Marinelli could tell you who that is."

I said that was a good idea, and Lansky said that if I was going to see Marinelli, I could go ahead and take something downtown for him. "You'd be doing me a little favor, that's all," he said. "It's right here."

He got up and went through a desk drawer. It only took him a few seconds to find what he was looking for and to seal something, probably money, in an envelope.

He handed it to me and said, "Give this to Marinelli. This time of night, you'll probably find him at that chop-suey place by his office. If you can't find him tonight, Monday is fine. Tell him it's for this week and next. Got that? This week and next week. Make sure he repeats those words back to you. Things have been confused down there since the mayor left, and I need to be sure this is handled properly."

He didn't expect a receipt. Fact is, Lansky almost never wrote anything down. Anything on paper in his handwriting could come back to bite him if the wrong people got their hands on it. As they said, he kept his business under his hat.

I tucked the envelope into my pocket with the book and told him I'd see him later.

Out on the street, the Majestic doorman had a knot of people gathered at the curb. Looked like he needed more than one taxi, so I headed toward the next corner to hail one for myself.

I hadn't got far when a car pulled up to the curb next to me. It was a big brown Olds Deluxe with four lights up front and big wooden spoke wheels. The passenger door opened. A guy in a suit stepped out and said, "Get in the car, Quinn."

He had a little automatic in his mitt.

"Fuck off," I explained and kept walking.

"This is about the pictures," he said. "If you want to take care of them and collect your six hundred dollars, you'll get in the car."

I stopped walking.

CHAPTER FIVE

I looked the guy over. He was medium height, making him taller than me, and built thick and solid. His hat shadowed his face, so I couldn't make out his features. I didn't know what was happening, but sure as hell I wasn't going for a ride with anybody.

I thought about where we were and what was close and said, "If you want your six grand, you'll put the piece away and meet me there." I pointed with my stick to a place a couple of storefronts down the cross street. He stood still, unsure what to do, then turned back to the car, looking for help. I walked away before they said anything more.

Light from the place, a diner called Allen's Lunch Room, spread across the sidewalk. I didn't look back, though I wanted to. Didn't matter how close the Oldsmobile was.

Allen's Lunch Room had big windows to the street, shiny tile walls, a counter down one side and booths down the other. Inside, there were less than half a dozen guys and a couple of countermen in white jackets. I slid into a booth near the front where I could watch the door. One of the countermen came over. I ordered black coffee and cherry pie while I waited and worried over the fact that somebody had been following me.

What the hell? How did these guys, whoever they were, know what I was about? My first thought was that one of the lawyers or somebody in the RKO office was in on it. Or maybe these guys just watched the Pierre Hotel. When Miss Wray left, in a big hired car no doubt, they followed her to my place. If they knew who I was and what I did, it wouldn't be hard to figure out the rest, including my ten percent. Then they tailed me. But none of that mattered, because I shouldn't have been there in that diner, not with Lansky's money in my pocket. I was ready to get up when the guy from the car sat down facing me.

Close up, in brighter light, I saw that he was younger than me with messy fair hair and an acne-scarred mug. His jacket elbows were shiny, his shirt cuffs were frayed, and his hat looked like it had been run over by a bus. He stared hungrily at my pie when the counterman brought it, and he ordered coffee for himself. A second guy got in the booth and shoved him toward the wall. I'd never seen either of them before.

The second guy was bigger, older, and horsefaced. His wrinkled suit had seen the same hard wear, and he stank of cigarette smoke. His tobacco pouch and papers were in his breast pocket. He had a whispery voice and a dead-eyed stare meant to frighten me. You knew right off, just by looking at him, that this guy liked to hurt people. He said, "You're Quinn, right? The go-between? You're gonna make sure we get our money."

I ate my pie. It was pretty good. The coffee wasn't, and it was too hot. "They haven't decided what they're going to do," I said. "The RKO lawyers. She wants them to pay. They don't."

The younger one loaded up his coffee with cream and sugar cubes until the cup almost overflowed. He slurped it down and added more. The older guy reached across him and grabbed the bowl of sugar cubes and put it down in front of himself where he could dip into it. He put a cube between his yellow front teeth and whispered around it, "Yeah, well, you better see that they say yes. We'll make contact again tomorrow. No funny business with the payoff. It's simple. We want it in ones, twos, and fives. No twenties, they're too hard to break."

"Yeah, no twenties. That's what you'll do if you know what's good for you," the younger one said, his eyes bright at the thought of so much money. He reached across for another sugar cube and the older guy brought a hand up fast, like he was going to backhand him. The kid cringed and flinched away and brought up an arm to shield himself. The sight of him doing that brought up somebody I hadn't thought about for a long time, Oh Boy Oliver. Oh Boy grew up in the same building with me. His old man was nice enough most of the time, but whenever he got loaded, he'd backhand Oh Boy just like that and Oh Boy would jerk back with the same flinch. It made me mad when I was a kid and it still did.

The older one said, "Be in her hotel at 6:00. We'll call."

"You're missing a trick," I said and waited. I had no idea what I was talking about, but their showing up like that and thinking about Oh Boy had put me off balance and I wanted to do something, even something small, to do the same to them.

It seemed to surprise them that I said anything. The younger one glanced over at the older guy. The older guy stared at me. Finally, he said, "What are you talking about, missing a trick?"

"You should have some of this pie. It's pretty good."

He said, "Don't get smart with me, asshole." He was loud enough that the countermen and the other customers looked at us.

"I'm not getting smart. I'm recommending the cherry pie. It's good. I mean it."

The first one believed me. He wanted a piece of pie. The older guy got more pissed and growled, "The bitch will be ruined if those pictures get out. People know she's a common whore, she's finished."

"Yeah, finished, they'll lock her the fuck up," the younger one said, and they both sniggered. He went on, "You make goddamn sure they know we're serious. We don't get our money, we'll plaster the whole fucking city with those pictures. We got a hunnert of them, you tell 'em that."

The older guy sucked on another sugar cube. "She'll get what's coming to her, all right. They always do. We know what we're doing."

I thought, *Damn, these dopes really do believe it's Miss Wray in the pictures. They're just as dumb as they look.* Best leave it at that. But were they just idiots or did they believe what somebody told them? It was also interesting that they didn't care that I could identify them, but then if they knew who I was, they knew I wouldn't go to the cops. Still, it's hard to predict what stupid guys are going to do, so I slipped my knucks onto my right hand.

When the counterman came back with the coffeepot, I gave him a quarter. I told the two guys not to worry, I'd tell the lawyers exactly what they told me.

The older one twisted around in the booth and grabbed my forearm as I stood up and went past. "Don't fuck this up. We mean business." He gave me another cold-eyed stare and smiled. "They don't fork it over, you're in the shit."

He whipped a steel sap out of his coat pocket and snapped it at my knee, the good one. He was too close and too fast for me to dodge it, but my stick was beside my leg and that's what he hit. It still hurt like hell and pissed me off, so I threw my coffee in his face, and gave him a quick shot to the ear with the knucks. The younger one looked like he was trying to go for the automatic, but he was jammed against the wall.

One of the countermen yelled something. I said it was okay and we needed somebody with a mop.

Then I leaned close where only the older guy could hear me and said, "Listen, you dumb fuck, you want to rough up the go-between, you do it *after* you've got the money."

I stepped back from the booth. Everybody else in the place was staring at us. Both countermen were hurrying toward us. I pocketed the knucks, held up a hand, and said, "It's all right."

The older guy had sugar and coffee all over his face and a trickle of blood from his split ear.

I peeled a buck off my money roll and dropped it on the table. "Here," I said to the countermen, "Give that one a piece of that cherry pie. It's really good. And some coffee for this one."

Out on the sidewalk, I turned back toward the lights of Central Park West. I hadn't gone far when I saw the big Olds parked on the other side of the street. I stopped in a shadow and waited. A few minutes later, the two idiots came out of Allen's and jay-walked across the street. The kid was stuffing pie into his face as he hurried behind the older guy.

When they reached the other side of the street, the back door of the Olds opened and a third man got out. All I could make out was a dark shape and the orange glow of a lighted cigarette. At first, it looked to be in his mouth, but as the two guys talked, he took it out and waved it around. I could hear voices but couldn't understand any words. They stood there in the street for about a minute. For all I could tell, he might have been reaming them out or telling them that they did a hell of a job.

The three of them got into the backseat, and the big car headed uptown. I went back to Central Park West and caught a cab down to Mulberry Street.

That late, Marinelli wasn't in his office or the chop-suey joint Lansky had mentioned. I knew there was an Italian place he favored over on Broome Street, but there was another beanery where Marinelli might be found, Celano's on Kenmare, and it was closer. Bingo.

I spotted him at a table with two other guys. When he saw me, he motioned for them to leave. I checked my coat and hat and made my way across the big, noisy, smoky place. But the noise was different. It didn't have the same slaphappy energy that you felt a few years before when they were making a lot of money. Now, everybody knew that the reformers were on the way, and they were trying to figure out how to stay out of sight and still turn a buck.

Marinelli was a big guy with the easy offhand gab of a seasoned pol. His father had worked as a translator for the newly arrived *paisans*, so early on, Al learned how to make himself useful. He started out as a port warden and alderman. Eventually, he was in charge of the inspectors who counted votes in city elections, and he had a hand in choosing people who sat on grand juries. A very useful guy indeed. When Charlie Luciano was looking for a fellow wop to keep an eye on things in Tammany Hall, he chose "Uncle" Al to work among the micks. He was my regular contact when I was handling business for Charlie and Lansky.

Marinelli was sitting behind the remains of what had been a good-size porterhouse. I looked at it and thought that was what I should've been doing—slicing into a steak upstairs from my place in the Cruzon Grill, and if things were even a little bit slow, I'd tell Connie to take the evening off and join me, and that made me think about whatever had Connie in such a lather. What the hell was I going to do with her?

Marinelli finished the chunk he was chewing, cut another, and said, "What are you doing here? Didn't expect you until next week." He spoke with the low murmuring voice that he used when he was talking in private. Guys at the next table couldn't make out a single word.

"Yeah, I know," I said as I sat and slipped him the envelope under the table, "but some other business came up and I had to see Lansky tonight. This is for this week and next, got that?"

He grunted and tugged at the envelope. I held on to it. "Got that?"

He frowned as he chewed. "Yeah, I got it. Two weeks," he said, palming the envelope.

I felt the weight of responsibility float away. Maybe the abrupt change in routine had got to me more than I understood, and it felt terrific to be rid of the thing. You see, in all the years I'd been doing this work, I never missed a meeting. Sure, a lot of lines got crossed and somebody didn't show up where I expected him to be, and sometimes other guys tried to hijack me and I was late, but in the end, I always delivered. Always. It would be a hell of a time to ruin my record.

He washed his steak down with a gulp of dago red.

I said, "This other business I mentioned, you might know something about it."

"Yeah, how's that?"

"Suppose a guy came across a stash of dirty books, 'art' picture books, real good 'art' picture books, who would he talk to about unloading them? Carlo?"

You see, after we knocked off Maranzano and Charlie took over, he handed over his peepshows and pinball machines to Carlo Gambino. He kept the slots for himself.

"How many books?" Marinelli asked.

"Can't say. I've only seen one and been told there's more, but who knows? It's not my racket. Before I do anything, I gotta be sure I'm not horning in on somebody else's territory. Is anybody else peddling stuff like that?"

He chewed and thought and shook his head. He allowed that you could find some higher-quality stuff, real hardback books and the like, in some stationery stores, but nobody was making payments to him to make sure the cops left them alone. The truth was, he said, that the market just wasn't that big or profitable. I said he was probably right. The whole business didn't smell right.

He pushed his plate away. "It's not really your line of work anyway. I hear you're going legit."

"I'm trying to, but they're sure as hell making it rough on me."

"I know. It's a hell of a thing. Now I've got this prick LaGuardia breathing down my neck. He gets in office, who knows what the fuck will happen."

Uncle Al looked around the big room at all the guys who were trying to figure out what was going on and if they were making a living today, would they still be able to do it tomorrow. He leaned across the table and for the first time, his voice got louder and guys at the next tables turned to listen. "It started with that goddamn Roosevelt and now the fucking reformers are crawling out of the woodwork. A hell of a thing, just a hell of a thing. I mean, think about it, what did we do wrong? Nothing. We gave the people what they wanted. They voted the right way and we made jobs for them and their kids. Yeah, we took our cut, but fair's fair, right? Isn't that what made this fucking city great?"

"It was just too good to last," I said, and he nodded his head.

CHAPTER SIX

I collected my hat and coat and went out to Mulberry Street to hail a cab. My first thought was to follow my original plan and look for Charlie at Polly Adler's new place. But the meeting with the two dumb-ass blackmailers—and their cigarette-smoking boss, if that's who he was—made me think that it might be a better idea to stop by my place and pick up a .38. But, thinking they were done with me for the night, I changed my mind. When the taxi pulled over, I told him to take me to Polly's address on Fifty-Fifth and to let me know if he noticed anybody following us.

He asked if I wanted him to shake them and I said, no, that wasn't important. I just wanted to know if anybody was interested. Nobody was. The cabbie was disappointed.

For a time, Polly had probably been the most famous madam in the city, and that's saying something. She had strong competition. But I knew her before then. Hell, I knew her before she was Polly Adler. I couldn't have been more than ten or eleven at the time. She was older. Here's how it happened.

* * *

When I first met her, she was Pearl Davis. I don't think Davis was her real last name, but everybody called her Pearl. She was an immigrant from Russia. She wasn't the prettiest girl you ever saw, but she was funny and curious and she was always in the middle of things. She was also busty and short. Truth is, at four-foot-eleven, she was one of the few women I've ever known that I could honestly say, "I towered over her."

Anyhow, she had been working as a seamstress at a dress factory when her foreman took a shine to her and asked her out. The first time they were alone together, he made a pass and she said no. Then he knocked her out and he knocked her up, and when she told him about it, the bastard fired her.

She dug up the money to take care of her immediate problem but had a hard time finding another job, and she spent about a year living hand to mouth in a ten-dollar-a-month mouse hole down on Second Avenue. I guess it was worse for more people in the Depression, but Pearl's year of being broke came at a time when it seemed to her like everybody else was flush with cash and that made it damned hard to take.

Now, the night she told me most of this was several years later. We had been drinking and she probably said more than she meant to. I listened a lot.

For her, the bad times ended in January, 1920, when a friend took her to meet a dress manufacturer who lived up on Riverside Drive. She said the place where he lived with his family was maybe the nicest apartment she'd ever seen. He didn't have any work for her, but while she was visiting his place, she met one of his acquaintances, Kitty Robinson, a tall, blue-eyed blonde about Pearl's age. Kitty was an actress and singer who'd just arrived in town from Chicago and had already landed a part in a new Broadway revue that was about to start rehearsals.

Kitty and Pearl hit it off, and before long, she was inviting Pearl over to her place, which was every bit as high-toned as the dress manufacturer's, nine rooms done to the nines. Better yet, Kitty palled around with all the beautiful, witty show business people. The two girls got along so well that Kitty invited Pearl to move in and keep her company until her mother arrived from Chicago in a few months. Pearl took her up on it and thought it was all pretty terrific until she got to know Kitty better.

That's when she found out that her friend liked to relax at "hop parties," where she partook of a pill or two of opium in a nice warm pipe. At first, Pearl thought it was just something that Kitty did from time to time, and it would certainly stop when Kitty's mother arrived. I don't know if she really believed that or not, but she learned different.

Kitty's mother showed up with a young lounge lizard gigolo in tow. She called him "Dad," and both of them dove right into the hop party whirl. Pearl tagged along.

One of their favorite places was another vast Upper West Side spread where an older woman named Melissa Louise lived. Melissa Louise was the mistress of a Wall Street financier, and she was so well heeled that she made the rest of them look like bums. Besides the apartment, she had a car, a chauffeur, a two-hundred-dollar-a-month allowance, and, she claimed, a hundred-thousand-dollar trust fund that was hers whenever she decided that she wanted to leave.

At Melissa Louise's place, they'd close the transoms and put damp towels under the doors of the drawing room. That's where the lady of the house would stretch out on a big fur rug while her guests reclined on the divans that surrounded her, and they'd all hit the pipe. All but Pearl.

Both Kitty and Melissa Louise warned her against the stuff, and so she never indulged. Though Pearl never said so, I got the idea that it wasn't so much her welfare and problems with the law that led them to keep her away from the pipe. They needed somebody who was straight to look after them. That's how Pearl and I met.

You see, at the same time she was moving into the world of

the upper crust, I was living in a building in Hell's Kitchen with Mother Moon. Oh Boy Oliver lived there too. Now, Mother Moon was either my aunt or my grandmother, we were never sure which exactly. Before she married a Chinaman, she was Mother Quinn, and my father had been told to find her when he came to America from Ireland. He did that, and he and my mother moved into her place. Then after he left and my mother died, Mother Moon raised me. She taught me how to steal and who to steal from, how to run and how to fight when I absolutely had to, and she hired me out to Rothstein as a messenger. She also loved her pipe. On those days and nights when she was not in the mood to stretch out in the Sans Souci opium den, she'd give me money and send me over to the place on Third Avenue to buy a can and bring it home. Pearl did the same for Kitty and Melissa Louise, and that's where we met, back at the office with a Dutch door where the old man who ran the place kept the supply that he'd dole out to a few old and trusted customers.

The sign on the street said that the Sans Souci was a music hall, and they did have some kind of entertainment. There was also a restaurant and a casino. The opium den was around back and in the basement. But if you wanted to pick up a tin of the best-quality stuff, you had to call ahead and see the old guy.

That's what I was doing one evening, waiting in an alcove off the main hallway and outside the office, when Pearl showed up.

She was not happy to be there. Melissa Louise told her it was completely safe and provided the car and driver and said that everything had been arranged, but the Sans Souci was not in the best neighborhood, and Pearl had hoped that part of the city was behind her.

Chinese waiters and other guys hustled through the hallway. It was narrow, crowded, dim, and thick with incense and tobacco smoke. A few of the guys glared at us suspiciously, but most paid us no mind. Pearl crowded in next to me. Even though I was just a kid, I was about her size and color. She said, "Is this the place for . . ."

"Yeah," I answered and rapped twice quick on the door. "Mr. Ung, you've got another customer."

The top part of the door swung open, bumping into us, and I could see Mr. Ung perched on his tall stool in front of a rolltop desk that took up most of the room. There was a little five-tael can of opium on the desktop. Mr. Ung gave Pearl the once-over and said, "Who you?"

Pearl stood as tall as she could, handed the old guy an envelope, and said, "Miss Melissa Louise called. I'm expected."

He sniffed and snatched the envelope. He said, "You wait," and started to pull the door shut.

I grabbed it and held it open. "Hey, that's mine," I said, pointing to the can.

He gave me a mean look, handed it over, and slammed the door. I could've left then, but I could tell the girl wanted me to stick around, so I pocketed the dope and introduced myself. "Don't worry about him," I said. "They wouldn't let you in if they didn't know somebody was coming. First time?"

"Yeah."

"How much are you picking up?"

"Three cans of"—she looked at a slip of paper—"Li Yun."

I told her that was the good stuff and the cans would fit in her bag, and she should be sure to keep it closed and tucked under her arm.

She shot me a skeptical look and said, "I may be new to this, but I'm not stupid. Besides, I've got a driver right outside. I'm not worried."

Like hell she wasn't worried. Pearl knew her way around some rough parts of town, but being in a place like that for the first time, she could use a little company, even a smart-ass kid like me.

I waited until Mr. Ung came back and checked the labels to make sure it was the Li Yun, not some junk he was trying to foist off. But I guess Melissa Louise was on the level. Pearl stuffed the cans down deep, clutched her bag, and held onto my arm as I led her back out by the restaurant to Third Avenue where her car and driver were waiting. She said, "Thanks, kid," and I didn't see her for a while after that.

She went back to Kitty's place, Kitty's Mom and Mom's Gigolo, and things went south.

Heroin and cocaine had been replacing opium for some time because they were easier to handle and more profitable, and people got a bigger kick out of them. There were only a few old holdouts like Mother Moon who stuck with the pill and the pipe. Kitty started shooting heroin.

Pearl was looking for a way out when she met a bootlegger named Scoodles Jerome at one of Kitty's parties. He told Pearl that he was having a fling with a society dame who was married. They were looking for someplace nice where they could while away an afternoon. He said he'd pay the rent if Pearl could find the right apartment and make herself scarce for a few hours from time to time.

It turned out to be two bedrooms furnished on Riverside Drive. Pearl moved in, and for a few months everything was terrific. Maybe Pearl caught a few more movie matinees than she might have, but that was okay. She still thought it was a sweet deal. Then Scoodles and his squeeze called it quits. He asked Pearl if she might know of a new squeeze. Just doing a favor for a friend, you understand, nothing more than that. She asked around and, sure enough, a cute girl named Fran, from back in her first days at Kitty's, said she was interested in a little hubba-hubba.

Things worked out so well that some of Pearl's other friends asked if they might help to entertain Mr. Scoodles. She said yes, and pretty soon he was spending two or three nights a week at her place. Pearl told me later that it was the best time she ever had in the business.

Scoodles was a nice-enough guy. I knew him because he worked with Lansky and Charlie every now and again. He thought Pearl's setup was so great that he'd show up most evenings about six with bags of chicken from the rotisserie down the street, and jugs of dago red, and they all had a fine old time. Eating chicken, drinking red, screwing, eating chicken. Since it was so informal, Pearl could still convince herself that she wasn't involved in selling sex. And, she kept telling herself, this was only temporary, anyway, a way to earn enough to go into some kind of legitimate business.

Then Scoodles invited some of his pals over. More girls told her they were interested. Before she really knew what she was doing, she was pocketing a hundred dollars a week, big money in those days, and she was looking for a larger place. Two bedrooms just wasn't getting the job done.

Now, the truth is that Pearl wasn't doing anything that hundreds of other guys and girls weren't doing all over the city. The difference was that through Scoodles, she met Charlie and a lot of other guys in the booze business, both the guys like us who sold it and the politicians and cops who got their cut to let us sell it. They had wallets full of cash and they were ready to spend a little extra or a lot extra, if the girl was pretty enough and energetic. And Pearl, as they say, had a good eye for young talent.

It didn't take long for word to get about that Pearl had the best girls and the highest prices. Sure, she was busted from time to time, but the charges were always dismissed and it didn't hurt her business. She got taken up by the literary and show business crowd, too. That's when she changed her name to Polly Adler, and the phrase "Going to Polly's" came to mean more than ripping off a quick slice. A lot of guys went to Polly's to play cards and backgammon, and to be seen and to talk about who they saw there. I visited once or twice myself, in my younger days, when I was flush with dough and the sap was rising. She served good booze and good food, and she charged top dollar for everything. She was fond of saying that her place was a combination of a gentlemen's club, a speak, and a harem.

Whenever there was a big nightclub opening or the like, she'd doll up three or four of her classiest heartbreakers and make a big show of parading them around. That always boosted her traffic, but she was careful. You didn't get into her place unless she knew you. Or you were recommended by the right guys.

I got out of the cab at Fifty-Fifth Street and Madison. The lobby of Polly's building was flanked by storefronts. Inside the lobby, I gave the colored elevator operator my name and said I was there to see Pearl, no, Polly Adler. He said she was entertaining visitors in a private party. I told him to call anyway and tell her I was there. He went behind his desk and, frowning at me, dialed the phone. After talking for a minute or so, he told me to wait, and took the elevator up.

Polly was with him when he came back. She was wearing a nicely tailored skirt and jacket that made her look like a well-heeled schoolteacher. Her hair was done up nice and in her high heels, she was almost as tall as I was. Damn, it was good to see her again. It must have been at least a couple of years since I'd been to one of her places or she'd been to mine.

"Hello, Jimmy," she said and hugged me. "Sorry to keep you waiting, but I had to be sure you were you. Charlie's here and he don't like to be disturbed."

I said that was good, I needed to talk to him, and we went up to her place.

She had the second floor. All of it.

There were twelve rooms to the place, and she wanted to show off all of them, except the ones that were being used. She'd just moved in and it was all new to her. Her taproom looked like the army had decorated it with red, white, and blue, stars and stripes, and the like. The mah-jongg room was Oriental red and gold. She told me that the bedrooms were peach and apple green because peach brought such a warm look to the complexion. I remember that the dining room was huge, and the main room was gray with green satin curtains that she was really proud of. I said hi to Charlie "the Bug" Workman and another guy I didn't know who were smoking and looking bored, while Charlie Lucky was enjoying himself in a peach bedroom. Three of her girls who were sitting around put down their magazines and perked up.

"All this furniture," Polly said, making a sweeping gesture, "that's Louis Seize."

"Oh yeah," I answered, "Louie says what?" It was an old joke with us.

She slapped my arm and said, "Goddammit, you're still an ignorant thug with no culture."

Truth is, the first time I said it at one of her fancy west side places, I had no idea what she was talking about. It was years later that Marie Therese explained that "Louie says" was French "Louis Seize," for the sixteenth guy named Louis who was the king of France and had fancy furniture named after him. Go figure.

"Yeah," I said, "I'm an ignorant thug with no culture. No drink, either."

"Cynthia," she said, "a cognac for Mr. Quinn."

Cynthia got up and went to the taproom. She was Polly's main assistant who took over running the show when they got busy. Since she wasn't as pretty as some of the other girls who worked there, she wasn't as popular in the sack, but she came to Polly from the nightclub business, and everybody liked to talk to her.

Polly and I sat down in the mah-jongg room, and Cynthia brought me a brandy. She said, "Hello, Mr. Quinn, nice to see you again. Everyone has good things to say about your place. Are you going to continue after . . . ?"

"Looks like it, thanks."

After she left, Polly said it had been a long time since I'd been in. "I hear you're keeping company with a pretty barmaid."

I said it was true, and she said it was time I settled down, and I said it wasn't that serious.

She got a funny look in her eye and said that she'd heard different. We talked about this and that for a few more minutes. Then Polly stopped, and I could tell there was something else on her mind. After a second or so, she said, "Do you remember the woman I told you about, Kitty? I was living at her place when I met you?"

"Yeah," I said, "the one with the Mother and the Mother's gigolo."

"That's the one," she said and lowered her voice even though we were alone. "I saw in the papers that she was arrested on a narcotics charge, and then a songwriter who knew her back when I was staying in her apartment, he told me that when they booked her, she was living in Chinatown with a Chinaman, working the street. He said she'd wasted away until she didn't weigh more than fifty pounds, if you can believe it. Fifty pounds! Two weeks later, she was dead."

"No kidding?"

"I know what the hard stuff can do to people. Enough of my girls have gone through 'the cure,' but for her, of all the girls I've known, to die from it, that's hard to take. Such a goddamn waste. I'm not saying that she was destined to be a Broadway star or anything like that, but she was so young when she got here and she got a big break right away. Millions of pretty girls come here and never get close to that kind of thing. Anything could have happened for her. And then to wind up like she did. I don't know, I still can't say that it was completely her fault. Maybe she never had a chance."

I was sitting there not knowing what to say to that when Charlie walked down the hall and stopped when he saw us.

"Jimmy, what the hell are you doing here?" He strolled in and shook hands. Polly said she'd get him a drink and hurried away.

Charlie settled in the nicest chair in the room and fired up a cigarette. He wore a dark gray pinstripe, a bright silk tie, and polished black wingtips.

As I'd explained to Lansky, I told Charlie about the picture book, the movie, Detective Ellis, and the studio lawyers. He'd heard of *King Kong* so he knew what I was talking about. I didn't mention the two guys who'd braced me at the diner. I just said, "So they figure that these pictures will embarrass the studio and the studio will fork over six Gs to keep 'em under wraps. When I take a look at the book, I see that at least a couple of the pictures were taken here in the city, and I think the book looks like something your guys might be handling with the peepshows and magazines and slots. If it is your guys, I'll tell the lawyers to pay up."

Polly brought his drink and left. Charlie ignored it. In the years since we knocked off Maranzano, he'd taken over the rackets, but all he really did was to skim the cream and then divide up the rest of the pie and try to keep guys from horning in on other guys' territories. He didn't have anything to do with that "boss of bosses" stuff. As long as the dough was rolling in, it was easy to keep the guys in line. Lately, it hadn't been so easy, but as far as I knew, he still had control over the Forty-Second Street neighborhood.

He shook his head and said, "No, I haven't heard about anything like that, and if one of my guys tried to put the arm on a movie studio without telling me, I'd have his balls. But this book, you got it with you? Let me take a look."

He got out his glasses and studied it more carefully than Lansky but not as much as the lawyers did.

When he reached the end, the picture of the girl with her dress ripped open, he said, "I know this girl. She wasn't a blonde, but I'd never forget those tits."

"Did she work here?"

He shrugged. "Probably. Can't say I really remember. What do you care anyway?"

"I don't. As long as you and Meyer aren't part of it, it's just a job. Pick up a little pocket money for an evening's work."

He took off his glasses and stubbed out his smoke. "We could all use some of that."

After Charlie and his guys left, I tried to find Polly but she was tied up on the phone. Cynthia was in the taproom. I showed her the picture of the girl on the Empire State Building. That was the one that had the best view of her face. Cynthia recognized her right away.

"Sure," she said, "that's Nola. Wow, she never had a wig that nice while she was here."

"That's a wig?"

She gave me that look that women give and muttered, "Men . . . Yes, it's a wig."

"Who is she? Where can I find her?"

"Let's see, she left about a year ago, I think. Let me get her card."

Polly kept a three-by-five card file on all her girls. Filled up a drawer. She had a lot of staff turnover.

Cynthia came back with the card. She said, "Yes, she was Nola Revere when she was here, and that was from February to May last year. I remember her but not very well. She was quiet, I think. Pretty, you can see that. Didn't use drugs, not much for booze, either."

"Was she friendly with anybody in particular?"

"I think she and Daphne may have gone to the movies together once or twice."

Daphne? Last seen at the door to the stairs in the Grand Central Building. What did that mean?

"What's this about anyway?" Cynthia asked.

"I'm not sure," I said, and looked over her shoulder at the card.

I could see the name Nola Revere printed on the top. Most of the three-by-five card was filled with numbers—dates and amounts of money, I guessed, a record of Nola's earnings, loans from Polly, and the like.

I reached for the card. She pulled it back and said, "No, Jimmy. Only if Polly says it's okay."

I said I'd wait. Cynthia said Polly was probably going to be on the phone for some time, and another party was expected soon, a big one. It was about to get very busy.

I said thanks and left.

*　　*　　*

I caught a cab on Madison and told him to take me back to the speak. On the way, I thought about what Polly had said about Kitty. Shacked up in Chinatown and dead before she was thirty. That was a hell of a thing, and then the rest of her story came back, how Kitty came to be in New York in the first place. Polly told it to me on the night I mentioned, when we'd been drinking. It must have been around '25 or '26. We were in bed, in the little office she kept as her private room back at the Majestic.

She said that after she left Kitty and Kitty's Mother and Kitty's Mother's Gigolo, she didn't hear from them for almost a year as her business grew. Then, one afternoon, Kitty's Mother showed up at her place and said everything had gone to pieces. Kitty was completely hooked on the hard stuff and had moved in with her supplier. Then Kitty's Mother's Gigolo forged a check, cleaned out her bank account, and took a powder.

Polly said that was terrible. What could she do to help? Kitty's Mother then surprised the hell out of her by asking if she could come to work for Polly. She was old compared to most of Polly's crew, but she still had her looks, and she swore she was clean. So Polly had her doctor look her over, and Kitty's Mother moved in. When the supplier kicked Kitty out, her Mother and Polly got the girl a cheap room and gave her enough cash each week to manage her habit.

Kitty's Mother explained that this really was all her fault. Kitty's real father died in the Chicago suburb where they lived when Kitty was just a little kid. Straightaway, Kitty's Mother fell for a sharpie named Hull. She admitted that she was blindly jealous and possessive of the guy, but he seemed to be just as head over heels for her, so that was fine. And he was crazy about little Kitty to boot. Doted on her every day, tucked her in every night. Things were great until Kitty started to grow up. When she was twelve, she looked sixteen. One evening when the tucking took longer than usual, Kitty's Mother became suspicious, went upstairs, and caught Hull in bed with Kitty.

Enraged, Kitty's Mother decided that it had to be the girl's fault and kicked her out then and there. Kitty took her sixteen-year-old figure and twelve-year-old voice into Chicago and started singing in restaurants and clubs. Once she was on her feet, she tried to get back in touch with her Mother, but no. By then, Hull had hit the road and Kitty's Mother had found Husband Number Three. She still blamed her daughter for everything.

So Kitty headed for New York, landed her part in the Broadway revue, and decided to try to reach her Mother one more time. As it happened, Husband Number Three hadn't lasted very long. And when the new Gigolo said he'd love to see the Gay White Way, Kitty's Mother finally said yes, and they moved east.

It must have been about then, as I remember it, that I told Polly that was the craziest and most terrible story I'd ever heard. She rolled over and lay on top of me and whispered, "That's not the worst of it." You see, Kitty tried to clean up, and Polly paid for her to take the cure. She knew it wouldn't stick, but Kitty got well enough to ask Polly if she could come to work for her, just for a little while, until she could get back on her feet and back into show business.

Polly said she shouldn't have done it, but she agreed. Within a couple of weeks, word got out that she had a mother and daughter working together in her place, and they attracted a different kind of customer, guys who were willing to pay a lot more to see them in the sack together. It only lasted for a month or so until Kitty's Mother moved back to Chicago and Kitty went back to the street. But the night Polly told me the story, she said it was one of the few things she had done that really made her feel dirty.

Made me queasy, too, and I had reason to remember it later when my business with Miss Wray was working itself out.

CHAPTER SEVEN

When the taxi dropped me in front of the speak, I checked the parked cars. No Olds.

I knocked on the door. Fat Joe Beddoes unlocked it and snarled, "There's some fucking newspaper guy to see you."

By then, it must have been close to midnight. I saw that the crowd was on the thin side but lively. Democrats, no doubt, happy their man was about to take office.

Arch Malloy was working the tables. Connie was with Marie Therese behind the bar. She gave me a quick smile before she remembered that she was mad at me and frosted over. I still didn't know why. I hung up my coat and hat and stopped at the bar. Connie said, "Saxon Dunbar is waiting to see you, and one of those lawyers who was with Miss Wray has called four times. His number is on your desk. 'No matter the hour,' he wants you to call him."

"That's what he said, 'no matter the hour?'"

She nodded and I asked how business had been while I was

gone. She said good and asked if I'd found out anything about the pictures.

"Not what I was expecting. When I'm finished with this guy, come up to the office and I'll tell you all about it. And ask Vittorio to make me a sandwich. I'm starving. Something hot. Didya eat yet? No? Tell him to make two."

She answered with a sly look that was almost a smile and said, "Whatever you say, Jimmy."

Saxon Dunbar held out a hand and got up from his seat at my table in the back. As usual, it was covered with the day's newspapers, four or five of them. I bought a lot of the papers in those days. Customers brought in more, and everybody who worked in the place gave me the ones that were left lying around. By that time of night, my table was a mess. He had dug out his paper, the *Gotham Comet*, from the stack. Looked like he'd been reading his own column and marked it up with a fountain pen.

Dunbar was a tall, narrow-shouldered guy with a cheviot suit, tartan plaid bow tie, smudge of a mustache, and a British accent. His column was called "Dunbar's Rialto." It was gossip and news about Broadway, moving pictures, nightclubs, and speaks. He was about half as popular and powerful as Winchell in his heyday. All the guys who wrote that kind of stuff could cut deep when they wanted to, but it always seemed to me that Dunbar took more pleasure from it, saying that somebody or other was Red or lavender.

I recognized him from the caricature that ran over his column, and I saw him around here and there. Even though we knew a lot of the same mugs, he'd never given me the time of day, and that was the first time he'd ever been in my place. But then, he never wanted anything from me before.

He shook my hand and went into his pitch, "I've heard a lot about you. Glad to finally make it official. Nice little place you've got here. I must admit that I didn't completely believe it when I heard that you serve only the McCoy. How do you manage?"

Connie came over before I could answer. I asked for a short brandy and another of whatever the ink-stained wretch was drinking. Rum and ginger ale with a cherry, as it turned out. She brought the drinks, and he danced around for a few more minutes, talking about this and that. There had been a time just a few years before when I'd have been pleased as punch to have Dunbar in my place, hoping that he'd say something wonderful about it in his column. Then after the free publicity, I'd have to turn away dozens of famous folks every night and sell twice as much of the most expensive booze as I did. But things didn't work out that way.

Jimmy Quinn's was a neighborhood bar. The gang guys who had a taste for the good stuff came around, and the cops who could afford it had always found their way in, too. But the lime-light eluded us, and the place was popular enough without being so busy that we went crazy. Maybe I was lying to myself when I said that it didn't bother me, but I don't think so. I just didn't have the white-hot ambition that drove guys like Lansky. I made a living, and enough interesting things seemed to happen to keep me from getting bored. Yeah, I lacked a private library, but I'd get around to that by and by.

When he finally decided to get to his point, Dunbar cut his eyes back and forth, making sure nobody was listening in on him and lowered his voice. "I've been told that you are in possession of some extremely graphic and embarrassing photographs of a certain leading lady who's the toast of the town right now. Is there any truth to that?"

He smiled, looking like we were both in the know.

My first reaction was simply to lie and say that I didn't know what he was talking about. It figured that he'd been tipped by the two dimwits from the diner. On orders from their boss, the guy in the backseat of the big Olds. What were they trying to do? Just tighten the screws on the studio? Again, it figured that they didn't know what they were doing.

When I didn't answer, Dunbar got chummier. "Look, I understand you're caught in the middle on this business, and I don't have all the facts yet, but I smell a good story here and I'm willing to do whatever I have to do to get the scoop. I know she was here tonight. They were still talking about her at the bar when I came in. Fay Wray."

That, I could work with. "Sure, she was here. So?"

"How are you involved with the photographs?"

I decided to play dumb. "I don't know how to answer that. Exactly what are we talking about?"

"All right," he said, starting to get tired of my act. "Since you read the column, you know that I spend most of my evenings at Jack and Charlie's 21. I've got press agents and publicity men fighting with one another to get a mention for their clients. Tonight I got a call on the telephone they keep at my booth. It's not a published number. Only a few significant people have it. The man who called told me that he has seen nude photographs of Fay Wray, and not just nudes but pornographic nudes. She's trying to buy them back and you're the middleman."

He paused, and I could see that he was trying to judge my reaction. I tried not to give anything away, but I probably did.

He went on, "Given that sweet little face and disposition, it may be hard to believe, but this isn't the first time around the track for this little filly. Some 'artistic' photographs that she posed for when she first came to Hollywood came to the surface a couple of years ago. The studio swept them under the rug, but people knew. And that was before it became so unhappy for her at home. Yes, things are stormy at the Saunders household, and it's no surprise that she's fed up with him, the way he acts. Believe me, she's not doing anything that he hasn't done already. Sauce for the goose, you know."

I nodded and he continued, "The story I was told tonight is that she learned that her husband, John Saunders, had some fluff on the side. They're really a mismatched couple, you know. He's ten years older than she is, frightfully good looking, glib, smooth, worldly, knows exactly how to dress and talk. Rhodes scholar, Oxford, Magdalen College, veteran of the Great War. She's from some Hicksville in western Canada. She's had a few decent roles, but just barely. The little lady is damned lucky to have landed this one."

He paused and winked like we both understood what he meant.

"Then while she was working on the *Kong* picture, she decided that she needed a little jungle love and set her sights on one of the sambos who played the natives. They spent a lot of long nights on the set. She wasn't as discreet as she might have been, and someone on the crew got the pictures. I'm sure there's more to it than that, but for now it's all I have. The salient point here is that she's willing to do anything and pay anything to get them back."

Salient? I'd have to look that one up.

He stopped, gulped his rum, and fished the cherry. "Of course, anyone could say that. When I asked for proof, he said I should talk to you because you are going to handle the money. You'll be making the payoff to the blackmailers tomorrow."

I reminded myself that the best lies are almost true. "You're misinformed," I said. "Yeah, I met Miss Wray tonight. If you know anything about me, you know that I don't talk out of turn. Anything between her and me stays between her and me. I'll be speaking with her. Maybe tonight, tomorrow, I'm not sure. When I do, I'll tell her that you want to talk to her."

Trying to hide his eagerness, he turned his glass and coaster in a circle and spoke slowly. "Yes, do that. And though she doesn't need to be reminded of this, tell her that I'm going to follow through on this with or without her cooperation. I mean her no harm. Truly. I can be her friend, if she'll let me. I just want a good story."

"Okay," I said, "I'll pass the word along."

"And I can do the same for you. Be your friend. You may not think that you need it now because you seem to have cornered the market on good liquor in this part of town. A year from now, that won't be the case. Every other bar and nightspot on the street will have the same bottles that you've got."

Then I had to give him a look of my own. "You think I haven't figured that out a long time ago? Come on."

"I can help you stand out from the pack."

He stood up. "But that's not something we need to worry about at the moment. The lovely Miss Wray is our concern. Here's my number at 21." He produced a card and handed it to me. "If we handle this properly, it can be extremely profitable for all of us, Miss Wray foremost. I'll be in touch tomorrow, and if you learn anything, you really should let me know about it first."

After he left, I dug out the copy of the *Comet* he'd been reading. In his doodles, he'd turned his caricature into a devil with horns and a forked tongue.

Arch Malloy had moved behind the bar with Marie Therese. I went to the empty stool at the back corner, motioned him over, and asked if he'd noticed a couple of guys he probably hadn't seen before. "One of them's a kid—messy hair, bad complexion. The other one's older, horse faced, whispery voice. Had coffee stains on his shirt. They didn't order anything expensive."

"Ah, yes," he said, "those two. Nursed a couple of beers for an hour. Didn't tip." Arch had been with us for a few months then. He was an older gent, another mick, but he'd been in New York so long you hardly heard it in his voice. He was one of those guys who read everything he could get his mitts on, and he loved nothing better than to sit back and talk about this, that, and the other. I enjoyed his company, and I've got to admit that if we'd been left alone, not a damn thing would have been accomplished at the place. Arch would spend the whole day jabbering on and on. But he was a good worker, and he'd been spending most of his time going through our inventory in the cellar and doing whatever was needed upstairs in the evening.

"They didn't talk much," he said, smoothing his soup strainer with a knuckle. "The boy was antsy. The older gent chain-smoked. Can't tell you anything else about them."

"They got in. Fat Joe must know them, or they mentioned the right name. Ask him about it if you get a minute. I'll be in my office."

Up in the office, I went to my dictionary and looked up *salient*. Prominent or conspicuous. Good word, but I wasn't sure he'd really used it right.

Then I saw the notes that Connie had left from the RKO lawyer wanting me to call him back "no matter the hour." *To hell with that*, I said to myself. *I'm not going to talk to anybody until I've had something to eat.* That's when the phone rang.

I shouldn't have picked it up. The lawyer said, "Jules Bennett Grossner here. What do you have to report?"

"Grossner," I said. "You're the one with the regular glasses. Right." He was also the one who was so concerned with the long-distance charges to California.

He snorted at the mention of the other guy's specs. "Yes, Shreve and his pince-nez. Were you able to learn anything tonight? Are any of your . . . associates involved?"

How much to tell him? On her way out, Miss Wray's friend Hazel said to talk to her first. And I still thought that someone in the lawyers' office might be in on it, so I said, "No, none of the guys I work with know anything about it. And nobody's making payments to Tammany to handle this kind of stuff. You'll hear from them tomorrow, probably. The guys with the books. You gonna pay them?"

He didn't say anything, and I got the idea they were still trying to figure out how to weasel out of parting with any cash.

"Let me know when you decide," I said and hung up.

I was still worrying over everything when Connie bumped the door open with her hip and brought in a tray with two grilled cheese sandwiches and a couple of cups of coffee. She put the tray on the table by the divan, pointed to the sandwich closest to me, and said, "That one's got the extra mustard." We dug in.

Vittorio from the Cruzon Grill upstairs made a hell of a grilled cheese. He sliced the bread thick and browned it up just right. The sandwich had a French name and he objected the first time I asked for mustard on it but he came around.

Between bites, I told Connie that Lansky and Charlie had nothing to do with the pictures, and that the guys who were trying to shake down the studio had tailed me from the speak to Lansky's and I'd talked to them in a coffee shop.

"You've seen 'em," I said. "I had an idea they might try to needle me, so I described them to Malloy and he said they were here, a kid and an older guy. Nursed beers at the bar."

She sat straighter. "Those two! I knew there's something hinky with them. They were giving me and Marie Therese the eye the whole time they were here."

"They say anything? Try anything?"

"Of course not. Frenchy saw what they were and took over that end of the bar."

I asked what she made of them and she shrugged. "At first I thought they were just the usual lonely guys, but there was something more. I don't know, nasty, strange, something about them. A lot of guys come in and spend the whole time looking you over and undressing you with their eyes and pinching your butt, but those two, especially the older one, they were more serious. And I'm not just making this up now that you're telling me who they are. Marie Therese said the same thing. Ask her."

"I told Malloy to ask Fat Joe why he let 'em in. We'll get something."

She finished chewing and asked what was going on. "I don't get it. You say these guys have got dirty pictures of Miss Wray, but they're not Miss Wray. That doesn't make any sense."

"I know it doesn't, and what's even crazier is that the two hinky guys seem to think that the pictures really are of Miss

Wray. The kid doesn't know from Shinola, and the older guy isn't much smarter. My guess is they're doing what they're told, but, here, take a look for yourself." I held out the book. "I warn you, they're pretty racy."

She gave me another look, then took the book and went through it. I think that the last picture might have shocked her a little, but except for a faint blush, she hardly let it show. She was smiling when she handed the book back and said, "It's a very good wig, and she does have a nice figure."

"Not as good as yours." She gave me another look. "Well, it's not."

"Don't try to sweet-talk me," she said, half smiling.

"I'm not. I'm trying to figure out why you're mad at me." And, boy, was that the wrong thing to say.

The half smile vanished and she said, "Just stop, you're only making it worse. I've got to get back to work." She left without saying anything else.

I finished my sandwich, went over to the desk, and found the number of the Pierre Hotel in the telephone book. I called and asked for Ruth Rose, the name Miss Wray was registered under. The hotel operator told me that the line was in use. I told her to send a message to the room that Jimmy Quinn was on the way.

Before I left, I opened the safe and stowed the dirty book. Since so many people seemed to be interested in it, I decided it should stay there. While the safe was open, I took out the Banker's Special. It was a Colt .38 with a two-inch barrel, a nice little piece. I checked to make sure there was an empty chamber under the hammer and slipped it into my coat pocket. You hardly noticed the bulge in a properly constructed suit like mine.

The Thursday night crowd was still happy, noisy, and thirsty. As I was putting on my topcoat and hat, Fat Joe hauled his big lazy ass out of his chair by the door.

"Malloy says you want to know about those two fucking guys that was here tonight."

"Right."

"They was fucking cops. Well, one of 'em used to be, anyway."

"You know them?"

"Yeah, but not for a long fucking time. The one guy used to come in when Carl owned the place, before you jacked up the fucking prices sos a regular workin' guy can't even afford to come here no more."

"This cop, he got a name?"

"Sleepyhead Trodache. Worked the fucking Vice Squad with Chile Acuna."

"Acuna? Did he get shitcanned when that bastard got it?"

"That was a fucking setup. Those whores had it in for him."

"My ass. They didn't call him 'Chile Acuna, the human spittoona' for nothing."

That seemed to offend Fat Joe, and he started sputtering more about the raw fucking deal those guys got until I told him to shut up.

"Look, I don't care what happened or if he came here when Carl owned the place. I own it now, and he doesn't get in. That's it. Right?"

Fat Joe grumbled and cursed and said something that sounded like he agreed. I went out to the corner and caught a cab to the Pierre. Again, I told the cabbie to keep an eye out for a tail. He didn't see anything and neither did I. There was no sign of the Olds. Not then.

CHAPTER EIGHT

Riding uptown, I worried over what Fat Joe said.

When he testified a few years before, Chile Acuna was the guy who put the Seabury Commission on the front pages of all the papers. You see, Chile was the main stoolie who set up the innocent landladies and nurses to be framed as hookers and railroaded through the Magistrate's Court. Got his start working as a translator for the cops in the Spanish neighborhoods. When he became a stoolpigeon, he'd go to a rooming house, say, and tell the woman who ran it that he was looking for a place to stay. Once they were in a room alone, he'd signal the vice cops outside. They'd bust in. He'd show them some money and say the woman had "exposed her person" to him. Sometimes the cops would beat up Chile a little to scare the woman. Once they had her in Magistrate's Court, they'd milk her dry, just like they did with the real whores.

When Chile sang like a crooner to the commission, he fingered about forty or fifty cops that he'd worked with. And the funny thing is that he only ratted on them because the cops double-crossed him and kicked him out of their racket. I didn't recall seeing the name Sleepyhead Trodache in the papers, so it was likely that he resigned before Chile appeared in court. He wasn't the only one. A lot of vice cops quit before they were fired or brought up on charges.

At the front desk of the Pierre, I told them I was there to see Miss Wray. They didn't believe me and they were pretty damn snotty about it until she told them to send me right up. Then they offered to have a bellboy escort me. I didn't need that, but on the way to the elevators, I had a thought and stopped by the concierge's desk. You see, the Pierre is a classy operation. They'd never let a couple of stumblebums like Trodache and the kid in the front door. I couldn't see them walking in and handing over a package that got to Miss Wray. But maybe somebody remembered something about whoever did bring it.

The concierge was a chunky-looking number who sized me up right away as somebody who wasn't important. When I told him I was working with Miss Wray, his opinion of me went up but not much. All the time I was talking to him, he was busy with other things.

"She got a small package about this big," I said, showing him with my hands. "Thick, brown paper wrapping."

"Miss Rose has been receiving a great number of items." He didn't even look up.

"Maybe you or somebody else will remember this one. It came in this morning. If you can tell me anything about who brought it, I know she'll appreciate it."

He nodded and that was that. I was dismissed.

The first thing I noticed about the place was all the damn flowers. Hell, you couldn't miss them. There were big bouquets on every flat surface, and the smell was enough to knock you over. Miss Wray still looked worried and wound up. She was still wearing the same outfit, too, and she kept sitting down and getting up and pacing and sitting down again as we talked. Her suite was about eight floors up on the corner overlooking the park to the west and south. Her view was probably about as good as Meyer Lansky's, but she was on the other side.

There was a moderately well-stocked bar, but it looked like she was sticking with the champagne. She offered me a glass, but I said no, hoping she'd try to ply me with something stronger. She didn't, dammit. She said Hazel was on the phone to her sweetie in California and asked what I had learned.

I took off my hat and coat and settled in an armchair. The card on the tub of roses on the table next to me said they'd come from her dearest friend Gary Cooper. She paced to the ice bucket, poured a thimble drop into her glass, and perched on the edge of the sofa close to me.

"I've been asking around," I said, "and I found out a few things."

She leaned forward, eyes wide, staring at me with an intensity I wasn't used to seeing in beautiful women, and said, "Tell me everything."

Without going into needless detail, I said that none of the guys I knew were in on this deal. "I don't know if the name Charlie Luciano means anything to you. . . ." She shook her head. "He's the biggest bootlegger in town and he takes a slice of just about any other sort of illegal activity that folks like to indulge in. He doesn't know anything about the book, and none of the guys who work for him do either."

"Is that good?"

"Not really. If we were dealing with Charlie's guys, we could probably be sure that they would take the money and turn over the rest of the books. Probably." Sure, they'd keep a few, but I didn't tell her that. Instead, I got to the important parts and told her that I'd been braced by a couple of guys who said they had the books and knew enough details that I believed them.

That's when she interrupted, "But how did they find you so quickly?"

"I wondered the same thing myself and I can see two possibilities. First, after they sent you the book and the demand for the money, they watched the hotel, and when they saw you leave, they followed you to my place. Knowing who I am, they figured I was going to be the moneyman, and so they followed me when I went out. Or somebody inside the lawyers' office or one of the studio executives is in on the deal and tipped them off. You know more about the studio than I do. What do you think?"

Looking more worried, she sank back into the sofa. "I really don't know any of these people"—she paused—"but, you know, I've been thinking that whoever took those pictures must have seen our sets and costumes, and I don't know how that could have happened because the production was kept about as secret as it could be. They didn't want anyone to know anything about it. This isn't like any other picture I've ever done. The cast did most of our work years ago. I've made two more pictures since then. Or is it three? Golly, I'm not sure. It took that long to work out all of those effects and they were afraid word would get out and somebody else would get their big creatures on the screen before we did."

"But somebody could have seen the photographs and drawings."

"I suppose so, if someone on the crew let them in."

But that wasn't what she was really worried about, so I told her that I might know who the two guys were. "Looks like it's a guy named Trodache, an ex-vice cop who has some experience with this kind of thing. I'm not sure that's really who he is, but we'll work that out by and by. The funny thing is that when he and his partner, a younger guy, were talking to me, they sounded like they believed that it really was *you* in the pictures. What I'm saying is, they don't know what they've got, and if they don't know that, there's probably a lot more they don't know. And there's a third guy involved, too. Didn't get a good look at him, but let's figure he's the brains. Any of that mean anything to you?"

She shook her head. I swear, the whole time I'd been there, she didn't blink.

"Anyway," I said, "the guy said they'd be in touch tomorrow about the money. Did the lawyers say anything more to you about whether they're going to pay?"

"No."

"One of the lawyers called me tonight wanting to know what I learned. I asked him what they were going to do. He didn't answer."

She stood and paced behind the sofa. "They'll pay or I'll have their jobs. What did you tell him?"

"Not as much as I'm telling you. Just that it's not one of my known associates, as the papers might put it."

She sat back down. "Oh, dear, this is not going well."

"No," I said, "and there's something you'll like even less."

Tired of waiting, I went over to the bar, found a glass, and poured myself a tot of the studio's brandy. It wasn't as good as mine. I sat back down and said to her, "Do you know Saxon Dunbar?"

Her face went white and her voice was strained. "No, don't tell me that he knows. If he sees those pictures, it's all over." She got up and started walking again.

"It's not that bad. He hasn't seen anything. He was waiting at my place when I got back. Somebody, and it's got to be the guys who braced me, called him and told him about the book and that I have a copy. Like I said, these guys don't really know what they're doing. You ask me, all they want is the money and they're afraid the studio won't pay. That's why they're trying to put more pressure on me. And it sounds like they fed Dunbar the same line about the pictures being you. And, I've gotta say, that's where I get lost in all this. I mean, anybody can see that it's not you, so why do you care anyway?"

She kept walking. "You don't understand. It's my husband. He's . . . He can be extremely jealous. And something like this, well, we've got to be sure that John doesn't find out, that's all there is to it."

"Okay," I said. "Would it make any difference if you knew who the girl in the pictures is?"

That stopped her. "It could change everything. Do you know her?"

"I've got a name, not a real name, of a girl who used to work for Polly Adler. Luciano, the guy I told you about, I showed him the book and he thinks he knows her."

She sat back down, chewed on a thumb knuckle, thought for a moment, and said, "This is astonishing. Hazel! Come here, listen to this."

I heard the sound of a handset hanging up in another room and Hazel came trotting in. "What is it?" She sounded worried.

Miss Wray said, "We may finally have some good news. Mr. Quinn thinks that he knows the woman in the photographs." She turned to me. "Can you bring her here?"

"No, all I've got is the name she used when she worked at Polly Adler's. She left there some time ago, I don't know exactly when or why. I might be able to find out, but I'll need to spread some cash around to get answers."

She asked how much. I said a hundred in ones, fives, and tens ought to do it. She told Hazel to call the concierge and have it sent up.

Now, I've got to admit that impressed me. I knew some guys who could lay their hands on large amounts of cash on short notice, but I'd never been around anybody who could just say "bring me money," like she was asking for a glass of water, and it happened. I guess if I'd thought about it, I'd have realized that RKO was probably going to take it out of her next paycheck, but I didn't think about that. Hazel made the call downstairs. I drank the acceptable brandy and tried to act like this kind of thing happened to me every day.

Miss Wray laid a warm hand on my knee. "What will you do now?"

I checked my watch. It was two in the morning. Things would be warming up down at Fifty-Fifth and Madison. "I'll go back to Polly's and see what else they can tell me. If I learn anything, I'll call in the morning."

"No, please, you must learn all that you can and then come straight back here to tell us."

"All right, if it's that important."

There was a soft tap on the door. Hazel hurried to answer it. A bellboy handed her an envelope. For a moment, she was unsure about what to do, but she opened it and gave him a buck.

After he left, she handed me the envelope and said, "Is ninety-nine dollars all right? I think I've got some money in my bag."

I told her it was fine and got ready to leave.

"One more thing," I said to Miss Wray, as I put on my topcoat. "Earlier tonight in my place, you said that I wasn't what you expected."

She nodded, still not giving anything away.

"What did you mean? It's flattering as hell to think that Jimmy Quinn's is so famous that Hollywood movie stars talk about it, but I'm not buying that. Why would you expect me to be anything?"

She drew out the moment longer than she needed to, then said, "You know my husband. Good night, Mr. Quinn."

I had no idea what she was talking about.

Out in the hall, the bellboy who brought the cash was waiting for me. He was about fifteen years old by the look of him, and not much taller than me.

"Excuse me, sir," he said. "I, ah, heard you talking to Mr. Phillip downstairs about a package for Miss Wray."

"Yeah?"

"I didn't handle it myself, you understand, but I could ask around, you know, check with some of the guys who work days. I mean, if you was interested in flowers and telegrams, nobody could help you, but we didn't deliver many packages."

I said okay and gave him another dollar, then made it two. Spread the wealth. "Yeah, ask around. I'm Jimmy Quinn. I'll probably be back tomorrow night. You learn anything before then, leave a message in Miss Wray's room."

CHAPTER NINE

The same gray-haired colored man was working the elevator when I came in. He cut his eyes at me as he called upstairs. I guess he didn't see many guys visiting twice in one night.

He hung up the house phone, still giving me the eye, and said, "This way, sir."

I winked at him and said, "They can't get enough of me." He didn't think it was funny.

The place was a lot busier than it had been a few hours before. Polly was haggling over payment with a guy who was with a group of visiting firemen. They'd set up a phonograph in the mah-jongg room where three guys were dancing with a couple of girls. A projector was running in the dark library, and some of the others were watching a stag movie and yelling and stomping, making idiots of themselves. I got a drink and found Cynthia in Polly's office.

I sat at the chair opposite the desk. She fitted a thick stack of bills into a cashbox, put it into a bottom drawer, and locked it. I counted eight cards on the desktop, one for each girl who was working, and two that were turned up on edge in the card file for the ones that were available. I knew Polly's system. Usually when they got busy, nobody bothered with the cards, but whenever Cynthia was in charge, she kept all the girls and their times straight.

Her smile was forced, but she made it look real. She said, "I certainly hope you're here for the right reason, but I'll bet you still want to know about Nola. Well, the answer's the same as it was before. I can't tell you anything unless I get the word from Polly, and she's probably going to be tied up for some time. These firemen . . . Jeez."

"Now, Cynthia," I said, sounding reasonable as I slipped a sawbuck under her hand, "you know that Pearl, I mean Polly, and I are old friends, and I'd never ask you to do anything she wouldn't like, right? Just tell me what you can about this girl, what was her name? Nola Revere."

She tucked the bill into her bra without missing a beat. "Well, I suppose there's no harm . . ."

As Cynthia put it, nobody knew Nola's real name or expected to. Judging by her accent, they thought she might be Polack. She said she'd worked in some dancehalls and she was so popular she decided she could do better. That led her to Minsky's burlesque, but she didn't like it there and a friend told her that Polly Adler's place was the best in town. She certainly had the figure. Her face was all right, but it was the figure that did it. As Charlie said, nobody forgot those tits. She started filling in on weekends. When one of the regulars left, she moved in and lived there from February to May.

"Why'd she leave?" I asked.

Cynthia shrugged. "Who knows? She waited until an afternoon when most of us were out, and then she packed up her clothes and left. The maid who was here said Nola told her to call a cab and left with her suitcases. All she left here were a few cosmetics."

"Is it unusual for a girl to take off like that?"

"No, happens all the time. We have a lot of turnover."

"Yeah, I know," I said. "Hard to keep good help." That made me think about Connie again, and I worried over whatever was making her so moody. What the hell was eating her?

"You said Nola hung around with Daphne. Where is she, anyway? I haven't seen her around." After that afternoon in the Grand Central Building, the last time I saw Daphne was in Charlie's place at the Waldorf Terrace a year or so ago.

"She left, too."

"Took off like the other girl?"

Cynthia shook her head. "She got out of the business, and it was good that she did. She and Polly had been on the outs. Daphne was the most popular girl here. She wanted more and Polly wouldn't give it to her. Don't tell Polly I said that. Anyhow, Daphne met a rich guy and he set her up in her own place."

"No kidding," I said. "I wonder if she could tell me anything about Nola."

Cynthia started to say something but stopped and shook her head. "No, Daphne was as surprised as the rest of us when she left."

I could tell she was holding out on me and she was worried at the same time. Well, why not? Most of the cops and thugs who came into the place thought that their position and their money gave them the right to do whatever they wanted to the girls, Polly and Cynthia included. They didn't talk about it, but I knew they'd been roughed up and the place had been tossed more than once.

Hell, it was the same for me, only not as bad. After all, in the eyes of the law, we were both trading in something that was illegal—booze and cooze. I had it easier since I didn't really have to hide what I did. If anybody complained to the local precinct cops that there was an establishment selling alcohol a couple of blocks off Broadway, they'd be laughed out of the place. For Cynthia and Polly, it was different. Somebody made enough noise about whores—even in a place as nice as Polly's—the cops would have to do something. And if some of Dutch Schultz's boys got carried away and knocked a girl around, Polly couldn't go to the cops.

Cynthia knew that if I decided to be a hard-ass, there was nothing to do about it.

I thought Miss Wray's money would be more persuasive and slipped her another ten. It smoothly joined the first ten-spot in her bra.

"Look," I said. "I don't want to queer her deal. I like Daphne, you know that. I just need to talk to her a little, that's all. Hell, if she can help me, I'll make it worth her while. Even with this rich guy, I bet she could use a little folding money. What do you say?"

It turned out that Cynthia and Daphne had been pretty close pals, too. Polly and all the girls had been happy for Daphne when she told them that one of her regulars, a Wall Street banker no less, wanted a "more exclusive relationship." They congratulated her and gave her a nice send-off. Daphne called Cynthia a few weeks later and said they should meet down in the Village for lunch, and that's what they did.

Cynthia said, "She's got a really cute little place. Hot water, her own bathroom and telephone, the works."

I asked for the address and number. As she was writing them down, a worried look crossed her face and she said, "You got to promise me you're not going to make trouble for her. Daphne's a sweet kid. It was good for her to find this fellow. I'd hate it if you messed it up for her."

"I'm only interested in the other girl, and I don't even know if it's that important I find her. This sure is a screwy business that I've got myself into."

I didn't know how right I was.

Back out on Madison, I hailed a cab and told him to take me to my speak and to wait for me when we got there. I still couldn't quit thinking about Connie. If you'd asked me why, I probably couldn't have told you. Whatever the reason, I thought it would be good if she came with me to see Miss Wray again. If we weren't too busy. Or maybe I was just hoping that we'd finish the business and tell Miss Wray that, yes, we knew who the other girl was, and Saxon Dunbar wasn't going to screw her over, and Miss Wray would say that was great, and Connie and I would leave after ten minutes and spend more of Miss Wray's money on another cab back down to the Chelsea where Connie would invite me up to her room. Fat chance.

It was probably about quarter after three Friday morning when we got to the speak. The cabbie double-parked. I gave him a buck and he was happy to wait while I went inside and found that the damn Democrats were still whooping it up. Connie and Frenchy were busy behind the bar. Marie Therese was taking care of the tables. They needed help. I handed Fat Joe Beddoes another dollar and told him to give it to the cabbie and tell him I wouldn't be needing him. Then I headed upstairs to my office.

I called the Pierre, asked for Miss Wray's room, and Hazel answered.

I told her that I didn't have anything more, but tomorrow I'd talk to a friend of the girl in the picture book. Maybe tomorrow, I couldn't be sure.

"Fay would still like you to come over," she said, sounding pissed, like people didn't say no to Fay very often.

"I don't have time to talk," I said. " See you tomorrow. Maybe."

I shed my coat, rolled up my sleeves, and went to the basement where I helped Arch Malloy load a fresh keg into the dumbwaiter and send it to the bar. Then while Frenchy moved it into place, I stacked three trays of dirty glasses into the dumbwaiter and sent them upstairs to the kitchen of the Cruzon Grill. I ran the glasses through the washer and dryer and gave them a quick once-over with a clean towel before I loaded them back into the dumbwaiter and down to the bar.

Back in the basement, Arch and I stacked the night's empties, and he took boxes of cigars and the special ten-cigarette packs of Camels we sold upstairs.

It was sometime after four when we kicked out the last of the happy Democrats and started cleaning up. I took the night's cash up to my office. I made a quick count and was glad to see that it had been a very good night. Connie would do the real count for the books, but she usually didn't get to that until the next morning, so I locked up the cash in the safe with the dirty picture book. I considered taking the book with me to the Chelsea because I might want to show it to Daphne, if I could see Daphne tomorrow. But, no, too many people wanted to get their hands on that book. Better to keep it locked up. I went back downstairs and we finished cleaning up.

It must have been around five when Connie and I put on our coats and hats. She turned toward the front door, where we usually went out when we closed, but I locked it from the inside and said, "Let's use the back tonight. And, here, take this." I handed her the little Spanish .25 automatic I'd just borrowed from Marie Therese.

Looking surprised and concerned, she put it in her bag and asked what was going on.

We went to the back stairs and I said, "I don't know what's going on. Nothing about this business feels kosher to me. I mean, for openers, any fool can see that it's not Miss Wray in the pictures, so why would anybody threaten her with them? And why is she worried about them? She says her husband will be pissed off anyway, and that doesn't make any sense either."

"Sure it does," Connie snapped back at me. "Some guys will use any excuse to get a girl under their thumb. Blame her for things that aren't her fault, tell her she doesn't look like he wants her to, you know what I mean."

"Yeah, I guess you're right." We saw it often enough with our customers, swells and mugs, it didn't matter.

We went out the back door. I locked it and unlocked the back gate that opened on the alley behind the place. I made sure it was locked tight before we walked down to Broadway. I wanted to take her arm, but I wasn't going to let go of the Banker's Special in my topcoat pocket.

"And then there's the two idiots who braced me outside Lansky's place. They don't know what the fuck they're doing, pardon my French. But if Fat Joe's right and the old guy used to be a vice cop, then we've got to be careful."

She nodded. "Yes, I've heard about them."

"I don't know that they'll try anything, but they followed Miss Wray to our place and then they got in, so they know who you are. I told Fat Joe not to let 'em in again, but it looks to me like they're so damn stupid you can't tell what they're going to do. Makes them dangerous. So maybe I'm nuts to give you Marie Therese's piece, but maybe I'm not."

Connie forgot she was mad at me and put her arm through mine as we walked down Broadway and then turned toward the Chelsea. There was no sign of the Olds or the idiots.

"What are you going to do now?" she asked.

I explained that when I'd told her earlier that I was going to Polly's, I was trying to find Charlie Luciano to see if his guys had anything to do with the book and the shakedown. Nobody he knew had anything to do with it, but he knew the girl in the book. She used to work for Polly. Hearing that, Connie perked right up and asked why I hadn't told her.

"Things are happening too fast. Seemed more important to pay attention to Saxon Dunbar and the guys who are asking for the money the last time we talked." Then I explained to her that I met Pearl, now known as Polly, back when I was a kid. I didn't go into all the whys and wherefores.

"Tonight," I said, "this girl named Cynthia was filling in for Polly and she told me about Nola, the girl in the pictures. She flew the coop about a year ago, but there's this other girl, Daphne, who used to work for Polly, too, and she was a friend of Nola's."

Connie said, "That's too many names to keep straight if you don't know them."

"Not much easier if you do. Think of 'em as Polly the madam, Cynthia her assistant, Daphne the mistress, and Nola with the tits."

"You're such a silver-tongued devil."

"Anyway, tonight I learn that Daphne is out of the life. She found a sugar daddy who set her up in a place, and she might know more about Nola, so I'm going to talk to her. After that, if the lawyers decide to pay up, I guess I'll be delivering six grand for them tomorrow evening."

The lobby of the Chelsea was empty, like it usually was when we came in from work. Tommy, the night man, was snoring behind the desk. The elevator operator was asleep on his little folding seat. I gave him a tap on the shoulder, like I did most mornings. He rubbed his eyes and said, "Hello, Connie. How you doing?"

"Good, Nelson. You? How's Phyllis?"

They yakked away all the way up to the fifth floor. Phyllis was either his wife, daughter, or girlfriend. I couldn't tell, but it was somebody they'd talked about before, talked about a lot from the sound of it.

I waited by the door to her room as Connie went through her bag for her key. Some nights I was invited in. I suspected this wasn't going to be one of them. But after she'd opened the door and checked to see that there was nobody in the room and nobody else in the hall, she threw her arms around my neck and gave me a long hard kiss that would melt stainless steel.

She rubbed her thighs against mine, and after she felt the reaction she was looking for, she leaned back and smiled.

I said, "Does this mean you're not mad at me anymore?"

She pulled herself closer so she could whisper, "Hell, no, I just want you to know what you're missing," and she kissed me again.

"Goddammit, what is going on. I don't—"

She cut me off with another purring smile, and she touched my lips with a gloved finger. "Don't worry, you'll figure it out," she said.

She could be the most exasperating woman when she wanted to be.

CHAPTER TEN

On Friday I was up before noon.

Based on what Cynthia said, I figured I had a fair chance of seeing Daphne, so I strapped on my brace and took out one of the better suits. It was a new single-breasted from Brooks Brothers, dark gray, almost black, finished off with a crisp white pin-striped shirt and a burgundy grenadine tie. When you're my size, you don't dress sharp, you look like a damn kid. It was cloudy and looked to be cold but warmer than yesterday, so I went with the lighter-weight camel-hair topcoat, the one with large inside pockets. I packed up Miss Wray's cash, the Banker's Special, my notepad and pen, found my stick and hat, and set off.

I picked up a few of the morning papers and decided to skip the hash house on the corner where I usually got breakfast. Instead, I went back to the speak. Some of Vittorio's guys would be in the Cruzon kitchen early. They fixed really good strong coffee, and they didn't mind whipping up something for me from time to time. Turned out to be a nice-size omelet and fried pota-toes and spinach on the side. Hit the spot.

While I was eating, I read Freddie Hall's review of *King Kong* in the *Times*. Miss Wray had been wrong when she said he'd hate it. Hell, I was sitting right next to him in the theater. I knew he liked it as much as I did. I thought he gave away too much of the story, but it's hard not to do that when you're enthusiastic.

After I finished, I took the tray back upstairs, got more cof-fee, and settled behind my desk. I put off making any decisions about what I was going to do until I got through the rest of the papers. The truth is I didn't know what I wanted to ask Daphne or what she could tell me, but I promised Miss Wray that I'd see this through, so I picked up the phone and dialed the number Cynthia gave me.

Daphne picked up before the first ring had ended, like she'd had her hand hovering over the phone. She said, "Okay, I'm ready."

I recognized her voice, but she surprised me by picking up so quick and I didn't answer right away.

She said, "Harold, what's wrong? I'm ready to write it down this time. Go ahead."

"Daphne? This is Jimmy Quinn."

"Jimmy? What are you . . . How did you . . . Oh, fuck, not now. Look, I can't talk," and she hung up.

I had no idea what any of that meant. She sounded surprised and pissed off, but at least I knew she was there. So I decided on the approach I'd been considering and went down to the cellar for an expensive bottle of Chablis.

Connie was sitting behind the desk when I got back. The safe was open, and she was counting last night's take. She cut her eyes at the wine and gave me a curious look but didn't stop her work. I didn't interrupt.

When she finished, I held up the wine and said, "How much do we get for this? Twelve fifty, isn't it?"

She said yes and I peeled thirteen bucks off Miss Wray's money and told her to add it to last night's total.

Connie's eyebrows arched. "What's up?"

I put on my topcoat and slipped the wine into the inside pocket. "I'm going to tell Daphne, whose last name I don't know, that Miss Wray, star of stage and the silver screen, would like to know anything she can tell me about one Nola Revere, late of Polly Adler's establishment. The wine is for Daphne. If she's got anything to say that's useful, we'll settle on a price. I got a hundred from Miss Wray last night."

"What do you mean you 'got a hundred'?"

"When I told her I knew who the girl in the pictures was, I said I'd probably have to spend some money to learn more. She told Hazel to call down to the concierge for a hundred bucks. Ten minutes later, it was there."

"Are you making that up?"

"I swear to you that I'm not. They live in a different world than we do."

Connie whistled low. "Ain't it the truth."

I was almost out the door when she stopped me, saying, "You know, it might be a good idea not to mention Miss Wray right up front. Isn't she more interested in keeping her name out of this business than anything else? You might need to drop her name to impress this Daphne, but don't use it unless you have to."

It was my turn to give her a look, and she could tell that I was impressed. *Damn*, I thought and not for the first time, *she's smart, stacked, and pretty, that's a dangerous combination.*

Out on the street, I took time to check for the Olds and the idiots. Nothing. I got a cab down to Christopher Street and walked a block to Gay, a crooked little street, not much wider than an alley. You find them tucked away down there in the Village. Daphne's address was a narrow place with a fire escape over the bright red door and a tree growing up against the front. A paper tag on the doorframe read D. PREWITT

I twisted the bell in the middle of the door. A few seconds

later I heard footsteps and then a voice behind the door. "Harold?"

"No. Jimmy Quinn. Again."

She said something I couldn't make out.

I said, "Daphne, if you'll just let me in and talk to me for a few minutes, it could mean a nice piece of change for you. That's all I want, a little talk, and I'm ready to pay for it. I've got a five-spot in my hand."

The bolt snapped back.

I guess I should explain that when Daphne was working at Pearl's place, I mean Polly's place, she was out of my league. Charlie Luciano liked her a lot for a few months, and during that time, Charlie "the Bug" Workman was working as Charlie Lucky's driver. He was sent to pick Daphne up every day or so, and as I understood it, he decided to cut himself in on her action, too. The Bug was a dangerous man. You didn't say no to him and Daphne knew that.

She was one of the best-looking girls who ever worked for Polly. The first thing you noticed about her was her shining blond hair, a lot of it even though most of the girls wore their hair bobbed. She also had a big inviting smile and a fizzy laugh to go with it. The rest of her wasn't bad, either.

Daphne wasn't smiling that afternoon when she opened the door. Her worried look made me think that maybe the sweet deal she had with her sugar daddy wasn't working out so well. She looked at the fiver in my hand, cut her eyes up and down the street, and pulled me inside fast. The place was low ceilinged and small, not much wider than the front door and the double window beside it. The furniture was covered in chintz and plaid. In the front room, she had a fireplace, a nice radio and record player, and a telephone on a round wooden table. I could see the kitchen in back and stairs to the bedroom upstairs.

She was wearing a nice prim-looking suit and blouse, even more businesslike than the outfit she had on when I saw her in the Grand Central Building. Her shoes were businesslike too, and she had her hair pulled back. A pair of thick-rimmed specs and a copy of the Friday *Gotham Comet* were on the coffee table in front of the love seat. If I saw her on the street in those clothes and glasses, I probably wouldn't recognize her.

Her worried expression hadn't changed. "What the hell is this?" she asked.

I gave her the five, took the wine out of my coat pocket, and said, "Here, this is for you, just to prove that this is a friendly visit. I'm on the up-and-up."

She looked at the label and was impressed. Since it was me giving it to her, she knew it wasn't some kind of camel piss in a phony bottle. "Okay," she said, "I'm listening."

A calico cat ambled down the stairs, clawed its way to the top of the loveseat, and stared at me. It was not impressed. I took off my topcoat and sat in a chintz armchair. "What can you tell me about Nola Revere?"

Her mouth sagged open in surprise, and she dropped onto the loveseat. The cat jumped down beside her. "Nola? What kind of trouble has she gotten herself into?"

"Nothing. Maybe. She posed for some dirty pictures, and some people are interested in them. They asked me to help. I understand you and her were friendly at Pearl's, I mean Polly's."

"Dirty pictures, yeah, that's how she got into the business. She was just a dumb kid then. Guys could sweet-talk her into anything. I tried to help her wise up, but with some girls, there's nothing you can do."

Daphne repeated what Cynthia said the night before. Nola was a Polack. Her real name was Nadzeija but nobody could pronounce it, so she started calling herself Nola. Hadn't been in the country very long, and when Daphne met her, she spoke hardly any English. But she didn't need to talk at the Times Square dancehall where she first worked. And she hated it. The pay wasn't good, and she was on her feet all night. She picked up extra money finishing guys off by hand in the back room. A lot of them wanted more than that. Another girl from Poland told her they could do better as strippers, so they bought some costumes and got on at Minsky's, but before long, it was the same story. The early show was the standard coochie dance on the main stage, but to make real money, they had to work the late show downstairs in the basement where things went further. A lot further.

A guy she met there talked her and the other girl into posing for a set of pictures fooling around with each other. Nola told Daphne that he paid them twenty bucks up front and promised them another twenty after he saw how the pictures turned out. He wasn't sure they'd be any good because the girls laughed and giggled too much, but he still wanted Nola to come back by herself. But that was the last they ever saw of him.

I asked if Daphne knew who the guy was, and she said no, Nola didn't tell her and that kind of thing happened all the time. It didn't sound like those pictures had anything to do with the book, anyway.

After that, Nola took her ten dollars and bought a nice dress and went to see Polly. Polly could tell right away that Nola would be popular, but her girls were the best. There was more to working at her place than a girl washing a guy's works, unzipping a shift, and spreading her legs. Polly's best girls, like Daphne, could accompany gents to upper-crust functions and look and sound like they belonged there. So Polly asked Daphne to give the new kid a little polish, not that all the guys cared. You see, Daphne could tell that Nola wasn't that sharp. It showed on her face, and that helpless little girl routine, real or faked, really hit the spot with a lot of customers. Nola never got to be as confident and collected as Daphne and Cynthia—damn few of Polly's girls were—but she did fine for herself.

She and Daphne shared a bedroom when she moved to Polly's full-time and they got along fine. Nola loved the moving pictures and so they went to all the new ones. That's where she picked up a lot of her English from the talkies, but she was never comfortable with it. The main problem she had was the same one that all the girls had. During the day she was lonely. They couldn't go to the pictures all the time, and there were a lot of afternoons when Nola would talk about how homesick she was. Her family was somewhere in Pennsylvania. They wanted nothing to do with her, and she didn't like them, either. No, she wanted to move someplace where it was warm, and she was better than most of the girls at saving money. All of them said they were only in the life until they saved enough to open a dress shop or move to a small town or got their break in show business—that sort of thing. But none of them did it. Instead, they blew their cash on clothes or cosmetics or jewelry. Or cocaine, if they could hide it from Polly and Cynthia.

"So is that what happened?" I asked. "Did she save up enough to leave?"

Daphne settled back and scratched the cat's neck. By then, she was comfortable talking to me. "It would be nice to think so, but I don't see it. I wasn't there when she left. I was out of town for a couple of days. She hadn't said anything about leaving, so I thought maybe she got lonelier than usual, but the other girls said she went out with them. Nothing happened with any of the johns, and she wasn't the type to keep quiet if somebody got out of hand."

"Could she have got knocked up?"

"She didn't say anything to me and she would have, and besides, Polly takes care of that. Look, that's it, that's all I know about Nola. Girls walk away all the time. It's not that mysterious. There was this one kid, a nice-looking Polack guy that was stuck on her. He met her at this restaurant where she went sometimes to get some home cooking. She took me there once. I don't think he knew what she did, and the way she talked about him, he wouldn't have cared if he did. They could've run off."

I wasn't ready to let it go yet and asked, "You think somebody made her an offer like you have? Set her up in her own apartment?"

Her expression got darker. "You don't know anything about what I'm doing here."

"Sure I do," I said. "You found a place to land, just like I did with the speak. Good work if you can get it, right?"

She shook her head. "Maybe." Then she looked at her watch and said, "All right, it's past one. That means Harold isn't going to call, and he said that if he didn't call, then he wouldn't see me until Sunday."

Her mouth twisted into a rueful smile. She scratched the cat's neck with both hands and said, "Another exciting weekend, Andrew." Then to me, "You'll find a corkscrew and a couple of glasses in the kitchen. Let's see if this stuff is any good."

The kitchen wasn't much bigger than some closets. She had good glassware and the liquor in the cabinet was scotch, the McCoy, and not much else. When I got back to the front room, she'd taken off her shoes and loosened her collar. The calico cat was purring on her lap. I opened, tasted, and congratulated myself on choosing well.

I poured two glasses. Daphne said, "What do you know about crooks on Wall Street?"

I hadn't expected that. "Nothing, really. A few years ago I was part of Rothstein's Liberty Bond racket, but that was simple theft. I thought the guys who ran Wall Street had it fixed so they didn't have to break any laws."

"Me too. Now, I'm not so sure." She took a short sip and then a longer one and then she started talking.

Harold—she didn't tell me his last name—came into Polly's a little more than a year ago. He was an older guy, in his fifties. Balding but tall and not bad looking and not fat, not too fat anyway. He had a lot of cash to spread around and he didn't show off with it, just bought the better booze and eats that Polly put out, and tipped well, particularly to the girls he liked. Before long, he started asking for Daphne whenever he came in, and he even phoned ahead to make sure he could see her. As johns went, he was the best, usually just looking for a nice relaxed tumble in the sheets. He liked to talk, too, but none of the "what's a nice kid like you doing . . ." stuff. It was questions about what she did that day, foods she liked, what she wanted to do with herself.

A few months ago, he called and asked for something different. He wanted Daphne to come out to a private engagement at the Gay Street address. He wanted her for the weekend, which was not an inexpensive proposition. Polly snapped it up and told Daphne to pack an overnight bag. Since transportation came out of her cut, Daphne took the subway. Harold met her at the door with champagne and flowers. When she asked what the occasion was, he said they were celebrating his freedom. His wife was gone for the weekend, and he wanted to indulge himself by being with her without all the "distractions" at Polly's. He'd laid in food and drink for forty-eight hours and suggested that she head upstairs and get rid of those clothes.

For the rest of the night and the next day and night, they screwed and drank and ate and talked and screwed. He told her it was the best time he could ever remember having, and it actually made him kind of sad because he was afraid nothing would ever be that good again. Daphne didn't tell me what she thought of that first weekend. I'm pretty sure it wasn't what he said, but she must have been flattered.

As she was packing up, Harold made his pitch. He started with what she already knew or had figured out. He worked on Wall Street, survived the crash, and recently had some good luck while most other people were still hanging on by a fraying thread. He lived out on Long Island. His son had grown and left home and now he and his wife barely spoke to each other. She had her life, he had his. They didn't ask each other questions. Now he wanted to enjoy himself. Would she consider moving into this place? He'd signed the lease. He'd transfer it to her name if she'd like.

Right up front, he said he wasn't some romantic idiot. He didn't love her and he knew she didn't love him, but he enjoyed being with her. Though he didn't know exactly how much she made working at Polly's, he was sure he could make her an offer that was in the same neighborhood, and, as he put it, "you won't have to work nearly as hard or as often." There were no promises on either side. If she got tired of the arrangement, she was free to leave. Finally, he said, he knew he couldn't expect an answer right away, so she should think it over and let him know as soon as she made up her mind. He sincerely hoped she'd say yes.

Daphne moved out of Polly's place the next day.

At first, it was exactly what he said. They put her name on the lease. He gave her two hundred bucks and set up a bank account for her. She bought new furniture for the place. He came over for lunch whenever he could and sometimes in the afternoon. Usually there was at least one day on the weekend. But the loneliness was no different there than it had been at Polly's. She got Andrew the cat and that helped, but not much. She thought about going to secretarial school or working on a real-estate license but didn't quite get around to it.

She hadn't been there a month when Harold told her that he'd got a tip on a stock. It would be impossible for him to explain all the ins and outs to her, but there were reasons he couldn't buy this instrument—that was his word, *instrument*—but she could and it would be completely legal. He'd show her what to do. He gave her the name and address of a brokerage, and he told her who to ask for when she went there. He even told her the day and time she was to go there, saying that all these details were just to make sure that everything went smoothly. No, he swore to her, you're not doing anything illegal. Handling it this way just makes sure that everything is aboveboard. He told her to dress severely and to wear the glasses. He didn't want any of the men at the brokerage making time with his woman.

She did just as he told her to. It was a nice break from her routine. She got her first real hint that something wasn't on the up-and-up when she went to the brokerage and asked for the man Harold had named, a Mr. Deener. He was a younger guy who bolted up from his desk in a bullpen full of desks when he heard his name. He hurried over to see her, mopping his face with a handkerchief, and she could see just how nervous he was. But everything went just as Harold said it would. The name of the company, or whatever it was, meant nothing to her. As Harold said, it was an instrument. She gave it to the nervous Mr. Deener. She wrote a check. He gave her a receipt and a folder full of papers she didn't understand.

A week later, a messenger arrived at her place on Gay Street and had her sign for an envelope. Harold called minutes later and told her to wait until he got there to open it. When they did, she was shocked by the amount of the cashier's check.

By then, we'd worked through half of the wine. Daphne took most of it.

"How many more 'instruments' have you handled?"

"Fourteen."

"How much money?"

"Almost eleven thousand," she said. "It's in the bank. There was some extra business, fine print, when we opened the account. Nobody said so in so many words, but I think Harold can get at it."

"So he could be setting you up," I said.

"Maybe, but I can't believe Harold would hurt me."

Not as long as the gravy train is running on schedule, I thought. "How long do you think you can keep him happy in the sack?"

One corner of her mouth cocked up. "As long as I want, buster."

She knew that wasn't true. It was the wine talking, but we let it pass. She said, "What do you think I should do?"

"The first thing is to figure out what he's up to. Then once you've got the details, decide if he's marked you to take the fall. If he has, then figure out how to steal it from him before he steals it from you. I don't know anything about that racket, but we've got three or four regulars who brag that there's nothing about Wall Street that they don't know. You want, I'll ask around, see if I can learn anything."

"How much?" She looked and sounded skeptical, but the idea interested her.

"I'm getting ten percent for this business with Nola."

She drained her glass and muttered, mostly to herself, "I don't know."

I asked if they'd talked about how the cash was going to be divided, and she said Harold had started talking about it as "their" money, but nothing more definite. I asked a couple more questions, but she didn't want to answer, so I said that if she decided to do anything, she knew where to find me. I got ready to leave.

She poured the rest of the bottle into her glass. "You know," she said, "I've always wanted to ask you about that day."

"What day?" I asked, knowing exactly what she meant.

"That afternoon that old guy—what was his name?—Manzanaro got killed. It was in that same building. I didn't realize it was the same place until I heard about it later. Somebody said Charlie Lucky was behind it. And one night in Polly's, Vincent Coll was bragging that he had been paid by the old guy to kill Charlie. Then a little bird told me it was you who stopped Coll."

I shook my head and said, "Don't believe everything you hear from little birds. What were you doing there?"

She laughed. "That was a hell of a story. The guy I was with, he said he was a big shot and he was going to make me famous. He was going to make me a movie star. He said I was going to be in the greatest stag picture ever made. With a giant ape, if you can believe it."

I sat back down and said, "Tell me about him and his picture."

He told the girls that his name was Oscar Apollinaire. Daphne remembered he first showed up a couple of years ago in the spring, when Polly was still working out of the Majestic over on the west side. That's when she was a favorite of the literary crowd, Benchley and those guys. This Apollinaire character fit right in with them. He was a real dude who sported brightly colored vests—bright red paisley, blue and silver flowers, that kind of thing—along with the fez and the Vandyke. Like a lot of that bunch, he was more interested in lounging about, drinking, and holding forth on this and that in the parlor than in running to a bedroom to dip his wick. As long as he paid for his drinks, Polly and the girls thought he was pretty terrific.

He said he was a Polack and had taken the name Apollinaire to honor his countryman who had become a famous poet in France. Daphne said he and Benchley shared a laugh over that, but nobody else got it. She sure didn't. Neither did I. Daphne also said that he didn't sound like he came from Poland or France. From his accent, the closest he'd been to Europe was an East River pier.

What she noticed about him was the way he always seemed to be standing back a step, away from everybody else. Even when guys were taking their time in the parlor, they liked to sample the merchandize, you might say. Engaging in a leisurely feel, having a girl sit on their lap, slipping a hand up under a hem to squeeze a thigh. That was part of Polly's place. But Oscar Apollinaire tended to stay off to one side or in a corner, watching all the girls, focusing on one and then another and taking notes and drawing sketches on little cards that he always had in his pocket. When Daphne asked him about it, he said he was working on other projects and was considering which girls might be right. Daphne figured she wasn't one of those special girls since he never went with her.

I interrupted then and asked if this character had anything to do with Nola, both of them being Polacks.

She said, "No. Oscar went for girls who were younger and thinner than me and Nola, and I never saw them together. In fact, now that I think of it, I guess I haven't seen Oscar since that day we saw you, or the next time, I guess, before Nola came to Polly's."

"Yeah," I said, "Tell me about that day."

She was about to have another drink of wine but stopped and said, "What's it worth to you?"

She already had the first five I gave her, and most of the wine, but I thought she was about to get to the important part, so I put another five on the coffee table. She smiled and scratched the cat.

After months of having nothing to do with her, Apollinaire gave her his card and made an appointment. He arranged to meet her for lunch at Rudolf's, a Midtown speak that was too high hat for my taste. He told her to dress like a secretary and to tone down the makeup. He said he wanted her "inner beauty" to show through.

"Yeah, 'inner beauty,'" she said, "When a guy starts talking like that, you're in trouble."

But it didn't happen like that, at least not at lunch. They were in a private booth, and he had a bottle of bubbles waiting when she showed up. As she was tucking into her lobster Newburg, he went into his delivery and asked if she'd ever thought about being in pictures.

She laughed and said no, she'd never had any acting lessons and wouldn't know what to do. He said, "The hell you haven't. Don't you act every night at Polly's when you're jollying them up in the parlor and later when you're telling them how great they were and it's never been better? You don't call that acting?"

That's when she began to suspect that maybe he'd seen more of her and her work than she knew. After all, Polly didn't tell the girls everything, and she catered to some demanding tastes. Word was that Polly could make arrangements for guys—and women— who liked to watch. But before Daphne could think about it too much, Apollinaire said she was just the girl he wanted, and he was willing to pay her three hundred dollars for an afternoon's work. That was more than she made in two months at Polly's.

"Keep talking," she said.

He told her that he had a small studio where he made special films, silent one-reelers "of the highest quality for only the most discerning clientele." Daphne said that Apollinaire always used words like *clientele* instead of *customers* if he could. That's the way he talked. The films were never shown in theaters, he said, only at exclusive, very private screenings. Some prints were available for sale to collectors, but he controlled distribution. The new film, his greatest, would be her entrée into the world of entertainment. She probably didn't know it, but the truth was that a lot of the stars got their start in the picture business that way.

Daphne put down her fork and said, "Thanks for lunch and drop dead."

She had seen Polly's dirty movies and knew just how crappy they were. He agreed with her and then lowered his voice and said, "Take a look at these," and handed her a book of pictures. It was about five by seven inches, bound with heavy copper staples. The title on the cover was *The Real "It" Girl*.

"I tell you," she said to me, "at first I thought I was really looking at Clara Bow. The girl in those pictures looked exactly like her, the round face, the little nose, the cute black wig, the middy blouse she wore in *It*, even those eyes, my God, those eyes."

Daphne thought the first shots of the girl standing and showing a lot of leg might have been from the moving picture, but things got racier as she turned the pages. The fake Clara shed the blouse, and in the last one, she was about to take on two guys.

Apollinaire said that she could see from those that he wasn't making the shit they showed at Polly's. He was making "real" moving pictures just like they did in Hollywood. Then he got really warmed up, Daphne said, and claimed that his pictures were actually better than the studios'. His costumes, his lighting, his cameras and lenses were as good as theirs and his treatment of his subjects was much more daring. He showed his clientele what they really wanted to see and took them where they'd never gone before.

Now, he wanted her to join him in his next project, *The Eighth Wonder*.

His enthusiasm sounded real enough, but she was more interested in the three hundred. He smiled and said the next step was for her to meet his silent partner, and they set off for the Grand Central Building, which was not what she expected. Even though he bragged on his high-class production, she figured this would lead to a nasty little hotel room with a nasty little partner who'd try to get her into the sack. But, no, they went up to a nice office on the sixth floor.

At first, she thought the office was empty because there was no light coming through the frosted glass door, and there wasn't a secretary or anybody else in the outer office where Apollinaire told her to wait. He hurried through another door and closed it. A few minutes later, just long enough for her to start getting nervous about the nasty little partner again, he came back and told her to come with him. They went down a dim hall past other doors to a big conference room. The curtains were drawn and it was dark except for a green banker's light on a long table. She could tell there was a man at the far end of the table, but she couldn't see his face.

Apollinaire said this was the girl he'd told him about, and she could tell from the quality of his voice that the guy at the other end of the table was in charge. He controlled the money. The guy hit a switch and another light came on beside her.

"Take off your blouse," he said.

She shook her head and said, "Not until I'm paid."

Now, there are some girls, given that situation in a fancy room with a man of considerable means who sounded like he was used to being obeyed, I wouldn't believe them if they said they refused to doff their duds. But not Daphne. Daphne was one of the most popular girls in the city. She could set her terms.

Apollinaire sucked in his breath but didn't say anything. After a moment, the man at the other end of the table said, "Very well, then. She'll do. You may go."

"Oscar hurried me right out," Daphne said, "before the guy had a chance to change his mind, I guess. And everything changed about him. He was walking faster and almost bouncing. When he saw there was a crowd at the elevator, he was too impatient to wait and said we'd take the stairs. That's when you saw us."

I remembered that part.

She said, "And you know what's funny, he said—"

I interrupted, "Wait a minute. Go back to the office and the guy at the other end of the table. Do you remember anything else about him?"

She thought a few seconds. "The office wasn't far from the stairs, almost right across the hall. That's all. The guy was kind of short, I think, not as short as you, and stocky, and he wore round glasses. I could see the reflection."

"Did you get the job?" I asked, though I figured he found his girl in Nola.

"No." She waved her hand like she was brushing him off. "Oscar set up another meeting and wanted me to go with him to take some test pictures and try on costumes at his studio, but I told him I wasn't doing nothing until I saw some real money, not just promises. He started backtracking, saying I didn't understand how the business worked. First he needed to make sure that 'the camera adored me.' Yeah, that's what he said, 'the camera adored me,' can you believe it?

"But anyway," she went on, "maybe I was being a chump, but I agreed to go down to his studio. But I'm not that big of a chump. I took a gun and I made sure he never got me where I didn't have a way out. His place was in a loft down in the middle of Chinatown, and that's where it really hit the fan."

She said that she'd never be able to find the place again. They took a cab to Chinatown and then walked down those streets that are too narrow for a car, and finally into a building and up some stairs to a door with three locks. Apollinaire's "studio" turned out to be one big square loft with a skylight. Most of the place was filled with carpenters' equipment, paint, and canvas for making sets. There were a lot of electric lights and a camera on a tripod near the skylight.

He had a dozen or so pencil sketches tacked up on a wall. They were wild jungle scenes with dinosaurs and a giant ape, and he showed her one drawing with a tiny woman up in a tree. He told her that was what she'd be doing. Daphne didn't understand what it was, because nobody had seen *King Kong*. Hell, I guess they had just started making the real movie. To her, the stuff about the dinosaurs and the giant ape was completely nuts. She didn't see how that could have anything to do with what Apollinaire was talking about. How was he going to get dinosaurs into that loft? So he explained that he wasn't going to try to have a giant ape because the ape wasn't really that important, the girl was important. That's what his clientele wanted to see. Actually, he thought the whole idea of a giant ape was just plain screwy and he didn't know how they were going to do it in Hollywood, so he was going to use a guy in a gorilla suit.

When he explained exactly how that part of the picture was going to work, she told him no deal and walked out.

She said, "Oscar could spin out a good line. The guy was a hell of a salesman, and even though I had a feeling he'd string me along with promises of that three hundred as long as he could, that didn't bother me. I knew I wouldn't take my clothes off or spread my legs until I had the money in the bank. I mean, I wasn't born yesterday. But then he told me about the guy I'd be with and there was no getting around it."

"What do you mean?" I asked.

"He tried to tap-dance by telling me this guy is just perfect for the part. He's really a great actor in Cuba. Yeah . . . Cuba. They all say that, don't they, but hell, I know what it means. I may be a whore, but I've got my standards. I don't care what you pay me, I'm not going to fuck a spade."

I never heard her sound so offended. But I wasn't surprised. A lot of Polly's girls came from the South, and the truth is, from what I heard, most of the girls felt the same way about colored guys. Not that the problem came up much at Polly's. At least, I never heard about it.

Daphne said that afternoon was the last time she saw Apollinaire. I considered telling her about Nola taking the part, but first I needed to know something else.

"You said this joker Apollinaire showed you a book of pictures of a girl who looked like Clara Bow, and he said they came from a one-reeler he made. That day when you went to his studio, did you see that movie or any movie? Were there cans of film sitting around?"

"No, I asked about that, and he said he kept his pictures in another workshop. The camera on the tripod looked like a movie camera, but what do I know from movie cameras?"

I figured that the guy really did make movies, but I still couldn't be sure. "You said that this Apollinaire gave you his card. Still have it?"

She said she thought so and opened a drawer in the round telephone table beside the love seat and found a cigar box. She took out a stack of business and personal cards and went through them. She pulled one out and handed it to me.

"Now, here's the funny thing I've been trying to tell you," Daphne said. "That day in the Grand Central Building . . ."

"Yeah?"

"Well, we opened the door and there you were, and I said 'Hello, Jimmy' and you said 'Hello, Daphne. Take the elevator' and Oscar closed the door. Remember?"

"Yeah," I said again, wondering what she was getting at.

"Well, right after you left, Oscar said 'I know that guy. That's Jimmy Quinn.' So you must know him, too, right? What? You don't?"

She must have seen the confusion on my face. Sitting there in her place, I didn't know what the hell to say. It felt almost like the chair was moving under me, and the hair on my arms and the back of my neck was standing up. Yesterday, Miss Wray said that I wasn't what she expected, and now this guy who somehow stole her movie claims that he knows me. That's not something that happens to a guy every day and it spooked me.

Daphne said, "It must be because you're neighbors," and that brought me back around.

"What do you mean?"

"Look at the card," she said. I did and I got even more spooked, a hell of a lot more.

The name Oscar Apollinaire was printed in the same blue ink as the words in the picture book. On the back, handwritten in pencil was "222 w.23/rm.624."

It looked like an address, and if it was, Oscar Apollinaire lived in the Chelsea.

CHAPTER ELEVEN

Still chewing over what Daphne said, I hailed a cab and told him to take me to the Grand Central Building. It was about quarter past three.

So this Oscar Apollinaire was behind the book, and the book must be meant to promote a stag picture, just like they used lobby cards to advertise the next pictures they'd be playing in real theaters. But why the hell would he be trying to put the squeeze on RKO, and what was this movie? I decided I didn't know enough yet even to ask the right questions, so I quit thinking about it.

As we drove uptown, I realized how many cabs I'd taken since last night. Give me somebody else's money to spend and I was Diamond Jim Brady. That's when I noticed all the guys on the street who were out of work. I hadn't seen them at night, but in the middle of the afternoon, they were hard to miss. Shuffling along the sidewalk or sitting on park benches staring at nothing or waiting in soup lines, there were a lot of them. Working nights, it was easy for me to forget what it was like for those guys.

I was lucky. The speak wasn't going to make me a millionaire, but I never missed a payroll. And as much as I didn't like that goddamn Roosevelt was ending Prohibition, somebody had to do something.

I hadn't been inside the Grand Central Building for two years. For the first few days after the Maranzano business, I didn't want to be around any investigation, but the truth is I just didn't have a reason to visit such a high-rent neighborhood.

I took the elevator to the sixth floor and walked down the corridor. The building was quiet and there weren't many people around. Maybe it was because that was the day before the inauguration. In my line of work, Friday afternoon was usually jumping. The place had been a lot livelier when I cased it for Meyer and Charlie. The office across the hall from the stairs had a frosted glass door with THE MARY WILCOX FOUNDATION FOR WAYWARD GIRLS written in gold leaf. I couldn't see any lights on the other side, but I tried the door anyway. It was unlocked. The first thing you saw when you came in was a big portrait of Mary Wilcox on one wall with black ribbon around the frame.

The outer office was bigger and tonier than Maranzano's, with chairs in a waiting area separated from a couple of secretary desks by a waist-high railing. There were three doors behind the desks, one of them open double doors leading to a hallway. I was the only person in the place, but a man's overcoat had been tossed over the divider, and there was a small suitcase on the floor next to it.

The Wilcox Foundation was one of those antivice, good deeds groups that popped up every few years or so to make the city a better place to live. As far as I knew, it was one of the few that most normal people didn't hate. While the Committee of Fourteen and the Citizens Union and those guys were trying to stamp out sin wherever they could find it, the Wilcox Foundation was meant to help the women and girls who got caught up in the Magistrate's Court business, no questions asked. After the Seabury Commission got that settled, you didn't see the foundation mentioned in the papers anymore, but it still had a couple of places downtown where dames who were in a bad way could get three hots and a cot.

That Friday, the office had an unused empty feeling and I wondered if anybody was still working there. Wondered why the door was unlocked, too. I stood there without doing anything for a full minute or so, long enough to decide that I was probably alone in the place. Or if there was anybody else there, he wasn't making any noise. I didn't either.

Moving quietly, I went past the desks and into the hallway. It had been cool in the outer office, and it got colder the farther I went from it. There were unmarked offices on either side. I tried each door and found them locked until I got to the end. The door on the right was open. It was labeled PETER WILCOX. I pushed it the rest of the way open and went inside. It was too dark to see anything until I found the lights. The office was nothing special: an average-size wooden desk and nice big rolling leather chair, telephone, shelves partway filled with notebooks and manila folders, a few framed photographs on the wall of Peter Wilcox and city officials. I recognized him from the papers. He looked a lot like Theodore Roosevelt with a thick neck, lantern jaw, bulky upper body and bottlebrush mustache. He didn't smile much in the pictures in the paper, or on his wall.

He was one of those guys, you saw his name in the papers all the time in stories about reforming city government and eliminating corruption, but never in the headlines. He'd be down a few paragraphs.

I turned to the doors on the other side of the hall. That was the conference room where Daphne and Apollinaire met his partner, who figured to be Peter Wilcox. It was a long carpeted walnut-paneled room with four tall narrow windows on one side and a table in the center with two rows of green shaded banker's lights. There were chairs on both sides and a high-backed chair at the end where I guessed the big cheese would sit when they conferred.

I was trying out the high-backed chair when I heard a door

open and voices in the outer office. I guess I should've thought about making myself scarce but, hell, I hadn't done anything. Just to be safe, I took out the Banker's Special and put it on my lap and slipped the knucks on my right hand. All I could see at first was the light I'd left on in Wilcox's office across the hall.

The voices got louder. The only words I could make out were, "This way."

I heard the sounds of something bumping into furniture and a bleating animal cry. I thought it was a sheep, but what the hell did I know from sheep? There were curses and more banging and bumping until two men and an animal staggered into the light. I still couldn't make out what it was, but it was about knee height to the men and it didn't want to be there. They had a rope around its neck, and it took both of them to drag it to the door. It balked and they struggled until one guy got behind and pushed while the other yanked on the rope and they got it through the doorway and into the office. When they got into the light, I could tell that it was the two idiots, the kid with the pistol and bad hair and the older guy, the vice cop that knew Fat Joe. What was his name? Trodache? His face was still red from the coffee I threw at him.

They were followed by a man in a suit. I only got a look at his profile and saw that he was a young fellow with round glasses, a downy mustache. Not tall, not short, smoking a cigarette. He had the overcoat tucked under his arm, and he was carrying the suitcase. Once the two guys had the animal in the office, he followed them in and shut the door. After that, they had a lot to say to each other but I couldn't understand any of it and the animal quieted down. All I could see was the line of light under the door.

I got up and walked back down the long table to the door. Along the way, I cocked the .38. The office door opened outward. I figured I could get close enough to hear and they might not see me behind it when they left. And if they did see me and object, I could shoot them. Or, if I had time, I could duck back in the conference room.

When I got to the door, I heard two of them arguing. It was

Trodache, with the whispery voice, and the young guy who, I guessed, was the boss, the one I saw with the big Olds the night before. I couldn't make out what Trodache was saying, but I could tell he was asking for something. The other man had a crisp, educated accent, easy to understand. "Don't worry," he said, "They're going to pay. Six thousand means nothing. And if they don't, it doesn't matter. We'll go back to the original arrangement, but this will be better. And remember, we've got to take a look at the other place before you call them tonight."

Trodache and the kid said things I couldn't get and the boss answered, "No, he won't be back until Sunday at the earliest and this is for me to worry about, it's not your concern. Go on. You know what you've got to do. I'll meet you at six."

I stepped back into the conference room. Moments later, the two idiots came out, and the door slammed fast behind them, like the other man had pushed them out. As they walked away, the kid said, "This is so fucking screwy I don't believe it."

The older guy croaked, "Think about the money," and they left. I heard the frosted glass door close.

For several seconds after that, I couldn't tell what the hell was happening on the other side of Wilcox's office door. It was completely quiet for a long time, then I heard bleats and moans and squeals and groans and grunts and a lot more banging around, much more violent than it had sounded coming in. The pace and intensity got quicker and more excited, and the bleating rose to sound like a terrified scream. It was almost human in its fear, but I knew it was the animal. The frightened sound seemed to go on for hours, but it couldn't have been more than minutes, long painful minutes, with more loud thumps of things being knocked over.

It ended with a long screech and a tearing sound and a satisfied moan that was human. Definitely human. Then the smell hit me. I knew it right away from the slaughterhouses down on Gansevoort Street.

I also knew that whatever happened next was going to be bloody, and I tried to clamp down on my shallow breathing and racing heartbeat. *Be cool,* I told myself. *Don't hurry, don't hesitate.* I made sure my finger was outside the trigger guard. Again, silent seconds stretched out until the door swung open and the third man stood there, his back to me, looking into the office. He wore a brown tweed suit. I could only see the collar of the suit until he took off the overcoat, and folded it carefully, keeping the blood-smeared front away from his hands and clothes. He put the coat in the suitcase, then took off the gloves I hadn't noticed, and put them in the suitcase, too, and snapped it shut.

The smell of blood and shit and offal was rank.

I couldn't see past the man into the office. His breathing still sounded as ragged as mine had been. He took time to straighten his tie, adjust his cuffs, and smooth his hair back with his hands. He picked up the suitcase, reached in to turn off the lights, closed the door, and left.

A few seconds later, I heard the frosted glass door shut again. I eased the hammer down on the pistol and forced myself to open the office door and turn on the lights.

It was a goat, not a sheep, with curled horns. It was hanging upside down on the leather chair. The guy had tied the rope around the animal's back legs and pinned the rope with a knife driven into the top of the chair. He'd killed it by cutting the throat and slashing it open from stomach to sternum. Another blood-streaked knife was buried in the middle of the desk. The guts and other messy stuff were smeared around the second knife.

Scrawled large in blood on the wall were the words *BROTHER BEAST.*

The smell alone was enough to make me dizzy. I wanted to scram out of there fast but settled down and strolled out like a guy who wasn't in a hurry.

Back when we killed Maranzano, it took four guys with knives and guns to finish him off, and even then, it wasn't easy, the old man put up a hell of a fight. I didn't see the body, but I saw the photographs. It was pretty bad. The goat got it worse.

After the business with Miss Wray saying her husband knew me, and Daphne saying that this Apollinaire knew me, the slaughter of the goat meant I was in the middle of something I'd never seen before, and it scared me worse than anything ever had.

CHAPTER TWELVE

So what do I tell Miss Wray and the RKO guys? That's what I was thinking as I settled behind my desk in the office. It was getting close to five o'clock by then, and the Democrats were making an early start of it. The bar was jumping. If it got much busier, as it tended to on Friday, we'd need extra help. I was reaching for the phone to call the kitchen when the thing rang. It was Grossner, the RKO lawyer. He sounded honked off.

"I've just learned that you've been in contact with the extortionists. Why didn't you tell us?"

"I had other things to do. Have they called? You decide to pay 'em?"

"No, and I can't say that I care for your attitude. We're not paying you to—"

"You haven't paid me anything yet. After you do, you can give me orders and I might listen to you, but don't count on it. For the moment, I'm working for Miss Wray. Take it up with her."

He backed off right away and said perhaps he'd been too

hasty. "We all want Miss Wray to be happy. I understand that, and even though we haven't agreed to their demands, we do have the money ready. Since they sent the book and the demand to the Pierre, we assume they'll call here. You should be here, too."

I said I'd be there in half an hour and told him to have them send up a corned beef sandwich.

That got him honked off again and he sputtered, "I'm not going to order a sandwich for you."

"Okay," I said, "then make it an hour" and hung up.

Vittorio's guys didn't have any corned beef, but there was some steak left over from lunch. They put some horseradish on the bread, too.

When I finished, I went downstairs. They were two deep at the bar, all the booths were filled and most of the tables. I went to the back corner of the bar and motioned Connie over. We had to lean close to hear each other.

I said, "It was an interesting afternoon. Daphne had a lot to say. I'll tell you all about it when we can talk, but the important thing is that it looks like the picture book is advertising for a stag movie based on *King Kong*."

That surprised her. "I never heard of such a thing. How could they do that?"

"Search me. But I might have a line on the guy who made the picture. Could be that he lives at the Chelsea, one floor above you."

That really surprised her. "You're kidding."

"If I'm lyin', I'm dyin'. Now they want me to go back to Miss Wray's hotel. If those guys who were in here last night call, they'll want their money tonight. Sounds like the studio is willing to pay up, so I might be busy. But I'll try to get back early, and maybe we can pay a visit to this guy. Daphne said his name is Oscar Apollinaire. And she said he knows me. That I can't figure at all. The name mean anything to you?"

"No," she said, "but I can ask Nelson."

"Nelson?"

"The elevator operator. He knows everybody in the building. Want me to call him?"

"No, ask him when we wake him up."

There was no sign of the Olds on the taxi ride up to the Pierre.

Miss Wray's suite was still lousy with flowers. It looked like more had arrived since I was there last night. One table had been cleared, and right in the middle of it, she'd put one white rose. The card leaning on the pot read CONGRATULATIONS! SEE YOU SOON, CARY.

Miss Wray looked terrific. She was dolled up in a long dress made of heavy blue silk with some kind of pattern woven into it, and a necklace with a diamond that would fill a shot glass. She was still pacing the room, and she'd switched from champagne to tea.

Detective Ellis was getting chummy with Grossner and Sleave in a far corner of the room. The lawyers were decked out in white ties and tails. Grossner got up as soon as he saw me. A fourth guy in a regular suit sat at a desk beside them. He was scribbling serial numbers from a stack of bills. He wasn't paying much attention to that, because all the time we were talking, he was turning to listen to us.

Grossner strode over and said, tugging at his coat, "All right, Quinn, what have you learned?"

I took off my topcoat and hat and went to the bar to pour myself a brandy. Then I said, "Miss Wray, do you want everybody to know this, or do you want to talk it over in private, just you and me?"

Grossner and Sleave started to say something until she held up a hand. "Go ahead," she said and gave me a wink they couldn't see. "I trust your discretion."

"It looks like the guys behind this are an ex-vice cop named Trodache and a kid. I don't know his name. Ellis, do you know Trodache?"

He shook his head, and his quick scowl told you everything

you needed to know about his opinion of vice cops. I asked the lawyers if the name meant anything to them and they said no.

"Trodache and the kid must have followed Miss Wray to my place last night. I went out after we talked and they braced me on the street."

Grossner interrupted me, "You're sure they're behind it?"

"They knew about the six thousand dollars, and they said they had more books. But they're not in this by themselves. There's a third guy, a younger guy. He was in the backseat of their car, and he's got to be the brains of the outfit."

Sleave, the lawyer with the pince-nez, said, "Is this the way these matters are normally handled? I mean, I thought these blackmailers or extortionists would want to keep their identity secret. How did you learn this man's name? Did he tell you?"

"No. After they left me, they went back to my place. Fat Joe knows Trodache and let 'em in."

I saw they didn't understand. "Fat Joe, the doorman. He probably told you to fuck off last night. Sorry, Miss Wray. He wouldn't say it to you."

Hazel came in and sat next to Miss Wray on the sofa. "He certainly did not."

"By giving me the business and then showing up at my place, they're letting us know that they're a step ahead of us. And why do they care if we know who they are? They didn't kidnap anybody, they've got dirty pictures. The monsignor gets steamed up about it but nobody else. What have they done?"

Nobody could answer that.

"The girl in the pictures used to work for Polly Adler under the name Nola Revere. She left Polly's without telling anybody why. Maybe she posed for the pictures before then. Maybe it's why she left. That I can't tell you."

I decided not to mention the Wilcox Foundation or the stag movie for the moment. But Sleave still had questions.

"Still, how did they steal our copyrighted material? Those costumes and sets were kept under wraps."

"Maybe they saw the lobby cards and posters like I did," I said. "Maybe somebody working on the picture told them what it looked like, I don't know. But there's something else. Trodache and the kid think that the girl in the pictures really is Miss Wray. What do you make of that?"

Nobody said anything. Then Miss Wray said, "Oh, come now. How could anyone believe that?"

I shrugged and said, "Seems to me it's possible they didn't have anything to do with taking the pictures. Maybe they bought 'em or stole 'em from whoever did."

"That doesn't matter to me," she said, her voice hard and serious. "I want them destroyed. Does everyone understand that?"

She stood up and stared at the lawyers and said again, louder, "Does everyone understand that?"

They nodded and I went on. "And then there's Saxon Dunbar."

At the mention of the name, the guy copying the serial numbers stopped what he was doing and stared at me. The lawyers didn't know who I was talking about. I said he was like Winchell and they understood.

"He came in my place last night, a few hours after you were there, and said somebody called him and said there were naughty pictures of Miss Wray floating around, and she was trying to get 'em back and I was the go-between." Again, I decided not to go into the rest of it about Miss Wray's other "artistic" photographs or her problems with her husband. But what about the rest of it?

"Now, here's what's strange," I said. "The guy who told Dunbar about the pictures also said that they were taken on the set where they made the movie."

Miss Wray's big eyes got bigger. "You mean he suggested that I . . ."

"Yeah, with one of the black guys."

Hazel jumped right up and said, "That's just . . . just . . . impossible. There were too many of the crew members on the set every night, and the only time the colored people were there was when we shot the altar scene and the rampage. You weren't even there that day."

Miss Wray couldn't say anything and just stood there with her mouth open until she laughed.

Grossner paid no attention to either of the women. He said to me, "What did you tell him?"

"That Miss Wray had been in my place and I met her and anything that went on between us was private. If he knows about you and Sleave, he didn't say so."

Sleave stepped in front of Grossner and declared, "All right, that's enough. This situation is becoming increasingly unpredictable. No more discussion. We're going to pay them, and Quinn and Detective Ellis are going to make sure that every bit of this horribly offensive and repulsive material is destroyed. The very idea of one of those savages and Miss Wray, it's unthinkable. When they call, we agree to pay and we end this. Detective, are you agreed?"

Ellis got up from the sofa where he'd been listening and said, "I'll talk to Captain Boatwright to make sure I'm covered this weekend, but I don't see why I couldn't be with Quinn when he makes the payoff."

Sleave said, "Do you believe what he told us about this ex-cop and Dunbar and the salacious story? Can we trust him?" He turned to me and said, "No offense, Quinn. Your reputation and your associates precede you."

Ellis gave me a thin little smile. He knew I wasn't telling everything I knew. "Yeah," he said, "you can trust Quinn. For now."

I asked how we'd get the books and Sleave said that could be worked out when they called.

Grossner clapped his hands together and said, "Excellent. We are agreed. Now, we have another engagement at the RKO offices and we're late already. It shouldn't take more than a couple of hours. You and Quinn can stay here and wait for the call. Miss Wray, are you ready?"

She held up a finger and said, "One moment. Mr. Quinn and I need to talk."

The lawyers stewed in their boiled shirts and tails. She guided me into a sitting room and closed the door. "What else did you learn today? I know there's more." She put a hand on my arm and nailed me with another wide-eyed look. It got warmer.

"First, like I told them, this afternoon I found out that the woman whose name I told you, Nola Revere, that's her in the pictures, for sure. And it wasn't the first time. It was some other photographs like that that got her into the business."

"Have you located her?"

"No, she quit Polly's and nobody's seen her since. But I may have a line on the guy who took the pictures. Oscar Apollinaire. The name mean anything to you?"

She shook her head.

"It looks like he's not the third guy who was with Trodache and the kid. Maybe he told them the pictures were really of you and sold them, or maybe they stole them. There's a chance I can find this bird later tonight, but it's too soon to say anything, and that's not what's really eating you right now, is it? You're more worried about what Dunbar might write in his column than the pictures?"

She thought before she answered. "Yes, I suppose so, but we can't deal with one and not the other."

"Suppose I could get Dunbar to lose interest."

"But how?"

"Leave that to me."

She said, "That would be wonderful," and smiled like an actress.

I said, "And when this is over, we'll sit down and you'll tell me about your husband and how he knows me." She stopped smiling.

Back in the flower room, as Grossner helped the women with their coats, Sleave came over and said, "Quinn, I hope you understand that I didn't mean to be insulting when I questioned your trustworthiness. We simply don't know you. We're really not used to dealing with situations like this, and your methods are, well, unorthodox. We do appreciate your help."

"I'll appreciate it more after you pay me, but it's okay, no offense taken. I don't know you and I don't trust you, either. I'm working for Miss Wray."

Surprised, he said, "You don't know her either. But you trust her?"

"Sure, I know her. I've been to Skull Island with her."

The way he looked at me, he didn't understand.

After they left, I poured another brandy for myself and gin for the detective.

Ellis knocked it back and said, "What else do you know?"

I guess I could've mentioned that I just saw a goat being slaughtered in a Midtown office building, but I didn't know what the hell that had to do with anything else so I just said, "Not much. I'd like to know more about Trodache."

Ellis muttered, "Goddamn vice cops. I'll find out about him, and there's a kid, you say? I know a couple of guys who worked with the Seabury investigation. If I can't get them, I'll have to find his file, and I won't be able to do that until Monday. And how the hell are we supposed to make sure the books are destroyed? Does anybody know how many there are?"

I found my stick and put on my topcoat. "That's not up to us. Let them figure it out. By the way, what're they offering you?"

He picked up his coat. "Retainer, nothing much. They're calling it 'law enforcement liaison' with their people in California, or some such shit."

Ellis and I were at the door when the guy who'd been copying the serial numbers got up and said, sounding nervous and edgy, "Uh, excuse me, gentlemen, you're not leaving, are you? I was told that someone would be here all night to handle the extortionists' call."

I got my first look at him then. He was about my age and taller and plumper. His suit was new, his collar was too tight, and he had extra pomade in his dark hair. I asked him who he was.

He said, "I'm Abramson. Public relations. I'm, uh, new. What do I do if they call?"

Ellis said, "Tell them you've got the money ready and they should call back later."

I gave the kid one of my cards with the office number. He took it and said, "Mr. Quinn, I couldn't help but overhear that you've been talking to Saxon Dunbar, and I just want you to know that, well, since I haven't been with the company very long, it would be a real leg up if you could introduce me to him. I know that *King Kong* doesn't need any help right now. We're selling out ten shows a day, but in a month or so, a little story about a star standing up for herself might be a nice little pick-me-up for the picture."

"But what if we just pay them?" I asked. "That's not 'standing up for herself.'"

"What really happens doesn't matter," he said, almost laughing. "It's the story we make of it."

CHAPTER THIRTEEN

Things had settled down by the time I got back to the speak, and I wasn't as spooked as I'd been at the Grand Central Building. A fair number of the Democrats were taking trains down to Washington for the inauguration, and so the crowd was light for a Friday night. It sounded different, too—not as jazzed, and a lot of people seemed to be talking about banks and holidays. Must have been about eight o'clock.

Frenchy said there had been no sign of the two guys, and there weren't any messages for me but he thought Connie had taken one on the office phone. Connie and Marie Therese were together behind the bar. Judging by their chilly expressions, I was back in the doghouse. I went around to Connie's end of the bar where we could talk and asked what had happened since I was gone. She was still giving me the shoulder and said I'd find the message on my desk.

Maybe I was tired and maybe I was still a little spooked too, but I said, "Dammit, what's the matter with you?" And I was loud enough that people turned to see what was going to happen next. Surprised, she stepped back quick and I couldn't read her face. I thought maybe I'd scared her and that was the last thing I wanted to do. But I was more embarrassed that I'd let anything show in front of customers. I wanted to pound the bar but didn't. So I went to the office and fumed.

This was ridiculous. I still didn't know what the hell I'd done to make her so damn mad and that made me even madder. I wanted to peek through the blinds over the window down to the bar, but I knew she'd be looking to see if I did. Dammit! She had me acting like some moony kid.

I collapsed in my chair and glared at the note on my desk. Saxon Dunbar called an hour ago. *Settle down*, I told myself. *Straighten out your mind. Quit thinking about the goat and the blood. Quit thinking about Connie. What are you doing? What are you trying to do? What comes next?* And when I thought about what came next, I thought about Miss Wray and the six grand for the pictures and the ninety-nine dollars she already gave me.

I found my notebook and started by counting taxi rides. Since she gave me the money, I'd spent seven on fares and tips, then twenty to Cynthia at Polly's to find Daphne, and ten to Daphne, and twelve fifty for the wine, rounded up to thirteen. That came to fifty bucks. Damn, it's easy to burn through somebody else's money.

I was still stewing about Connie, so I went on with the busywork that I needed to do if the screwy little plan that I had in mind was to work. First, I straightened up the room. Not much, not like anybody had really gone over it, but I threw away the morning papers and stacked the rest on the table. Used a bar towel to take care of the dust that furred the back of the divan, the leather chair, the tables, and my liquor cabinet. I took extra care with the leaded glass shade on the lamp. It was on the cabinet and I didn't use it much. That night I turned it on and took out bottles of good scotch and gin, and three short heavy glasses.

Then I dusted and polished them and arranged them so the light hit them just right and glowed through the bottles.

It looked great until I remembered that Dunbar drank rum.

I went to the cellar and took my time going down the steps. Truth is, with my knee, I'm slow going down any stairs and that gave Arch Malloy a few seconds to put away his book and look like he was working.

When I got to the bottom, he was loading two cases of booze into the dumbwaiter. The copy of *The Story of Philosophy* he'd borrowed from me was open on a chair. He'd got farther into it than I had or probably ever would. I asked him where we kept the rum, the really good stuff.

"And what, precisely, would you be looking for?" he asked.

"I don't know. Precisely. Never developed a taste for it myself. Have you?"

He closed the dumbwaiter and sent it upstairs. "I sampled quite a bit of it when I was in Cuba. Most days, it was all we could lay our hands on, what with the war and all. As for quality, well, memorable it was not, but it did what we wanted it to do, and I counted us lucky to have it."

He went to one of the taller stacks of shelves, kicking a short stool in front of him, and climbed on it. "Let's see. I believe this is where I moved the more exotic specimens."

He pulled down a wooden crate and then got down a second. "If you can tell me what you're needing this for, perhaps I can make some suggestions. Or perhaps we could sample three or four."

I pulled out a dusty fifth of dark Bacardi's and said, "I'm looking for something that will tempt a rum drinker."

"Yes," he said. "If I'm not speaking out of turn, could it be that you're referring to that unctuous Limey scribbler Dunbar who recently graced us with his presence?"

Unctuous. That was another one for my list.

Malloy took out two more bottles. "This, they say, is a higher quality of Bacardi than the one you've got there. At least according to the invoices, you pay more for it. I've found that I cannot tell the difference, but it's been so long since I tasted either, we should not take my word for it. Now, where are the glasses? Ah yes, here."

He produced a couple of glasses, cut the seal around the neck of the bottle with his knife, and thumbed the cork out. I poured. We tasted.

"Arch," I said, "are you married?"

If the question surprised him, he didn't show it. "I was. In Ireland. She died."

I said I was sorry to bring it up and he said, "No, that was a long time ago, and I suppose her passing is the reason I left and why I'm here. Let's try that one you've got."

We did and he was right. I couldn't tell a difference.

"Did you like being married?"

"Most of the time. I'd do it again if I could find a woman who'd have me, but that's increasingly unlikely. Now, this third bottle, it is something different entirely, a rarity in my experience."

As Arch cut the seal, I saw that it was a square clear bottle filled with greenish-amber hooch. After he wiped the dust off, it had a warm inviting look. The label was Spanish.

Arch said, "I believe the proper term for this is rum infused with absinthe. I've heard of it but not sampled." He wiped out our glasses and poured. It had a strong sharp smell, and the first taste numbed the tongue. Arch said that he needed another small sip before he could render a judgment. I passed. This would do for my purpose.

"Yes," he said, holding the glass to the light, "just a touch of the Green Fairy. I'm guessing that your inquiries about the late Mrs. Malloy have something to do with the romantic straits in which you and the lovely Miss Nix find yourselves."

Straights? That didn't seem right. Another word to look up. I tell you, listening to Arch was an education. "That's one way of putting it," I said. "I've done something to put her back up and I can't figure what it is."

"I'd tell you that I'd ask Madam Reneau, but she won't talk about Connie. She thinks of the girl as a daughter."

Madam Reneau was Marie Therese, and I knew he was right.

"But I can give you one small piece of advice. You say you've done something to anger her. I certainly did many things that angered Mrs. Malloy in our few years together, but as I look back, it seems to me that more often than not, it wasn't that I did or said something to cause the dustup. It was that I had *not* done something. So perhaps you should approach it from that direction. Is there something you promised to buy for Connie, or a thing that you said you'd do and then, inexplicably, forgot about?"

I picked up the square bottle and said that I couldn't think of anything like that. Still, I worked on it, and as things turned out, Arch was right.

Back in the office, I put the rum on the liquor cabinet to one side, behind the gin but close enough to the lamp to catch the light. I called the bar and told them to send up a bucket of ice, seltzer, ginger ale, and four glasses. Connie brought them. I was going to say that I was sorry for raising my voice, but she was still giving me the silent treatment, so I just told her to put the stuff on the cabinet and to send Dunbar up when he arrived.

She nodded and left without saying a word, and that got me steamed all over again. I took the dirty picture book out of the safe, put it on my desk, and turned it over. The thing was held together by two thick copper staples that were easy enough to pry apart with a letter opener. I took off the back cover and lifted the pages out over the staples. The shot of the girl on top of the Empire State Building was still the one with the best look at her face. I tucked it and the one of her in the diner under my blotter and locked the rest of the book back in the safe.

I can't say why I took such care with it. The thick heavy paper that the pictures were mounted on had something to do with it. That and the clarity of the photographs and the careful printing of the text meant that somebody had put a lot of work in on it, and so the craftsmanship made me think it might be valuable and not something you'd just throw away. That got me wondering about this Oscar Apollinaire again, assuming he was the craftsman in question. I really wanted to talk to him.

But that was for later. First I needed to talk to Saxon Dunbar. I found his card and called his number at 21.

He picked up on the first ring. "Talk to me."

I told him who I was and said that I'd come into possession of something he wanted to see. He said he'd be there in twenty minutes. It took him twice that because it was Friday night.

When he walked into my office, Dunbar had an extra bounce in his step and a mean twinkle in his eye. He found me with my sleeves rolled up and sitting at my desk with a brandy, reading Winchell's column in *The Mirror*. The liquor cabinet was behind me off to one side. He perched on the other side of the desk and made a production out of fitting an oval cigarette into a black holder and lighting up. I found an ashtray in a drawer.

I said, "Last night, you told me that somebody called you and said they knew about dirty pictures of Fay Wray. Is that right?"

"Yes, and that you had been engaged to arrange their return."

"Have you heard from them again?"

He shook his head.

"I don't think you're going to. What they told you, it's about half right. Now, for reasons that I won't go into, I couldn't say anything yesterday, but today things have changed. This is the way I heard it. Yesterday morning these guys, the ones who called you, sent some pictures to Miss Wray at her hotel and put the squeeze on the studio to keep 'em out of circulation. They said they had dozens maybe hundreds of copies and they wanted six Gs for them. RKO lawyers weren't sure what they should do, so they contacted the cops on the quietus, and one of the boys in blue suggested they all talk it over here at my place. Now, here's where they lied to you. The girl in the pictures, it ain't her."

I pulled the photographs out from under the blotter and passed them across the desk. He picked them up, gave them a quick look and then a second before he tossed them back, disappointed.

"This is ridiculous," he said. "Any imbecile can see that's not her."

"That's what the lawyers said, but Miss Wray was still upset and wanted the studio to pay up. Last night they put her off. Asked me to look into it and I did. Today they got her calmed down and she agreed there was nothing to worry about. If the guys call back, they'll tell 'em to shove off. And that's it, I guess. Except I'm out the six hundred bucks I would've pocketed for being the go-between."

He jammed the half-smoked cigarette into the ashtray, spraying tobacco and ash all over my desk.

I took a sip of brandy and said, "Of course, I couldn't say anything last night, but I remembered what you said about being Miss Wray's friend and my friend. Now I don't know how you handle your business since most of the time I can't figure out who you're writing about when it's 'Who was that man who was spotted coming out a certain Broadway Baby's digs on Fortieth Street?,' but I figure it would not help your reputation if you named names and got it all wrong."

He shrugged and fired up another smoke. "But it is such a juicy morsel and it's been months since I mentioned Rastus. Shit, shit, shit. But perhaps the evening's not a total loss. What's a man got to do to get a drink around here?"

I asked what he took. He said he'd have a taste of that rum. Make it neat. I poured a double.

When I gave him the glass, he smelled it, smiled, and sipped deeply. I topped off my brandy and put my feet on the desk.

He eased back in the chair. "You said they asked you to look into the pictures. Did you find anything?"

"Yeah, the guy who runs the back room at the Eltinge Theatre burlesque show said he bought 'em from a hophead photographer. Said this guy comes in every now and then when he's hard up with sets of pictures, usually girls and girls. Said they always sold fast and he got a buck apiece for 'em, if you can believe it. Times like these and guys will fork over a whole dollar."

Dunbar shrugged again. "Takes all kinds. But if only they'd been real. Imagine that! Then six thousand is peanuts."

"My guess is that some guy who knew about the movie saw the pictures at the Eltinge and figured he might be able to bluff the movie people."

Dunbar squinted at the pictures and said, "He certainly got them to look good. If he'd just found a girl who looked more like her, then I could do something with them. I see more of this lookalike material out in California. Short films, too, even some that are the genuine article. You wouldn't believe what some of the bitches who are on the cover of *Photoplay* did when they were working their way up, if you know what I mean."

"No kidding."

And he went on teasing me without naming names. I think he was disappointed that I didn't press him on it. He was working on his second drink when I went into my spiel about how I'd been thinking about what he said about everybody else having good booze after Prohibition ended, and I hoped he'd give me a nod or two in his column. By the time I poured his third, we were chummy as hell.

"Funny thing," I said, "the guy at the Eltinge told me that this hophead photographer finds his girls just like the movie director in *King Kong*."

Dunbar said, "What do you mean? Haven't seen it."

"In the movie, this guy Denham is looking for a girl to star in his picture but it's going to be real dangerous, see, and so he can't get any real actresses to go out into the wilderness with him so he goes out looking for any pretty girl who's so broke she'll take the job, and he finds Ann Darrow, that's the girl's name, trying to steal an apple. Well, this guy, this photographer, he finds girls by hanging around the places that help dames, like that wayward girls outfit, what's it called?"

"The Mary Wilcox Foundation, aptly named I must say. If there was ever a wayward girl, it was her."

"What do you mean?" I said. It wasn't what I was expecting to hear.

"Oh, this is a nice one," he said after another drink. "You know who Mary Wilcox was, don't you?"

"Sure, the high-society dame. She died a few months ago, right?"

"That's her. Wife of Peter Wilcox, upstanding pillar of the community, one of the city's most powerful bankers, hobnobs with Pierpont Morgan, etcetera, etcetera. Everyone thinks that he started the foundation because of the business that the Seabury investigation uncovered, and that may be true enough, but he named it after his wife because she was the upper crust's own Miss Roundheels, a real Flaming Youth."

His eyebrows arched. "A few years ago, she cut quite a swath through the city's eligible bachelors. It lasted until her husband got wind of it and had her committed upstate. The public story was 'nervous exhaustion,' brought on by her tireless good works, but the woman was a raging nymphomaniac."

"No kidding?"

"I know all about it, of course, but the family did a magnificent job of hushing up all the young sports who could have blabbed. Threats, bribes, plum jobs, you name it—whatever it took." He drank and sighed. "Another wonderful story that I must take to my grave."

After Dunbar had bid a sad farewell to his absinthe-infused rum, I put the pictures back into the book, fixed the staples, and stashed it in the safe. About twenty minutes later, my phone rang. It was Abramson, the kid the RKO lawyers left at the Pierre.

Sounding breathless and excited, he said the extortionists had called. I asked what they said.

"They want the money. I told them we have it but I couldn't do anything. They're going to call back in an hour and I can't reach anyone. What do I do?"

I said I'd be right there.

CHAPTER FOURTEEN

In the lobby of the Pierre, I checked the bellboys' station for the kid I talked to but didn't see him. He found me before I got to the elevators, and by the smile on his face, he had something. He rode up to Miss Wray's floor with me but didn't say anything until we were alone in the hall.

"A buddy of mine works the service entrance where the regular deliveries are handled. Mostly it's just the usual business stuff with messengers. He said they were twice as busy yesterday just taking care of Miss Wray's flowers. But he did remember the guy who brought in a package, on account of the guy making a big deal out of it being 'personal,' and it had to be handed to her and nobody else. Of course, they told him it didn't work that way and he left it with them."

I slipped him a single and held on to another one. "What can you tell me about him?"

He looked at the bill and back at me. I made it two. "Older man. Gray hair. Brown suit. Not one of your regular deliverymen. Nobody remembered seeing him before. I talked to a lot of guys back there. They were sure about that. And there's one more thing."

I gave him another buck. "He didn't take off his gloves."

I had to laugh. "Not bad, kid. With the two I gave you last night, that makes it five bucks for gray hair, a brown suit, and gloves. Hell of a racket you've got going here."

He tipped his little cap and said, "I do what I can."

The joint still stank to high hell of all those flowers, and coming on top of all the business with Connie and the con-artist bellboy, it made me even crankier. Hell, I wasn't cranky, I was pissed off. But that didn't bother Abramson. He looked relieved when he answered my knock. He ushered me in saying, "God, I was afraid they'd call back before you got here. Nobody ever said I'd have to do anything like this. I mean, at first it was really exciting to be asked to help in something this dramatic, you know, counting money and being responsible for it, but then Mr. Sleave and Mr. Grossner left me here and I realized that if anything goes wrong, they could blame me for it and there are so many things that can go wrong. What if they want *me* to meet with these criminals?"

While he was yammering away, I went to the bar, poured a brandy, and told him to drink it. "Look," I said, "you're a smart kid. You figured out that they've got you here to take the fall if this deal goes south, and that's good. You're on to them. So just simmer down and tell me exactly what the 'criminal' said. What did the voice sound like?"

He knocked back the brandy and coughed so hard I thought he was going to bring it back up. Eventually, he said, "It was an older man, I think, but he wasn't loud."

"Whispery?"

"Yes, whispery. He said, 'Do you have the money ready?' and I said we did but the men who are in charge aren't here. Then he said he'd call back in an hour and if there wasn't somebody here to give him the money, we'd be in trouble. He sounded mad. What do we do now?"

I went over to the desk where he'd been counting the money. It was in an open valise, ones, twos, and fives bound with rubber bands and paper bands. Beside the bag, weighed down by an empty inkwell, was a stack of Pierre stationery filled with handwritten serial numbers. I guess the lawyers figured they had to keep the kid busy doing something.

There was a phone on the desk, too. I got the hotel operator and gave her the number of Ellis's precinct. A sergeant put me through to him. The place sounded noisy, and I could tell Ellis was steamed. He said there was a change of plan.

"You heard about the banks, didn't you? Yeah, they're closing, a bank holiday they're calling it. Goddamn Commissioner Mulrooney ordered ten extra men to each precinct to protect the banks and post offices, the places people are trying to deposit money. I don't know when Captain Boatwright will spring me. For tonight, you're on your own."

I didn't like that one damn bit. Dealing with a mean ex-cop and a stupid kid didn't bother me. The slaughtered goat . . . That changed everything.

I asked Ellis if the lawyers had told him how to handle the payoff. "Did they say anything about handing over more copies of the book? Or do I just fork over the cash?" I looked at Abramson as I said it. He shrugged.

"Hell, I don't know," Ellis said. "Ask them. I'll call when they cut me loose."

I hung up. Abramson could tell something was wrong. I asked if he could get hold of the lawyers. He said they were at a dinner for the RKO muckety-mucks and couldn't be disturbed. He'd already left one message for them.

"And you don't know anything about getting copies of the books, either."

He got a helpless look on his mug. "I don't even know what

these books are that everybody keeps talking about. Can you explain it to me?"

"It's pictures of a dame who looks like Miss Wray, if she had forgot to put on most of her clothes."

"Wow," he said and flushed.

About ten minutes later the phone rang. The whispery voice said, "Who's this?"

"Quinn."

"Good, do you have the money?"

"Yeah, you got the books?"

"What?"

"The books. You said you've got dozens or hundreds of copies. You and the kid couldn't keep your stories straight on that part. You're not getting any cash until we get the books. That's the deal."

"Wait a minute," he said, and I didn't hear anything else for a while.

When he came back, he said, "We'll bring 'em."

"Wait a minute," I said and put my hand over the mouthpiece. I turned to Abramson. "You know Sleave and Grossner better than I do. If I agree to deliver the money without their okay, will they try to stiff me on my fee?"

He thought before he shrugged again.

"Well, hell," I muttered, "I know where they work. If they welsh, I'll shoot 'em." The kid's face went white and I realized he was scared of me. I took my hand off the phone and said, "Okay, it's a deal. And don't try to hand me any horseshit about meeting you in a cemetery at midnight or anything like that. Let's make it easy on everybody. Why don't you come here? Even though you look like somebody shit on you, I'll tell the desk to send Sleepy-head Trodache right up."

He hung up without saying another word. I guess he hadn't figured that I knew his name. Maybe I shouldn't have mentioned it.

Abramson looked even more worried. "I know I'm new to this, but this isn't how they do it in the movies."

Then it was my turn to shrug. The kid paced until the phone rang again.

Another man said, "Mr. Quinn?"

"Yes." The voice was calm and kind of theatrical or dramatic. I was pretty sure it was the young guy who killed the goat.

"I believe you're at the Pierre, isn't that right? Well, then, we're close. It's a short cab ride. Actually you could walk if you'd like, or I could send a car, but I suspect you would not be comfortable riding with my associate. No matter. I'm sure we can resolve this matter with no more unpleasantness. Just bring the money to 900 Fifth Avenue, the corner of Seventy-First, as soon as possible. We'll be waiting. Good-bye."

I told Abramson to get his coat. We were going to deliver the money. He didn't look to be happy about it and said he'd call the lawyers and leave them another message. On the way down to the lobby in the elevator, the day caught up with me. It seemed like a hell of a long time ago that Daphne had been crying on my shoulder down in the Village and not much that had happened since then made sense. I stewed as the cab took us up Fifth.

We pulled to the curb in front of a mansion. Abramson was popeyed when he got a look at it. I tipped the cabbie an extra buck and said, "Say, do you happen to know whose place this is?"

"Yeah, it's that banker, Wilcox. And thanks, pal."

There was a walled courtyard between the house and the sidewalk. An iron gate in the middle of it was unlocked. We went inside and walked around a fountain with a statue of an angel in the middle. The house was made of stone and looked to be four stories tall. It took up about half of the block. As we climbed the steps to the wide front door, I unbuttoned my topcoat and suit jacket and slipped my knucks onto my right hand.

At the door, Abramson hesitated and looked over his shoulder at me.

"Go ahead," I said and pointed to an ornate knocker shaped like another angel. It sounded loud when he rapped it.

The door swung open right away and we saw Trodache. I'd had an idea he might be there, and I wasn't surprised that he kept one hand behind his back. *Don't hesitate, don't hurry*, I told myself. He was bringing the sap around when I shoved the kid out of the way and jabbed Trodache right in the breadbasket with the tip of my stick. I had it in both hands and gave it to him as hard as I could. He doubled over, retching. I pivoted, reversed the stick, and caught him in the face with the crook. The steel sap clattered to the marble floor as he gagged and rolled into a ball. I gave him one more shot with the knucks to make sure he stayed down. He did. Then he threw up.

Abramson sputtered, "Why did you do that? What's going on?"

I leaned over and gave Trodache a quick frisk. Two pockets were empty. I rolled him over and found a set of handcuffs and a little automatic in a holster on his hip. I pocketed the gun and the sap, dragged him over to a heavy wooden chair against one wall, and cuffed him to the arm. He was a heavy bastard.

It took me a few seconds to settle down. I finally noticed that we were standing in a marble entry hall with another fountain in front of us. There were mirrors and paintings of mountains and oceans between the windows. It was almost as grand as Peacock Alley in the Waldorf. And it was cold. Outside, the temperature was around freezing, but it felt colder where we stood. You could see your breath.

The kid sidled up close and whispered, "Please, Mr. Quinn, what's going on?"

"I'm not sure. To tell you the truth, this is the first time I've done this myself. I mean I've handled a lot of payoffs where the interested parties want to keep it on the QT, but everybody knows who everybody is. Now, with something like this black-mail or extortion, whatever you call it, you figure that the guys who are doing the extorting would not want us to know who they are. But that doesn't seem to matter to these jokers. Maybe they haven't done it before either."

"Actually, I meant him. Why did you, uh, you know?"

"Sucker punch him? Because he was about to do the same thing to you. He tried it on me last night."

"Well, thanks, I suppose."

"And I just don't like him. But you know what strikes me as funny? Where the hell is everybody? I mean, a place like this, you'd figure there's a flunky for every room."

"I've given the staff the night off. This way." The goat killer was down at the end of the hall by an open door. He motioned for us to join him and went through the door. Abramson looked at me. He was scared.

"Come on," I said to him. "Let's get this over with."

As we walked down the hall, I slipped off the knucks and took out the Banker's Special.

He was in another library. Seemed like everyplace I went to in this screwy business had a library. This one was about four times as big as Meyer Lansky's. It was two floors tall with a corkscrew iron staircase leading up to a narrow iron gallery on the upper level. It had one of those ladders with wheels to reach the high places, and a wooden globe so big you couldn't have put your arms around it. But, like Polly's place, it looked like nobody had ever pulled a single book off the shelf. A fire in the fireplace did nothing to take the chill off the room.

The goat killer was wearing a black suit. Medium build, sandy hair. He was about sixteen, maybe less, it was hard to tell. He put a log in the fireplace and flung himself into a leather club chair. On the table next to him, he had a steaming bone-white teacup and a long Colt Woodsman pistol. I thought there was a resemblance to Peter Wilcox, and he acted like he belonged there and looked at me like he expected me to do what I was told. Hell, if he was in Wilcox's foundation and Wilcox's house, I was going to figure that he was a Wilcox.

I sat in a chair that faced him, cocked the .38, and put it on the arm. He must have seen the pistol, but he didn't react to it. Abramson stayed close behind me.

This Wilcox sipped the tea and eased back in the chair before he spoke. "You've brought the money."

I nodded. "What about the books? Trodache said you'd have them."

"Yes, the books." He hadn't expected me to ask about that and started lying, obvious from the way he looked and how he sounded not so sure of himself. "I . . . decided not to bring them. It would have been impractical, and besides, they don't matter. Once we have the money, they are no longer important."

He said it like that explained everything. "I can assure you that the remaining copies of the photo album will not be made public." He stopped and chuckled. "They will be burned. Now, I'll need to examine the money before we proceed. I would have Mr. Trodache take care of it, but he appears to be incapacitated."

Abramson hesitated. I told him to go ahead. He edged toward Wilcox, put the valise in his lap, and hurried back behind my chair. Wilcox leaned forward and stared at him all the way, focusing so intently on Abramson's face that it made him uncomfortable.

He pawed through the money, took out two of the banded stacks of bills, and held them up to the light. That seemed to satisfy him. He didn't bother to count, just snapped the bag shut, sat back, and said, "I believe, in this situation, the party receiving the payment keeps the container, isn't that right?"

"No skin off my ass," I said. "It's not my valise. Abramson?"

"Uh . . . It's mine, but I'm sure I will be reimbursed."

The guy said, "Then our business has been concluded. You may leave."

Abramson had hustled halfway to the door by then. I got up, keeping the pistol pointed at the floor, and was ready to go when I stopped and leaned on my stick. I waited until the guy noticed me and said, "I know I've got no reason to ask, but . . . why? I mean, you're the boss here. These two muttonheads are following your orders. Why are you doing this?"

He smiled. "There's no reason for me to tell you, but since you ask, I will. I'm going to punish my brother. For his many sins. And when he has suffered sufficiently, then I shall kill him."

He snatched the Woodsman up with a practiced hand and put three rounds through the wooden globe. The .22 slugs didn't move it, but he put in a nice tight grouping right in the middle.

"Good evening."

On the way out, we found Trodache on his knees next to the heavy chair. He was trying to unlock the cuffs and glared hard at me until he noticed the pistol. His face was a mess. I stepped up too close to him and he jerked back, his eyes shifting between the piece and my face.

I said, "I gave your boss the money. All of it. He says he's going to burn the rest of the pictures and I guess that's good enough for now, but if you come back asking for more, I'll find you. Understand?"

He muttered something and I said again, "Do you understand?"

"Yeah, shit, I understand. I haven't even seen any goddamn pictures. We just followed the bitch from her hotel to your place and then we followed you. Just like he told us to. Christ, this is a crazy fucking job."

I couldn't disagree.

CHAPTER FIFTEEN

There was a telegram waiting for Abramson when we got back to the Pierre. He said it was from Uncle Julie. When I asked who that was, he said it was Grossner, the lawyer. "Uncle" explained a lot. It was just past midnight.

The telegram said they would be back soon, and I was not to leave the hotel. Still pissed off about Connie and even more confused by what we'd just seen, I decided I needed a brandy. The stuff in their bar was cheapjack horse sweat in a fancy cut glass decanter. I called the concierge and ordered a bottle of Delamain. I told them to make it snappy and they did. I had a tot.

It did not clear things up for me. When I thought about him, I realized I didn't know much about Peter Wilcox. He owned the Ashton-Wilcox Bank—I knew that—and that meant he was rich. I mean, anybody who owns a bank is rich, right? I saw his name in the papers all the time in stories about reforming city government or eliminating corruption or doing good works. He managed to do all that without being a dickhead. Take the Foundation for Wayward Girls. Despite what Saxon Dunbar said, everybody knew that it didn't do anything to punish the dames who needed help or preach to them. It was just a leg up for them and their kids.

So how the hell would a guy like that have anything to do with a six-thousand-dollar shakedown? To him, six thousand dollars wasn't even peanuts, it was peanut shells. But Wilcox probably was involved in financing stag movies. Maybe this guy had something to do with a woman who'd been in one of them. But that didn't explain "Brother Beast" or the kid being in Wilcox's house.

I found the telephone and called the speak. Frenchy answered. He said it was still slow. I told him to get Malloy. When Malloy picked up, I lowered my voice so Abramson couldn't hear what I was saying and asked Arch what he knew about Peter Wilcox. Arch was one of those guys who knows a lot of stuff and liked to share it with everybody.

"Now that's about the last question I expected to hear," he said. "Let's see. His father, Learned Wilcox, founded the Ashton-Wilcox Bank with Robert Ashton. Ashton was considered the more cautious of the two. Learned was so openly rapacious, he gave other robber barons a bad name. Ashton-Wilcox made billions financing arms sales to warring governments. Peter took over when his father retired. When Pierpont Morgan called his friends to prop up the stock market in '29 to forestall the crash, Peter Wilcox was one of them. He's a widower. His wife died sometime recently, I can't say exactly when, but within the last year. He's been active with the Progressive Party and the reform Democrats. Big backer of Roosevelt. He'll have a prime seat at the inauguration in Washington tomorrow. What else do you need?"

"Does he have a brother?"

Malloy paused before he answered. "I don't think so, but I'll have to check to be sure. And what, I must ask, is this in aid of?"

"I really don't know. I'll tell you when I see you," I said and hung up.

I guess I could've worked on it more that night, but I'd done what they paid me for, or said they were going to pay me for, and I'd leave it to Abramson to tell them the rest. While I sat and drank and tried to get the memory of that damned bloody goat out of my head, Abramson went back to pacing and leafing through the pages of serial numbers that he'd copied and staring at the door to the suite. He perked up every time he heard the ding of the elevator bell and was waiting at the door when they finally opened it.

Seemed like everybody was talking together when they came in. I could tell that Miss Wray and Hazel were floating on a cloud because they understood how incredibly popular their big ape was. I think it finally hit Miss Wray that this wasn't just any other moving picture. This one was really special, more than anything she had ever done or most people in her business ever would do. When she thought about it, she still remembered the work, sitting in this big hand and screaming into a microphone for hours. I understood what it was because I'd been to Skull Island and to the top of the Empire State Building. And I realized right then in that room full of flowers that maybe the guy who made the dirty pictures understood that, too, and was trying to steal a little part of it.

Miss Wray's big smile disappeared when she saw me and remembered the other business I was taking care of. Hazel cracked a bottle of champagne and filled a couple of glasses for her and Miss Wray. Probably wasn't their first.

Abramson was ready to be the center of attention, and I was happy enough to stay in the chair with the good brandy. Sleave and Uncle Julie Bennett Grossner seemed not to understand when he explained that we took the cash to a Fifth Avenue mansion, or maybe they didn't believe him.

The kid had been through most of it when he said, "I really could not have handled this without Mr. Quinn. He anticipated that the ruffians would attempt to intimidate us and he was prepared."

Then they all crowded around me. I could tell how worried Miss Wray was, so I said, "There was really nothing to that. Things just got a little interesting for a few minutes. The important part is the other copies of the book, right? And the brains of the outfit said he'd burn them."

Uncle Julie frowned. "Do you have any reason to believe him?"

"Maybe I could've hung around and demanded that he turn them over, but I thought Miss Wray said she'd be happy if they were destroyed."

She spoke up. "That's exactly what I said, and if Mr. Quinn believes that he's settled the matter, I'll take his word for it."

"There's also the matter of my fee," I said, and everybody went quiet.

Sleave cleared his throat. "Yes, about that. It really does seem to us that six hundred dollars is excessive for what amounted to a few hours' work. Let's be reasonable."

"You're not going to stiff me," I said without raising my voice. "Just send it to the Chelsea Hotel."

He and Grossner started to say something else, but Miss Wray took over. "Gentlemen," she said, and they shut up. "I will take it as a personal favor, one which I am sure I will mention to Mr. Cooper, if you will see to it that Mr. Quinn is taken care of properly." She turned to me. "Actually, he and I also spoke of another issue . . ."

"It's settled," I said. "Completely."

"How nice," she said, and her smile was a wonder to see. "Mr. Grossner, I think a bonus is in order for Mr. Quinn, and it should be substantial."

Uncle Julie didn't know exactly what she was talking about, but he knew that Mr. Cooper was his boss. He said he'd see to it first thing in the morning.

Miss Wray said, "That's just wonderful, and thank you all so much for an absolutely delightful evening. I can't remember when so many people have been so nice to me, and now I'm exhausted and must say good night. No, Hazel, I'd like you and Mr. Quinn to stay for a moment more."

Hazel hustled the rest of them out. As soon as they were gone, Miss Wray said, "Saxon Dunbar, tell me about him." Hazel reloaded their glasses, and they sat perched next to each other on a sofa.

"That was easy," I said. "He was fed the line that the pictures were real. I showed him a couple of them where you can really make out the girl's face. He saw it wasn't you right away and lost interest. Somebody making cheap pictures based on the movie isn't a scandal."

Hazel chewed on a knuckle and cut her eyes over to see how Miss Wray was reacting. I wasn't sure either, but I could tell she wasn't completely happy.

Hazel chimed in, "Do you think they'll do what they said? Not send the pictures out to the magazines or columnists or demand more money?"

"The guy who's in charge is pretty strange, all right, but he says he only wanted the money, and I had a little talk with one of the other guys, so now he knows the score. He says he was just doing a job and I believe him. About that much, anyway."

Miss Wray said, "I suppose that's the best I can ask for." I hoped she'd leave it at that.

Before she could think of something else, I said, "Good. Now, tell me how I know your husband."

Hazel said, "Fay, do you want me to leave?"

She shook her head, gave me another look, and said, "Think back two years ago, the summer of 1931. It was unbearably hot."

I nodded, wondering if she was talking about the Maranzano business, but it had nothing to do with that.

"My husband is John Saunders, John Monk Saunders. Does the name mean anything to you? No? He won an Academy Award for *Dawn Patrol*. He wrote the script."

"Oh, yeah, I saw that. Nice picture." It wasn't as good as *Hell's Angels*, but I didn't say that.

"John also wrote a book entitled *Single Lady* about a woman named Nikki. It was a motion picture too, *The Last Flight*, and it was produced as a musical play here in New York in 1931. They called it *Nikki* and asked me to take the lead."

She thought it was going to be a perfect season for her and her husband and that made her feel a little guilty. While the rest of the country was trying to deal with cities full of guys looking for work, she was living in a thirty-dollar-a-day suite at the Pierre. The world was her oyster and her oyster was a bowl of cherries, you might say. She was a popular actress, and she'd be spending the summer with her husband. For a time, it was as fine as she thought it was going to be. They went out for a weekend with Alfred Steichen, and he took pictures of her. They threw a party for the cast of *The Last Flight* when it opened, but when she was rehearsing and on most other nights, John went out on his own to sample what he called "the complete New York speakeasy experience."

As soon as she said that, I knew who she was talking about and said, "Okay, now I remember him. He said that in my place. More than once as I recall. Good-looking fellow. Had some very nice tropical worsted suits. His face was sunburned or tanned, if that's what you call it." I remembered how his choppers shined when he cocked his head and smiled. Always at a woman. He never missed a chance to catch his reflection in one of the mirrors behind the bar, and he admired what he saw.

"Yes, that's John. What did you think of him?"

"He was my favorite kind of customer. He had money in his pocket and expensive tastes, and he brought friends."

I was so involved with the Maranzano business that I was not in the speak as often as I should have been that summer. The first night I saw Saunders, he'd already been in and both of our waitresses jumped on him as soon as he walked through the door. Who was working then? I thought it was Bridget and Dinah. And I remember how Marie Therese shooed them away and got giggly and girly over the guy herself, and I remembered how Frenchy narrowed his eyes when she did. For a month or so, Saunders showed up early, around four almost every afternoon, always dressed sharp. He usually had one or two boisterous pals with him, and by the time he left a couple of hours later, he had collected a few new friends who went with him "to the next watering hole," as he called it. He usually picked up the tab for the group and he tipped well, especially if Dinah had been waiting on him. She fell hard for the easy smile.

Most nights, that would be the end of it. He started at my place because we had the best booze, and we wouldn't see him any more until the next day. But a few times he'd show up again at three in the morning, after he'd sampled some of the gamier examples of the complete New York speakeasy experience. On those nights, he'd be all over the women. We'd make sure he had enough money to pay the fare before we loaded him into a cab and sent him back to the Pierre.

"No, seriously," Miss Wray said. "What did you think of him? I know that you impressed him. He said everybody knew you bought your liquor from Charlie Luciano. He said you were dangerous, one of those real tough little guys who doesn't say much and watches everything. And I know there were women, with John there always are, so don't bother with them. Before we married, he explained that he is simply oversexed. The other women mean nothing to him. He knew I'd understand."

She said it like it didn't mean a damn thing to her, but I didn't buy that, and I could tell that Hazel had heard it before and she didn't buy it either. But what did I think of her husband? That was hard to answer. Saunders and I only had one real conversation, and now that I knew about the flying movies he wrote, it made a little more sense.

It was around five in the afternoon and he was sitting at a table with two other men, one older with burn scars on his face and neck, and the other about Saunders's age, thirty or so, I guessed. The younger guys were telling flying stories. You could see them acting out what they were saying with their hands, making turns and banks and such. I can't remember if we were shorthanded that evening, but I wound up taking a tray of drinks to their table, the best gin all around.

As I collected the empties, Saunders said something along the lines of mine being the finest speakeasy in Manhattan. He'd heard that Jimmy Quinn's was the place to go for good booze and he'd been searching high and low for something better but he hadn't found it. After buttering me up like that, he asked me to join them. It wasn't something I did very often, but I made exceptions for big spenders, so I took a short gin with them.

Like most of the swells who wanted to talk, he asked if it was true that I was on friendly terms with all the gangsters in town. I said not all of them and changed the subject by asking how he and the men sitting with him knew each other. Saunders said that the younger guy and he had been in the air corps together. The older guy was a pilot, too, but he'd been overseas in France. If he told me their names, or his own, I don't remember. That got him talking about how close he was to the men he'd served with and how he literally cried on the wing of his airplane when he learned about the Armistice that ended the war and he wouldn't get to join the fight. He was training other pilots in Florida at the time and they had this special bond that only certain groups of men can form.

That led to one of them, I think it was Saunders, saying that from everything he'd heard, he envied men like me because we made our own rules. We had our own code and defined things by our own standards. He said that the air corps expected some things of him but he was really more concerned with what his fellow pilots thought, and did I agree that courage was grace under pressure?

I figured from the way he said it, I was supposed to know that phrase and I said, "If you put it that way, yeah, I guess I do. You see, there was this kid I grew up with named Oh Boy Oliver. Oh Boy was a normal kid like the rest of us, but his old man took to drink in a bad way and he used to smack the hell out of Oh Boy and his mom and his brothers. If you do that enough times to a kid, you make him scared of everything and that's what happened to Oh Boy. He'd jump away from his own shadow, but there was a time a few years later when we ran into an opportunity to make some good money by relieving some guys of some items they were transporting down near Atlantic City. We needed an extra hand and, even though he didn't really want to come along, we talked Oh Boy into joining us. It turned out to be more interesting than we thought it was going to be. When the shooting started, I was pretty sure Oh Boy would be the first to crap out, but I was wrong. He was so scared he was shaking, but once we mixed it up, he was right there next to me. Sure, after it was over, he was sick and he said he'd never do anything like that again, but, yeah, I guess I'd call that grace under pressure."

That led them into stories about flying, and by and by Saunders said, "You're not much of a man's man are you, Quinn?"

I don't know if he meant it to be as insulting as it sounded. The older guy noticed and was surprised. Saunders paid no attention to him. But, hell, I wasn't insulted. I've been hearing the same thing since I was a little kid. Saunders expected an answer, so I obliged and said it was true.

"You see, I didn't grow up with a bunch of guys. I lived in a tenement where there was a dozen families. It wasn't a bad place but it wasn't the Ritz, and when I got old enough, part of my job was to make sure that nobody bothered us. I mean, I earned a fair amount doing this and that mostly on my own, but when I was around the place, I was expected to make sure that the kids could play on the stoop or the roof without anybody messing with them or stealing from them, and that's what I did. I wasn't big enough to scare anybody, but I did know how to handle a pistol pretty good by then, so we didn't have much trouble. Shoot a few people, word gets around, you know.

"When it's guys you don't know, that's a different ballgame. You get a bunch of men's men together and they'll start goofing around and pretty soon it'll turn into horseplay and they'll start punching on each other and messing around with each other, and then one of them's going to look around and figure who's the littlest guy there. And he's gonna start picking on him. And that little guy's going to be me.

"Now, if there's any way I can run away, I will. An old woman taught me that a long time ago and it has served me well, but if I can't run, then I gotta do something, right? I mean, you just can't let a guy do whatever he wants to you. So you use your knucks"— I took mine out of my pocket and put them on the table—"or your stick"—I held it up—"or your pistol, depending on the situation. Then, if you handle it right, you don't have to dispose of a body later. So I try to avoid those situations, and I guess that means I'm not much of a man's man, but I don't hold it against those that are."

Saunders and his pal didn't know what to say. The old guy laughed like merry hell.

That's all I could remember of the conversation. I was quite a blabbermouth that evening, but I didn't mention any of it to Miss Wray. Instead, I lied and said, "Your husband tended to be quiet when he was in his cups. I liked that about him."

She drained her glass. I knew she didn't buy it. "And the women were all over him then. No, don't say anything. That's the way it always is for John." She'd had enough champagne to forget the "oversexed" business, and her voice was sad.

Hazel tried to change the subject. "Are you sure that we've nothing to worry about with those awful photographs?"

"No," I had to admit. "The guy behind all this is nuts, but I got the feeling tonight that he really is only interested in the money and now that he's got it, he won't bother you anymore. And there's one other thing . . ."

I knew I was making a mistake as the words fell out of my mouth. "I may be able to find the guy who took the pictures. Does the name Oscar Apollinaire mean anything to you?"

Miss Wray and Hazel looked at each other and shook their

heads. Miss Wray said, "I can't tell you how important this is to me. I must meet the woman in those pictures. No matter what those studio men say, if word of this gets back to John, he'll be furious. Sometimes the smallest, most inconsequential thing will set him off."

She focused on me. "At the end of that summer, when the play closed in October, John had been so successful at capturing the fullness of the complete New York speakeasy experience that he had to go to a 'health farm' in upstate New York for a week to recover."

I thought even a month might not have been long enough to do the trick.

She said, "It's funny, but now I remember that week I spent alone here at the Pierre as the most rewarding part of the trip. John had been disappointed that the play had not been well received, but I enjoyed it. I thought I did well, and that's where I met Cary, who was just wonderful. It was a lovely but bittersweet week by myself. You see, they had done much of the preliminary work on *King Kong*, and I knew that Mr. Cooper wanted to talk to me about it as soon as I returned to California.

"When John was ready to come back, I had the hotel hire the very best car they could find, not just a limousine but a Rolls-Royce, mind you. I wanted him to return in style. But do you know what he said when he saw the car?"

She paused, and I could tell that Hazel knew what was coming. "He said there were scratches on the door. Scratches. On one door. They ruined everything for him. Why hadn't I noticed that and demanded that they bring around another car? He sulked all the way back to the city."

She held out her glass and Hazel refilled it. "I couldn't believe it then and I can't believe it now. I know I shouldn't let it upset me, but it does."

Hazel put a hand on her shoulder. "Fay, don't do this to yourself." It didn't work.

"That's what happened over a few little scratches on a car that wasn't even his. You can imagine how he would react to those pictures! And I know something else about them."

By then she was swaying a little on the sofa. "The girl in the pictures, that's the girl he really wants. She's the girl he wants me to be."

Hazel said, "Now, Fay," and Miss Wray ignored her.

"Right after we were married, John said that he had the three things he'd always wanted. He was famous, he was rich, and he was married to a beautiful actress. But I've seen how he acts with other women, the ones he's attracted to, and they're all the same with their well-stuffed brassieres, the way he drools over them. That's what he wants me to be."

What she said squared with my memories of the man. Right then, I think, everything that had happened over the last two days caught up with her and the first tears came. Hazel put her arms around her.

I let myself out.

CHAPTER SIXTEEN

In the cab on the way back to the speak, I tried to figure out how everything I'd learned that day fit together, and I did a damn poor job of it.

For a while, I tried to put this Oscar Apollinaire character at the center. But I didn't know enough about him. It made sense that the picture book was promotional material for a real movie that he was planning to show at "very private screenings." That's what he told Daphne. But why would he use the book to put the screws to RKO for six grand? Simple, he wouldn't. Even if Apollinaire made the book, it didn't necessarily figure that he was involved with the extortion. Unless he had split from his "silent partner," Peter Wilcox.

Okay, so who was the guy who killed the goat? Not Peter Wilcox. The guy I saw was too young to be Wilcox. And if Arch was right, Wilcox was in Washington for the inauguration. And if Peter Wilcox felt the urge to slaughter a goat, he'd do it someplace else. That guy hated Peter Wilcox. Could he be Wilcox's younger brother? His twin, even his evil twin? Damn, that was a screwy thought, but why the hell not? Everything else about this was screwy. And one other thing I knew, whoever this guy was, he didn't have much trouble getting into Peter Wilcox's foundation office and his house. *And maybe I know something else*, I thought. *He needs money.*

But there was no reason to keep worrying over that. This was the guy who threatened to make the pictures public, and he clued Saxon Dunbar in on them, and now Dunbar wasn't interested, and the guy had been paid off. So, I figured that part was over for now. It was time to find Oscar Apollinaire and hear what he had to say. I hoped I wouldn't have to go far. It was late and I was getting tired.

It was a little after two Saturday morning when I got back to the speak. Things had slowed down by then. I went to the end of the bar and motioned Connie over. She gave me a look and said something to Arch. He was standing next to her and took his time walking over to me. Connie turned around and talked to Marie Therese. I started to get steamed all over again but forced myself to calm down and thought, why the hell not? Why shouldn't Connie be as screwy as everything else today?

Arch gave that little shrug that said *Women. What're you gonna do?* "Good evening, sir, I've been considering what you asked when you called, and I'm almost certain that I'd know if Peter Wilcox had a brother, but I cannot say with perfect certainty. I know a bit, but I've not made a study of the man and his family."

"It's all right," I said, "but if you could find out more by tomorrow, I'll put something extra in your pay envelope. I need to know about cousins, any close relatives, I guess, and his deceased wife."

"I don't have the particulars at hand, but if you could tell me why you need this research, I might be able to expend my efforts more efficiently."

"I wish I could, Arch. Oh, yeah, and there's something else. What does it mean when you sacrifice a goat? I mean, why would somebody do that?"

That got his interest. His eyebrows popped up, and his mustache bristled at the question.

"And one more thing, I know Connie's still pissed at me, but tell her—no, ask her—to call up to the kitchen and have them make a couple of sandwiches and coffee for us and bring them to my office. I gotta talk to her."

Arch said, "Go for the roast beef if there's any left. It was a little dry but very tasty."

"I had the steak a few hours ago."

"Then stick with the cheese."

"Done," I said and went upstairs to my office.

When Connie bumped open the door with her hip a few minutes later, she had a tray with one sandwich and one cup of coffee. She set the tray on my desk and said, "You wanted to see me?"

"No, I need to talk to you." I picked up half the cheese sandwich and dug in. "I didn't have time to tell you this earlier, but you should know what went on today."

She pulled up the chair and sat close to listen.

I told her about it all, including the business with the goat, which didn't bother her as much as I thought it would since she saw a lot of that being raised on a farm in California. I finished up with the guy on Fifth Avenue and how he said he was going to kill his brother.

Connie thought about that while she finished off the sandwich and the coffee. Then she said, "That's the craziest story I ever heard. We've got to talk to this Oscar Apollinaire. You said he may live in the Chelsea, right?"

In the elevator, Nelson said, "Hi, Connie. Apollinaire? Yeah, he's on six, in 624, I think."

It was about 3:30 in the morning then. We'd left Frenchy, Marie Therese, and Malloy to close up and gone back to the Chelsea.

Connie said, "What's he like?"

Nelson closed the doors. "Odd fellow. Sports a fez and fancy waistcoats. Keeps even more irregular hours than you two."

I asked if Apollinaire was in, and Nelson said he had gone up about an hour ago.

Then Nelson asked which floor. Usually we both got off on five, Connie's floor, and then I'd take the stairs down to three later. From time to time, we'd both get off at three, but that hadn't happened for a few weeks.

Connie said, "Five, please, Nelson. I need to freshen up."

That made me think that maybe she'd want to change clothes and I could help her with that, but, no. As soon as I took my top-coat off, she went into the bathroom. After a time and without my assistance, she did up her hair and put on a very nice white silk blouse.

I told her she looked terrific. She smiled and nodded and didn't say anything else. We took the center stairs up to the sixth floor and went down the hall to 624. I could hear dance music from a phonograph through the door. I rapped on the door with my stick and we waited. Connie was so jazzed and curious, she grabbed my arm tight and bounced on tiptoes. I kept the other hand in my coat pocket with the .38.

The girl who answered the door was not what I expected. She was young and dark and tall and slender. She wore gauzy harem pants and an unbuttoned gold lamé vest with nothing under-neath either of them. She had a silver chain with jangly coins around her hips and silver rings on her toes. The thick smell of hashish explained her dark pupils and pleasant smile.

She said hello in a dopey kind of voice, and I said we were looking for Oscar Apollinaire.

Her brow wrinkled for a second, then she smiled and twisted around, saying, "Baby, there's some people here to see you."

When she turned, the vest swung open. Connie frowned and blushed and looked down.

A man's voice came from another room. "Who is it, Honeybunch?"

Without answering, she strolled away from us and we could see the room. At first, all I could make out were the bright colors, orange, red, and yellow, in the flickering light. I thought it was from a fireplace like the one I'd just seen in the grand library, but this came from an electric fixture with a revolving colored shade. As my eyes adjusted, I saw that the room looked like the inside of an Arab tent, a Hollywood Arab tent with big pieces of silk hanging from the ceiling and the floor covered with carpets and cushions.

Honeybunch said over her shoulder, "*Entrez vous*, and please take off your shoes."

Connie and I *entrez*ed. She took off her shoes. I didn't.

As Honeybunch settled on a pillow and picked up her hash pipe, a man came in from the back. "Who is it?" he repeated, sounding suspicious and worried. He was bald and brown from the sun with a thick black Vandyke. Dress slacks, suspenders, and a starched white shirt. No shoes, no tie.

He took a long slow look at Connie before he turned to me. Then he said, "Jimmy Quinn, long time, no see," and held out a hand. I almost recognized the voice.

When he smiled, I saw the gap between his front teeth and remembered him.

"Well, I'll be damned. Bobby Colodny."

CHAPTER SEVENTEEN

The first time I met Bobby Colodny, I couldn't have been more than ten or eleven. I can't remember what I was doing that morning over on the west side near Tenth Avenue, and it's not important anyway. They still called Tenth "Death Avenue" around there, not because it was such a tough neighborhood but because there was a freight train that ran on street-level tracks. It went real slow, but kids goofed around and ran in front of it, and a few years before, one of them had slipped and the wheels cut off his head. So I was careful around there. But I wasn't prepared when I went around a corner and found a horse standing across the sidewalk in front of me.

There was a boy on its back, turned out to be Bobby. He yelled out in a loud voice, "Hey, kid, this is the Dummy Boys' street, and if you want to walk on it, you pay us a nickel." A bunch of kids behind him yelled at me to get the hell out of there.

Now, I don't know if they were real Dummy Boys. Yeah, the Dummy Boys were a gang that rode horses, but a lot of people had horses then. You saw about as many of them as cars on the streets.

Anyway, I was so surprised I stepped back, and I think they expected me to run away. But I didn't. I figured, *Okay, it's his street and I need to use it. I'll give him five cents.*

So I dug a fistful of pennies out of my pocket, counted out five, and held them up to him. He reached down, kind of surprised, and I went around the horse. The guys behind him didn't know what to do and just stood there as I hurried through them. I was past them when a big kid heaved himself up from a stoop and stood in my way.

He was a few years older, fat and wide, and he was holding an empty bucket of beer. By the way he smelled, it wasn't his first of the day.

"Hey, Colodny," he yelled. "Did this kid pay?"

The kid on the horse said I did, and they all looked at each other. I guess nobody paid them before.

The drunk kid said, "What're you doing here?"

I said I had business.

The kid called Colodny, still on the horse, said, "Ain't you the kid that works for the Brain?"

That's what some people called A. R. in those days. But not me. Truth is, though, I was kind of proud to be recognized that way. I didn't know the word had got around.

I answered by shrugging like it was nothing because I didn't really know what to say, and I had been taught not ever to say anything about A. R.'s business.

The big kid laughed real nasty and said, "The Brain, huh, well, what're you gonna do if we take your nickel and kick your little ass off our street anyway?" The other boys laughed with him then, but not Colodny. I saw that I had a clear street behind me, so I yelled back at the big kid, "It'd mean you won't get any more money off me, so that would be pretty damn stupid, you fat tub of lard."

The other guys laughed harder, making the big kid so mad he

threw his empty bucket at me. By then, I was halfway down the block. In those days, when I ran, nobody caught me. I sure wasn't worried about a fat drunk kid.

The next time I saw Bobby Colodny was a few weeks later on the same street. I stopped at the corner and was ready to take another route if those guys were still there, but the sidewalk was empty, no guys, no horse, no fat boy on the stoop. So I went on and I hadn't got far when somebody yelled my name. That stopped me because I didn't know anybody there. It was the kid I'd seen before, Colodny, without the horse. I was ready to run as he crossed the street. I saw that he was a few years older than me and a lot taller, with curly brown hair under a newsboy's cap. He had a wide gap between his front teeth.

He said, "You're Jimmy Quinn, ain't ya? Yeah, I thought so. Look, Delmar was outta line the other day, acting like he did, and you oughta know he ain't any kind of boss around here. He don't call no shots. Anything Mr. Rothstein needs in this neighborhood, you just talk to me. I'm Bobby, by the way, Bobby Colodny."

We might have said something else then, but I don't remember. That's when I first began to figure out that because I worked for A. R., other boys looked up to me, even older boys. When you're a short kid, that means a lot, but I didn't understand it well enough to let it swell my head.

The next time I saw Bobby was at the movies, and from then on, that's where I always saw him. Almost always. You see, he was like me, wanting to be the first to see the new pictures the first day they opened. We must have run into each other a dozen times in theater lobbies over the next few years. We usually didn't say much to each other because Bobby had a girl on his arm as often as not. When we did talk, we figured out that we liked the same kind of pictures and the same stars. And for Bobby, I remember it was always the women in the movies. I'd be lying if I didn't admit that was a lot of the attraction for me, too, but when Bobby talked about them, this dreamy look came over him and you could tell he was a man in love. Bobby was one of those guys, puberty hit him like a falling piano. He'd make a move on any girl who didn't run away from him and some who did. He told me once that he thought it was some kind of compulsion, he couldn't control himself. "Yeah," he said, "I get slapped plenty, but I get my ashes hauled plenty, too." He even snaked a girl away from me and knocked her up. He was just one of those guys who'd do that and not see anything wrong with it.

In the years after that, we'd run into each other in the penny arcades, too. By then, I was helping to move slot machines and pinball machines in and out for repair. Bobby was doing the same thing with peep show machines, the racy kind from the back rooms where they kept some of the slots, too.

That's what he did during the day. At night, he hung around the girls' dressing rooms at Minsky's and Eltinge's burlesque houses. He told me he did favors for them, buying them cigarettes, booze, marijuana, cocaine, soft drinks. Anything they needed, he'd find it. Any time I wanted, he said, he'd get me into the late show downstairs. That's where the real action was.

I'd have taken him up on it, but by then I was working with Lansky, Luciano, and Longy Zwillman stealing cars and driving liquor. After a while, when I hadn't seen him for a long time, I asked around and heard Bobby had left town and gone into the movie business.

That didn't surprise me. I mean, I liked the movies. Give me a couple of hours on my own, I'd duck into the closest theater and watch whatever was playing. But Bobby loved the movies, loved them as much as he loved girls, and maybe for him they were the same thing or close to it. Where moving pictures were concerned, he wanted to know everything.

So I guess it was about ten years later that I was seeing Bobby again in this crazy room that could've belonged to Rudolph Valentino. He didn't look like I remembered him, but a lot of that was due to the cue ball head.

He took a long look at me and I could tell that he was judging the price of the suit and he knew it wasn't cheap. His mouth widened into a sly gap-toothed half smile, and he said, "So it's Jimmy Quinn, the famous gangster."

I shook my head.

"Hell, if I know you, you're famous."

"But I'm not a gangster. I run a respectable gin mill."

He didn't care to argue the point and turned to Connie. There was no mistaking the wolfish look on his face. "And who is this lovely young lady?"

"She's Connie Nix. Connie, this is Bobby Colodny. He's from my old neighborhood, or close to it, anyway."

"Then who's Oscar Apollinaire?" she said as he took her hand in both of his.

"Yeah, Bobby, who's Oscar Apollinaire? That's who we came up here to see."

"You've heard of me, that's wonderful! It's my *nom de plume* or *nom du cinema*. Oscar Apollinaire is an *artiste* of the *avant-garde*." Sounded like Bobby had picked up a lot of French since he'd been away. He told us to have a seat and ushered Connie onto a low chaise where she almost had to lie down as she tucked her skirt under her legs. I took a chair. He sprawled across three big pillows on the floor.

He said, "I thought you lived here, too, and I've been meaning to look you up, but my work keeps me very busy."

"So I've heard," I said, and his eyes narrowed.

"What'd you mean?"

"We'll get to it by and by. First you've gotta tell me where you've been. I mean, for a while there, it seemed like I was seeing you every week or so at the pictures or the arcades, and then you were gone. What happened?"

"It's a long story. But where are my manners? Honeybunch, did you offer our guests a turn at the pipe?"

I said no thanks, and Connie shook her head.

"Gage? Cocaine? I've got some of Captain Spaulding's finest.

No? You never were one for the hard stuff, were you? Afraid I don't have any booze that's up to your standards."

"No, we're fine. Somebody told me you got into the moving-picture business."

He laughed and said, "Yeah, that's what I did all right, but not like you think. Did you ever hear of the Projectionists?"

Now, I've always found that people enjoy talking about themselves, and Bobby sure did. He left out some things that I was able to fill in, and it seemed like he couldn't decide whether he should tone it down to keep from offending Connie or if he should be racy to get her worked up. Not that it mattered, he was flirting like I wasn't there, anyway, and for a while Connie loved it. Honeybunch was more interested in her hash pipe and the music from the Victrola.

Bobby didn't mention his work with the naughty peep shows in the arcades, but that must have been how he met the Projectionists, Dieter and Gus. They were two older guys whose territory went to upstate New York and Connecticut and Rhode Island and down into Pennsylvania. They drove a Ford truck and showed stag movies to men's groups—lodges, veterans, unions, fraternities. Depending on what the guys wanted and the product they had on hand, they'd set up a screen and projector and run one-reelers for two or three hours. They got a hundred bucks, some warm beer, cold sandwiches, bad liquor, cheap cigars, and, if they were lucky, a place to stay for the night. When they were on the road, they slept outside. They never worried about the cops because the boys in blue were always invited. Bobby said in some towns, the preachers and priests didn't give them any trouble because they figured the pictures took some of the pressure off the local wives to do what their husbands were wanting to see.

At first, Bobby loved it even though Dieter and Gus piled the grunt work on him—changing tires, repairing broken films, cleaning up, and all that—while they got drunk. The way it worked was, the Projectionists would go out on the road for a few months and follow their circuit, bringing them back to New York when they learned that a new supply of pictures had arrived. Most of them came from South America and Mexico, with a few from France, Bobby said. They'd buy all they could afford, and then approach a few collectors in the city, rich guys who would shell out serious money for copies of the best stuff. Then they'd hit the road again.

After he'd been with them for almost two years, Bobby decided that he'd learned everything he could about that side of the business, all the things that could go wrong when you went to show a moving picture on a screen, from not having the right film to a tear in the screen to a balky projector. And, he said, by then the pictures they were showing had lost something.

"I mean, how often can you watch some fat hairy spic slipping the sausage to a blowsy broad when they're poorly photographed with the wrong lighting by some guy who has no idea of where to put the camera or what to do with it?"

That was all Connie could handle. As long as Bobby was just talking, she was fine but when he got specific, I saw the first flush spread across her cheeks and throat. She struggled up from the low chaise and said, "I'm sorry, Mr. . . ."

"Bobby," he said.

"Bobby then. It's been a long night and I'm exhausted." I stood up, and she said, "No, Jimmy, you stay here and catch up. I'll be just fine."

"No, I'll come with you just to be sure."

Bobby looked like he wanted to ask something. I said I'd be right back, and Connie and I left.

In the hall, she said, "Really, Jimmy, you don't need to do this."

I said, "I had to get a little rough with that guy Trodache. Like I said last night, he knows where we work, he might know where we live. So humor me. What do you think of Bobby?"

She smiled a little. "He certainly is, I don't know, exotic? We see a lot of interesting characters in the bar, but he's really something, and that room of his, wow. And he sure knows how to flatter a girl."

"Ain't that the truth. You better watch out for him."

"Don't be ridiculous," she said as we got to her room. She unlocked the door and I went inside with her. "See, nobody here," she said. "Nothing to worry about."

I said, "I worry," and put my arms around her and kissed her. She responded but just for a second before she pushed me away. I let her go and gave her a curious look. She looked right back at me, giving away nothing.

I said, "You've still got Marie Therese's pistol, right? You didn't give it back to her?"

Her expression changed then, getting serious. She said yes, she still had it.

"Keep it handy for a few days. I'll see you tomorrow."

Back up in his room, Bobby flopped back down on his cushions and said, thinking out loud, "Isn't that girl the sweetest little peach. I wouldn't mind a taste of that. Are you and her . . ."

"She works for me," I said.

"And?"

I shrugged. "We get along."

"From time to time, I host private soirees. In fact, I've got one coming up. Dress her up right and she could do very well for herself, double what she'd clear on a good night at your place, easy. A lot more if she was interested in it." He stopped like he'd just thought of something, and then said, "But where was I? Oh, yeah, Dieter and Gus, those assholes."

One night outside a town in south Jersey, when they were near the end of their circuit, Dieter and Gus really tied one on. Though Bobby didn't say it, I got the idea he might have helped them along. After both of them had passed out, he took their strongbox out of the back of the truck and got the key to it in Gus's shoe. He left them fifty bucks, the truck, the pictures, and the equipment and figured he was doing them a favor. He hoofed it into town and caught the first train heading west the next morning. He knew if he was going to learn anything about the other side of the picture business, he had to go to California.

"That's the source of the quality material, not the crap we were showing, I learned that when we were on the road. Guys want to see naked women screwing, it's that simple. But because I really like good movies, I was spoiled. I wanted a stag picture to look as good as a real picture. Okay, there was no way to tell a real story, but I knew that if I learned how they made pictures at the studios, I could make one that *looked* as good as theirs."

He said, "First, you need a beautiful girl. That's not as hard as you think. You can't swing a dead cat out there without hitting a dozen of them, and with the right makeup and clothes, you can make just about any girl look like you want her to. So I learned about makeup and hair dressing and costumes."

He did that by getting in tight with the guys nobody ever heard of, the guys who worked on the sets and made the backdrops and did the rest of the hundred little things you've got to do to make a moving picture that I never thought about. Bobby didn't say it in so many words, but I figured that he managed to get close to those guys the same way he wormed his way backstage at Minsky's, by supplying dope and booze and smokes. Working with those guys, he was able to see how all the little pieces fit together to make the kind of moving picture he imagined.

The first trick, he said, was light. He had to make light do what he wanted it to do. He told me to think about outdoor scenes. A lot of them looked so bright that you could tell what was happening but you couldn't make out any details, like when the Keystone Cops were chasing each other down dirt roads. That wouldn't do if you were trying to show a sexy woman's body. He said there was a guy who shot portraits of all the famous actresses. Maybe I'd seen them. The guy's name was Hurrell. And there was a Chinaman out there, a cameraman who could do incredible stuff with filters and frames to make a girl's eyes look better. And there was another guy who made these real arty, dreamy photographs. Their work was like nothing Bobby had ever seen and he wanted to capture that same satiny texture and glamour with naked girls. But it wasn't the same with still pictures and moving pictures. He had a lot to say about different kinds of orthochromatic and panchromatic film stocks that I didn't understand.

After Bobby thought he'd figured out all those things, he had to rent a camera and lights and a private place where he could build his sets. Then he had to find a lab that would develop his film without asking any questions. And he had to keep all of it secret. Once he had those lined up, he called a girl he knew, a tall girl who looked a little like Theda Bara but hadn't had any luck breaking into the business. She had developed a taste for cocaine.

Bobby said, "I thought back to the days when I first got in backstage at Minsky's, remember that time? Well, there was this one night, some of the girls were talking and didn't know I was there. One of them was saying how cute I was and how she liked me, and there was another one, an older bitch, who laughed and said, 'Yeah, if you get 'em when they're young enough, you can get them to do anything,' and they laughed with her, and she said, 'So work him for all you can before he wises up.' It made me mad to hear it, but, shit, the bitch was right and I didn't forget it. And it cuts both ways, don't it? A little flattery, a little money, a little gin, a little snort, my Theda Bara was ready to do anything I asked her to do."

He made a lot of mistakes on that first one, even with what he'd learned from the professionals, and wasted a lot of film, but he kept at it. At first, he tried to be the guy who was seduced by her, but that just didn't work. He had to be behind the camera. The only actor he could find refused to work without a mask because he thought he still had a chance to be a star. The girl though, she was fine. In some shots, you would think she really was Theda Bara.

"I look back on it now," Bobby said, "and compare it to the work I've done since and it doesn't look so great, but at the time, it was damned good. If it wasn't the best stag film ever made, it was a hell of a lot better than any of the shit I showed with the Projectionists, and I'm still damn proud of it."

"What did you do with it?" I asked.

"Brought it back home. What else would I do? That was the idea all along."

"Uh-huh," I said, like I wasn't buying it.

"What, you don't believe me? Come on then. I'll show you."

CHAPTER EIGHTEEN

Bobby got up from his pillows and pulled a key ring out of a blue-and-gold box on a table by the door. He said, "Honeybunch, don't touch anything," but she was busy with her pipe.

I followed him out into the hall and down to 618. He had to unlock two locks, one a heavy deadbolt, to open the door. "It may not look like much," he said as he snapped on a light, "but this is where the magic happens, or part of the magic."

To me, it was more impressive than his Arabian Nights tent in a different way. It was filled with stuff and smelled of ink and glue.

A workbench made of boards that had been nailed and screwed together ran along one wall. On the opposite wall there were shelves made of the same rough lumber. They were stacked with bolts of bright cloth, folded dresses, long wigs on model heads, shoes, cosmetics, and masks trimmed with feathers and fur. In the middle of the floor were a sewing machine and an easel and a drawing desk and dress forms and a big trash bin.

There was a typewriter on the bench, but most of the space was taken up by a hand-operated printing press with a round metal plate and a long handle, tubes of ink and rollers, a fat pot of glue, boxes of heavy paper and cardboard and envelopes, and a metal stapler almost two feet long.

"This is pretty impressive," I said and meant it.

Bobby sat in a chair by the press. I perched on the stool at the drawing table. "Yeah," he said, "I built the shelves and the bench. Funny, after I left Dieter and Gus, the first thing I learned about making moving pictures was carpentry. The second was sewing."

"I don't understand," I lied. "What does this have to do with movies?"

"You've got to have something to take a picture of. Sure, you need the girl, but she has to be in a place or a situation, and you've got to make that. Then she has to wear clothes so she can take them off. You see, you've got to create a world on the screen. The studios, they've got their own shops. They can make a western town or a French palace. I make mine myself. It starts with drawings. From those, I paint my flats and props. They ain't here, they're too big. And then there's the costumes. They're not like regular clothes. They just have to look good for the camera and come off easy."

"And the press?"

"That's for my promotional material." Until then, he'd sounded proud but not bragging. When he walked over to the press, his voice changed. This part of it, he really liked. "I can't do the billboards and newspaper ads they use, but I don't have to. My audience is smaller, but they pay more and they get a lot more than just a movie for their money."

"Not that I'm doubting your word, but I see all this stuff here and in your other room, but I don't see any moving pictures."

"I got another place for the rest of it, a loft down in Chinatown that no white man could ever find. But if you don't think my pictures are real, take a look at these."

He pulled a box down from one of the shelves over the bench

and took out a couple of picture books, the same size and shape as Miss Wray's.

The title on the first was *The Real "It" Girl*. It was the one Daphne described, the one he showed her before he took her to see his partner in the Grand Central Building. The second book was *The Fool and the Vamp*. Except for the black wig and a bra made of metal snakes, the girl didn't look much like Theda Bara, but there was no mistaking how she seduced her fool.

"Okay," I said. "How does it work?"

He said that when he came back from California with his first picture, he took it to a gentleman of his acquaintance, a fellow he got to know when he was with the Projectionists. This was a rich guy who shared Bobby's tastes in "the highest-quality exotic entertainment." He was a collector who bought the best movies and had a library of "masterpieces of eros." I didn't ask for his name. The guy was impressed with Bobby's movie and agreed to bankroll him.

Bobby said, "One of the big problems is just finding a place to develop the negative and make prints. With still photography, you can set up a lab in a closet, but it takes more with moving pictures, if you care about quality the way I do. So, first thing, we bought this little shop down on the Lower East Side. It used to do work with an animation studio when they were still in business. I can work there and not worry about nobody bothering me or turning me in to the cops. The regular work we take in is starting to make a little money, too."

Bobby made silent one-reelers that were quick copies of whatever was popular in real movies, but he didn't call them "real movies." The stories didn't mean much as long as the girls looked enough like Mary Pickford or Claudette Colbert or Clara Bow or Fay Wray.

Bobby's partner financed the first pictures and introduced Bobby to some of his like-minded blue-blood pals, and they formed the Oscar Apollinaire Société de Cinéma. "This is not some jerkdog outfit. The premieres are strictly black-tie or costumes. Catered, nothing but the best. The members are masked but not all the masks stay on all night. Some of 'em bring companionship, or that can be provided. I make up these photo books to build interest in every new picture. The members love 'em. Always asking for extra copies. Of course, the members can buy their own prints of the movies after the premiere, and I can arrange entertainment for their private parties."

"Sounds like a hell of a lot of work for one guy."

He frowned. "It is. I've had guys helping me but nobody I've been able to trust."

He looked like he was about to offer me the job, so I cut him off. "Where do you find the girls?"

"Cathouses and burlesque shows. That part ain't as easy as I thought it would be either. There's plenty of girls, but the ones who'll do it for fifty bucks are the ones you don't want, and the ones you want, they'll string you along forever before they turn you down. Ain't it always the case," he said and laughed.

"Quite an operation," I said to keep him talking. I could tell he was still looking for me to show him a little respect.

"The crash damn near did me in, and the year after it was grim."

"You don't need to tell me about that," I said.

"Now, I can't complain. We're doing all right. The one I've just finished is a two-reeler that's the most ambitious yet. I'd invite you, but things are busy at the moment. Some other time, maybe."

"Probably too steep for me anyway, but I wouldn't mind taking a look at one of your pictures."

"Like I said, right now, I'm booked solid. Talk to me in a week or so and we'll work it out. Now, your girl Connie, I could use her. I'm having a *soirée cinématique intime* in a couple of days. I've had to change the date once already, and I'm scrambling to find some last-minute help. Do you think she'd be interested? She'll be serving drinks and food. I'll pay her whatever you give her. If she's willing to do a little more, she could double or triple that in tips. What do you say?"

"It's up to her."

"I'll talk to her," he said, and I felt a nasty uncomfortable churn deep inside.

He stared at me for a few seconds, then said, "Now tell me what the hell you're doing up here."

I'd been waiting for that, but I hadn't worked out how much to tell, so I answered, "Last night, a lady, an actress, came into my place. You probably know who I'm talking about. She brought one of your picture books. It's called *Kong*. Somebody wanted six grand from her to keep it private."

His eyes narrowed then, and I could see his jaw clench and relax, clench and relax, as I spoke. "They said they'd get copies of it to all the papers. Even though it was clear that the lady in that book is not the actress, she didn't want those photographs being spread about. She wanted to pay the guys off, and after a bit of persuasion, the studio lawyers saw it her way. I agreed to be the middleman for them, but before I could do anything, a couple of guys threatened me. One of them's an ex-vice cop named Trodache."

When I said the name, Bobby cursed, "That cocksucking son of a bitch." He got up and paced the room, reminding me of Miss Wray a few hours before. "Spill it," he said. "What else?"

I told him that the man in charge was a strange young guy. Maybe I should've mentioned what went on with the goat in the Grand Central Building, but I didn't. I said the big cheese lived in a mansion on Fifth Avenue and he claimed that he was going to burn the other copies of the book, and he was doing this to punish his brother and kill him.

"His brother? You're sure he said his fucking brother?"

I nodded. Bobby mulled over that and said, "Trodache used to work for me. Can't trust him. He stole from me, and he never delivered what he promised." I could figure what an ex-vice cop promised to deliver Bobby. "How the hell did he get his hands on a copy of the book? Have you seen it?"

I nodded again.

"Do you have it?"

"No," I lied. "Why?"

"It has a number on the back. That'll tell me whose copy it is. But . . ." He paused and started talking to himself, trying to convince himself, "No, this doesn't change anything. It's still smooth sailing, nothing but smooth sailing."

When he remembered I was there, he looked up and said, "So Miss Wray has seen it. What did she think?"

"It embarrassed her. The RKO lawyers were interested in how you copied their costumes and sets."

"I'll just bet they were." He laughed, sounding pleased. "You see, I've got this guy at RKO who tipped me to it as soon as he heard about the production. He took pictures of the first drawings and sent 'em to me. The minute I saw the idea of a sexy blonde and a giant ape, I knew it was going to go through the roof. Of course, I couldn't do a big ape, but that didn't matter, the story's really about a sexy white woman and a big spade, and I already had the guy. A fellow with an enormous kidney stabber working a sex show up in Harlem. And besides, the girl's more important than him. That's what my audience is interested in."

I said, "What's the deal with the name, anyway? Oscar Apollinaire?"

"That's who I am now. Bobby Colodny was somebody else. He was a kid when he left here. What I'm doing now, he couldn't do. That's why I grew the Vandyke and shaved my head, so I wouldn't look like Bobby Colodny anymore. I've actually passed some guys from the old neighborhood on the street and they didn't even look twice at me, not even you."

I nodded and I could tell he was about to say something else about the Grand Central Building, but he read my look and said, "All anybody sees is the fez and the beard. Nobody from the old days knows I'm here. But now you do. And how did you find me?"

"Through your star, Nola Revere. I showed the book to somebody who knew her from Polly Adler's place. And I came across one of your cards with the address." No need to bring Charlie Luciano or Daphne into the picture.

"And you want to know if I had anything to do with Trodache putting the squeeze on Miss Wray?"

"Before I came up here, I thought maybe you did, but not now."

"Jesus, the last fucking thing I need right now is to get mixed up with a studio. I've got too much to do, and I'm not ready for them yet. There's a hundred things to be done before Sunday. You gotta understand, this is my business. I've finally got it to the point where I'm proud of the pictures, and I'm making some good money off them. You're not going to try to screw me over, are you?"

"It's not my game. I just told Miss Wray I'd try to find the guy who made the book and see to it that it wasn't going to be made public. She says her husband would go nuts."

Bobby sneered. "Her husband, hah, that second-rate phony."

Seemed like nobody had much use for Saunders. I got down from the stool at the drawing table. Bobby stood up too. Trying to sound like it didn't mean anything, he said, "Speaking of Nola, you wouldn't happen to know where she is, would ya?"

"Why do you ask?"

"It's nothing. It's just . . . Do you know where she is or not?" By then he wasn't trying to hide anything. This was important.

"No. Nobody I've talked to has seen her since she left Polly's. And that was when she went to work for you, right?"

He didn't say anything, and I could tell he was working out what I knew and who'd been talking to me. "It's not that important," he lied. "But if you run across her, tell her I'd like to see her."

I knew it was past time to leave and so did he, but we stood there sizing each other up for a couple of seconds.

He said, "Who'd've thought that a couple of guys like us from our neighborhoods would wind up here in the Chelsea? And, you know, this ain't the best there is. You wouldn't believe how it is out west. The sun, the ocean, all the space—it's nothing like the city. Sometimes I want to go back, but, hell, this is it for me. All the time I was out there and when I was on the road with the Projectionists, I wanted to be here." I knew what he meant.

As I took the stairs down to the fifth floor to check Connie's room, I tried to fit Bobby into the rest of this screwy business and didn't get far. Her door was locked tight, so I went on to my room on the third floor and sank into my chair. It was a hell of a lot more comfortable than the stool in Bobby's workroom. I considered another short brandy but decided it wouldn't help me think and I was pretty confused right then. I unstrapped my brace as I tried to work through what I knew. None of it fit together, and I knew I wasn't seeing all the pieces.

I thought about the last things Bobby said and wondered why he wanted to find Nola. That made me curious. Those pictures of her were at the center of this business, and nobody seemed to know where she was. Then thinking about Nola made me think about Connie and what Bobby said about her working for him. That made my stomach hurt, and I needed to warn her about him, but what would she say? And that led me back to Nola, and to Daphne and her sugar daddy in the Village, and the guy who killed the goat, and Miss Wray.

By then I was too tired to think about it, but I had an idea about how I might go after something else that Bobby said.

CHAPTER NINETEEN

I was up early on Saturday, early for me, anyway, and worked through what I was about to try to do.

First, I strapped on the brace and dressed down. Found a pair of denim pants in the back of the wardrobe, a flannel shirt, a beat-up leather jacket, and my Keds. Then I took a minute to look at the pistol and sap I'd taken from Trodache. The sap was steel. The gun was a cheap little silver-plated automatic with broken pearl grips. Looked like it had been through a lot of hands and purses. Trodache kept a round in the chamber. I unloaded it and put the gun and sap in my lockbox. Collected my hat and stick and loaded up my pockets with knucks, notebook, money clip, and the Banker's Special.

It was cold and cloudy when I went down to the diner at the corner for hash and eggs. The radio behind the counter was tuned to WOR, where an announcer in Washington was going on about all the people and microphones they had covering the inauguration, and the vast hordes of curious sightseers—common folk and sophisticated cosmopolites—who had filled the city. He mentioned the many prominent New Yorkers in attendance. I perked up when he dropped the name Peter Wilcox. He went on to say the network had portable pack transmitters mounted on the backs of announcers in the crowd. These guys would speak into hand microphones and the machines on their backs would instantaneously send their observations to the control stations and then to the networks. They also had guys in aircraft, including the airship *Akron*, with shortwave transmitters, and parabolic microphones to pick up the band music. I hadn't heard a radio guy so excited about something since the Lindbergh kidnapping a year ago.

I wrote *cosmopolite* in my notebook and finished my breakfast.

On the street, I didn't see the Olds or Trodache but decided it would be better to take the El, anyway. No need for a cab. I walked to the Ninth Street station and took a train to Mott and Grand Streets. Nothing unusual happened on the trip. No giant apes tearing up the tracks.

You see, it was about five years before all this happened, in the fall and winter of 1928, when I busted something inside my right knee. That was when A. R. was killed, too, but I'm not going to go over that again. The important part was that I couldn't walk without a crutch. Dr. Ricardo, a hophead who wasn't really a doctor but was as close to one as anybody I knew, told me about a guy down in Chinatown who could make a brace for my knee. With the brace and a stick, he said I would be able to walk almost like a normal guy. I couldn't run anymore, but I could get rid of that damn crutch and that meant a lot to me.

Funny thing was that the guy who made the brace was a Jap, not a Chinaman, and he also made my knucks. He was a blacksmith and toolmaker named Sam. Sam's father was a mean old man who taught me how to use the stick in a fight. Sam's son was a kid who translated for his grandfather while the old guy knocked me on my ass several times a day for two weeks.

I got off the El at Grand Street and crossed to Mott. The sidewalk stands were busy. I moved slower than the foot traffic, and I could hear the sound of more radios coming from one storefront to the next, all tuned to broadcasts from Washington. I guess there was nothing else on any station and everybody wanted to hear it as it was happening. I couldn't remember how many doors Ricardo had told me to count past the intersection, but I was sure I'd know it when I saw it, and I did. The green paint had faded, but there it was, two steps down from the sidewalk. The hallway behind it was still dim, long, and cold. I rapped on the door at the far end with my stick and smelled burning charcoal as I went into a room with two big doors that opened onto a courtyard.

The place had changed, Sam hadn't. He was still a big guy with massive shoulders. He wore a dark robe under a leather apron as he worked a piece of metal over a forge in the courtyard. But as I remembered, the walls of the room had been covered with handmade metal tools or weapons—I was never sure exactly what they were—and now the rough plank walls were almost empty. I guess the crash hit him just like everybody else.

He turned down the radio and squinted, trying to make out who I was. When he saw the stick, he recognized me.

"Jimmy San." He sounded happy, hoping I was there to buy something. I was.

We sat down inside, and I showed him how the bottom straps on the brace were wearing out where they folded. He said he could fix them, and I said that was good and I'd take a couple but it wasn't why I was there.

"Ran into a guy last night who said that he had a place here in Chinatown, a place where he makes moving pictures. It was in a loft, he said. Now, these are the kind of pictures that he has to keep on the private side. Yeah, *that* kind. He doesn't want to be disturbed. He also claimed that this loft was so secret no white man could ever find it."

Sam looked more interested. I'd been a good customer.

"I'd like to look at the place," I said and took a five out of my shirt pocket. "Can you help me?"

He said to wait and went out to the courtyard. A few minutes later, he came back with his father and his son. The old man used a stick and was every bit as evil-looking as he'd been five years before. The boy had sprouted and was taller than me. He wore dark slacks and a white shirt like he'd been working behind a counter in a store. The three of them yakked away in Japanese. Then the boy said, "Is this dangerous?"

"I don't know. I don't think so, but I don't know."

They talked some more, and the boy said, "Are you going to try to get inside?"

"I can't use a pick," I said, "and I don't have a key, but if the opportunity presented itself, who can say?"

They palavered some more. The kid said he'd need ten and another five to get through the lock.

I said, "Ten if we find the place. Do you know where it is?"

"No," the boy said, "but Grandfather knows someone."

"Yeah, I'll bet he does."

The old man cackled like a happy devil.

For the next hour or more, Grandfather, the boy, who was also Sam, and I weaved through the streets. The other Sam stayed at the shop. They walked so fast I had to work to stay with them. The old man kept turning around and waving his cane at me and repeating something that must have meant "Hurry up." Three or four or five times, we stopped at a storefront where they went in and left me on the sidewalk to cool my thumbs and twiddle my heels. If I hadn't done business with Sam before, I might have thought they were putting something over on me. I was familiar enough with most of the streets they led me down, and nobody looked like they were paying more attention to me than they needed to. I was seldom out of range of a radio for long. Seemed like everybody wanted to know what was going on in Washington.

I remember I was standing outside a busy chop-suey joint when I heard that bastard Roosevelt telling me that the only thing I had to fear was fear itself. What crap! I was not inspired. When they came out of the last shop, a teahouse, I think, they were arguing. They kept their voices down, but I could tell they weren't agreeing with each other. In the end, it seemed like the old man agreed with the kid.

Young Sam said, "We know where this place is. It's not in the best neighborhood, but we ought to be all right in the middle of the day."

"Sure, that's fine." It's been my experience that in Chinatown, the later it gets, the better your chances of finding trouble, particularly if that's what you're looking for. It's like that in most parts of New York, come to think of it.

"And we'll have to pay," he said.

"How much?"

"A dollar or two more, maybe three."

I gave him three ones. The old man snatched the bills away from his hand, and we set off. It took maybe another twenty minutes on narrower streets, and through a big open market building filled with strung-up birds, smelly fish, butchered meat, and vegetables and other things I didn't know. We went all the way through to the back where Grandfather talked to a Chinaman in a black suit. He was smoking a cigarette and leaning against a door. The old man slipped him a bill. The Chinaman didn't look happy about me being there but let us through into an alley.

We followed it until we came to another guy. He got another dollar and let us through another door. That put us inside a building in a hallway. Until then, we'd been hurrying, but the old man motioned for us to slow down. I slipped the knucks on my right hand. The place might have been an apartment house or a rooming house. I could hear more radios through transoms but not the noises you get in a crowded place like Mother Moon's or a tenement. The cooking smells sure weren't the same either.

The old man led us to a door that opened onto a staircase,

and the whispered argument with the kid started up again. The old man won that one. He pushed open the door, turned, and put a finger to his lips. We went slowly up narrow wooden steps. When the door closed behind us, it was almost completely dark and quiet. No more radios. We went up to the fifth floor where he pushed open a door to a short hall or landing with a freight elevator on one side and a metal door with three locks on the other. A dirty skylight overhead let in a little gray light.

The kid said, "Grandfather can open the door."

"You're sure this is the place I'm looking for?"

The boy translated, and the old man spat a lot of words back at him. Blushing, Sam said, "A white man with a beard rents the room. He pays more not to let anyone else in. He brings women here. No Chinese, only white women. Do you want him to open the door?"

"Is he going to break it in with his cane?" I asked, and the old guy's eyebrows shot up. Yeah, I figured he knew English better than he let on, but I said to the kid, "Do these stairs go on up to the roof?"

They nodded.

"Okay, first we find out if there's anybody inside."

We went up two more flights to another heavy door that was locked. Sam said the old guy could pick it for five. I told him to go ahead. There wasn't enough light to see anything, but I guess he worked by touch. I could hear the scratches of him working with metal picks. Less than a minute later, the door popped and we were on a flat gravel and tar roof in the shadow of a wooden water tank on metal legs. There was a big square skylight right in front of us. The one we'd seen from below was a few feet away. Sam and the old man edged toward the big skylight. I looked around.

The roof we were on was taller than any of the ones around it. A cracked wooden chair was under the water tank. Dozens of stubby hand-rolled cigarette butts littered the gravel around it. Looked like somebody had spent time there.

The peaked skylight was made of panes of wired glass that were cleaner than the smaller skylight. The edges of the metal frame were softened by thick coats of paint. I could see a gear wheel and ratchet mechanism that would open the glass panels, but the chain that would open it was gone and the two biggest gears were padlocked together. Even if you broke through a single pane, you couldn't open the skylight.

Down below us was Bobby's studio.

It took the old man a lot longer to work through the three locks on Bobby's door. I could tell that both he and Sam wanted to go inside, but I told them to wait outside. Hell, they'd done it enough times to me that day.

The loft was a lot like Bobby's workroom in the Chelsea with a cluttered bench attached to one wall. It was piled with big light bulbs, electrical cables, and tools. Pinned up on the wall over it were the drawings Daphne told me about, jungle scenes of dinosaurs and Kong fighting. But the first thing I noticed, right in the middle of the room, was the big black hand the girl was on in the last picture in the book. It was made out of lumber and wire and covered with black canvas and matted carpeting.

There were a lot of lights and screens mounted on metal stands facing the hand, and a wheeled platform with a tripod that looked like it was meant for a camera. Four fake tree trunks with leafy branches were behind the hand and there was a canvas flat painted to look like a jungle behind the tree trunks.

The fake stone columns that Nola Revere had been tied to were on their sides against one wall. I could see that they were made of canvas and plywood tacked to two-by-fours. The little table and a section of the wall in the diner scene were on the other side of the jungle flat. The white shower stall was in a corner.

At the end of the workbench was a mirror with lights around it and a lot of cosmetics.

I walked around, looking at all of it, and I realized that Bobby must have shot the whole picture right there. The backgrounds and props for all the photographs I'd seen in the book were in that room. Except for the one he took on top of the Empire State Building. How did that figure in?

You see, the one thing Bobby told me the night before that I didn't believe was that he made his movies in a Chinatown loft. I believed he was telling the truth when he said that the book was a come-on to get guys worked up over his next picture, just like the real movie guys did. But if he shot moving pictures of those scenes, how could he do it in one place? That seemed impossible to me. Now I knew, and I felt like a dope.

I tore a page from my notebook, went over to the makeup mirror, and wrote him a note.

Bobby,
Nice place. Hope to see one of your pictures real soon.
—J

I turned the mirror lights on so he'd notice the note and slid it between the mirror and the frame. Give him something to think about next time he came by. I was patting myself on the back for being such a clever son of a bitch when I noticed the dress.

It was a filmy thing crumpled up on the stool in front of the mirror. Light blue with a gold braided rope at the waist. Like the rest of the stuff, it was something I'd seen in the book, in the last picture. Nola Revere was wearing it when she was tied to the pillars and the guy in the gorilla suit was threatening her. The dress had been ripped open at the sleeves and from the neck almost to the hem. When I held it up, I saw that the material in the middle was stuck together in a rusty red knot.

What the hell did that mean? It gave me a nasty, greasy feeling, but at the same time, I knew that everything in that loft was part of an act, a trick to make me think that the phony thing I was seeing was real.

But that didn't make my stomach feel any better. I took one more look around the place and left.

Back on the landing, the old man charged me another five to relock the door. Maybe I didn't need to do it but, hell, a little breaking and entering between old friends is one thing. Not locking up after yourself is impolite.

Getting out of the place was easier than getting in. We went back through the alley and the open-air market, and from there it was only a couple of blocks to streets I knew. Going back uptown on the El, I thought over the stuff I'd seen in the loft and everything Bobby said the night before. I could see how most of it was part of the same story.

Bobby went off to Hollywood to learn how to make movies. He came back here as Oscar Apollinaire and impressed his fellow art lover Peter Wilcox to bankroll top-drawer stag films that he copied from popular Hollywood pictures. Somewhere the ex-vice cop Trodache was involved. Maybe he blackmailed women into performing. Then he and Bobby parted company on bad terms. But he still knew about Bobby's version of *Kong*, and he got his hands on a copy of the promotional book. When he found out that Miss Wray was going to be in town for the premiere, he used the book to pry six Gs from the RKO guys. But who was the guy in the Fifth Avenue mansion and what did he want? Maybe he was somebody who worked for Wilcox. Or maybe he used to work for Wilcox. Maybe he and Trodache got canned together and were getting back at their old bosses.

I was still working on that when I got off the train and walked back to the speak. I wasn't dressed for work, but I thought I'd check in before I cleaned up. I was just about to cross Ninth Avenue when I saw the kid, Trodache's dim-witted partner, on the sidewalk across from my front door. He was wearing an overcoat with the collar turned up, and he had his cap pulled down low over his eyes. Given what I'd done to Trodache the night before, it figured the kid wasn't there to give me a Good Citizenship award. But, hell, he could wait.

I turned at the corner and went to the alley that runs behind the speak. I let myself in through the back gate and the back door. The crowd was light for a Saturday afternoon. Connie was behind the bar. I went around to the business side where we could talk in private.

"Listen," I said to her, "tell Fat Joe there's a kid outside, the same kid who was in here the other night with that guy, you remember, the ones who gave you the willies. Yeah, well, the kid's hanging around across the street. Tell Fat Joe to keep an eye on him."

"What if he wants to come in?"

"Not now, maybe later. Anything else?"

"Yes." She gave me a big phony smile. "Your friend Daphne is waiting in your office."

CHAPTER TWENTY

Daphne had helped herself to a shot of the absinthe-laced rum. She was sitting on my divan in a tight silvery gray dress that showed off a lot of leg and cleavage. Her hair was done up more than it had been at her place on Gay Street. But she wasn't giving me the full treatment that had made her so popular when she was at Polly's. I took off my hat and coat and sat behind my desk and enjoyed the view.

Daphne knocked back half the rum. "She's in trouble, isn't she? Nola. What the hell's going on, really going on?"

"Why don't you have a drink, Daphne? Oh, I see you already got one. I told you what's going on. Nola posed for some dirty pictures. Some people wanted to know more about them and they hired me to look into it. I did."

"No, there's more to it than that. I talked to Cynthia at Polly's. She says the pictures have something to do with that moving picture everybody's talking about, the jungle movie. What gives?"

She wasn't slurring her words, but I thought she probably

wasn't used to anything as strong as the rum, and she was taking it neat. Most of the times I'd seen Daphne drinking, she had wine, and most of that was at Polly's, so it was probably apple juice.

I said, "It's hard to explain. Let me show you," and opened the safe. I took out the book and sat next to her on the divan as she looked through it. She flipped through the pages fast, her eyes wide, and when she finished, she tossed it onto the table like it was burning her fingers. "I'll be screwed, blued, and tattooed, the son of bitch Apollinaire got *her* to do it."

"Yeah, that's what it looks like. A couple of guys had the idea that she looked so much like the actress in the big movie that they could threaten the studio with bad publicity if these pictures ever got out."

Daphne snorted. "That's ridiculous. She doesn't look anything like Fay Wray. I do, but she doesn't, that's why he wanted me first."

"Sure it is. The guy behind it is an ex-vice cop named Trodache. Know him?"

"Only by reputation. The cocksucker got canned two or three years ago. Does he have anything to do with Nola?"

"Maybe, but I don't think so. I got the idea he doesn't know who she is. He really believes the girl in the book is Fay Wray, from the real movie. Do you know where Nola is?"

"No, that's why I came here, to find out what you know."

Daphne said that after I left her place, she started worrying about Nola. She hadn't really thought about her since she moved to Gay Street, but after what I said, she got guilty about it. She and Nola had been close. Even if Nola left the city, she'd let Daphne know about it. But Daphne moved out of Polly's about the same time Nola left, so maybe the girl didn't know how to get in touch. But when Daphne talked to Cynthia, she learned that nobody had heard anything from Nola. Then Cynthia told Daphne she'd figured out that the dirty pictures I showed her had something to do with *King Kong*, and Daphne got more worried.

"Now, after looking at the book, I'm really scared. What if Oscar didn't tell her about screwing the nigger until it was too late? What would he do to her?" She looked and sounded like she really was concerned for Nola. Until then, I'd figured she was trying to play an angle I didn't understand, but that wasn't it.

"I don't know what's happening," I said, "not all of it anyway, but maybe I can help you. You said this Oscar Apollinaire took you to see his 'silent partner' in the Grand Central Building. Tell me everything you can remember about that day, the guy, the meeting, everything. First, was he a young guy or was he older?"

"Older. He didn't say much, but his voice was deep and he was . . . assured and confident. Whoever he is, he's used to giving orders and getting what he wants."

"There's a younger guy involved, too, who's sort of like the guy you described, at least with the round glasses. Looks like Trodache is doing what this fella tells him to do. That mean anything to you?"

She thought and shook her head.

"Okay," I said. "Anything more about Oscar Apollinaire? Did you ever see him with Nola?" I didn't want to tell Daphne about the whole Bobby-becoming-Oscar business. That would only confuse things, and I can't say that I really understood it myself.

"No, I've been thinking about that ever since I talked to Cynthia, and I never saw them together, but there were a lot of nights when I was out on call while Nola stayed in."

"Did you tell Nola about Apollinaire's offer?"

"Maybe, but just talking, you know. It happened about a year before I met her, maybe more. Hell, I don't remember the dates."

I remembered the date just fine, but again I didn't say anything. "You said there was a guy who worked at a restaurant who was stuck on Nola and they might have taken off together."

She leaned back on the divan and said, "That was the first thing I thought of. The place isn't far from my apartment. I went there before I called Cynthia. The guy's still there and now he's moony over another girl. He said he hadn't seen Nola since the last time we were in together. He even showed me a picture of his new sweetie and, wouldn't you know it, she's a ringer for Nola. Same smile, same tits."

I got up, put the book back in the safe, and poured another tot of rum in Daphne's glass. I asked her if she knew Peter Wilcox.

"The banker? No."

"He wasn't a customer of Polly's?"

"I never heard her mention him, and when she lets down her hair, Polly can drop names with the best of them."

"So what are you looking for?" I asked. I suspected the real reason she came uptown to my place was that her sugar daddy hadn't called and she was lonely on a Saturday night. Hell, that was true for most of my customers, whether they had a sugar daddy or not.

"She's my friend. I want to be sure she's okay. When I talked to Cynthia, she said one of the other girls said she thought she saw Nola at Bergdorf's a month ago. I hope that's right, because it just makes me sick to think about what Oscar might have done to her. No, don't give me that look. Nola's like me. We may be hookers, but we've got standards. There's lines you don't cross."

My look had nothing to do with what Nola did. I was thinking about that red stain on the dress. "And why are you coming to see me?"

Daphne smiled, stretched out her legs, and crossed them slow, with a hiss of silk as her stockings rubbed together. "Because you want to find her, too. You want a taste, I can tell. What man wouldn't, after seeing those pictures?"

"I'm not a detective."

"But you're interested."

I shrugged. "True enough. You gonna pay the freight?"

She squared her shoulders, thinking we were playing on her ground now. "I'm sure we can work something out."

"One hundred up front," I said, thinking of Miss Wray's expenses.

That pissed her off, but she tried not to let it show. "Now, how can you act that way after all that we've—"

I laughed. "Don't bother, Daphne. Come on, we both know the score."

She started to say something but stopped and her expression changed. "It's her, isn't it? The barmaid. Yeah, that makes sense."

"I don't know what you're talking about," I lied, "but here's what I'll do. Forget about the hundred. I don't know what the hell is going to happen with this screwy business, but it ain't over, I know that much. If I find out anything about Nola, I'll tell you. If I see her, I'll tell her to call, okay?"

She stood up and smoothed her tight dress over her hips and cocked her head at me. She wasn't trying to be sexy. At least, I don't think she was. She said, "Yeah, that sounds like a square deal."

I walked to the door with her and said, "One other thing. There may be a kid out on the street. Wearing an overcoat, cap pulled down over his face. He's working with that shithead Trodache. If he looks like he's paying any attention to you when you leave, come back inside and . . . No, wait, here's a better idea. Stick around for a few minutes. Have one on the house and let me take care of him."

I went up the back stairs to the kitchen of the Cruzon Grill. The cooks were in the middle of their evening work, but one of them took time to slice open a long loaf of bread and load it up with some leftover ham and cheese and a lot of mustard. I had him cut it in half and saved the big end for myself. He wrapped the other part in butcher paper. I put it and a pint of milk in a paper bag and went out the front door of the restaurant.

The kid was still across the street, but he was keeping an eye on the front door of the speak. That was a couple of steps down from the sidewalk. The restaurant was seven steps up. He didn't notice me until I was in front of him. It was pretty damn cold then, and he was shivering in the threadbare overcoat and cap.

I had no idea what I was doing, but I remembered how he'd eyed my cherry pie in the diner and figured it wouldn't hurt to confuse him. And I'm embarrassed to say that it was right then that I realized I'd left the Banker's Special in my coat back in the office. If the kid wanted to play rough, I'd have to beat him up with my stick and a milk bottle.

He flinched back a step when I held the bag out to him, just like he did when Trodache threatened him in the diner. "Go ahead, take it," I said. "Just a sandwich and a bottle of milk. You look like you need it. I guess Trodache's got you out here to keep an eye on me. It's okay. Here, take it."

The kid was cutting his eyes from side to side like he was trying to decide which way to run. I put the bag on the sidewalk between us and took a step back.

"What's your name?"

He looked at the bag and back at me. I took another step back and leaned on my stick.

"I don't know what Trodache told you about last night, but he and the boss got the money. Yeah, the moving picture guys came up with the six thousand."

He had been eying the bag, but when I said that, his head snapped up.

"The pictures have been taken care of. We're square, right? Or have you still got some beef with me?"

He snatched up the bag, stepped back, and peeked inside. When he got a whiff of the ham, his lips twitched and he drooled a little, but I could tell he was confused and probably wouldn't do anything as long as I was there.

I said, "Look, I don't mind your hanging around. It's a free country. But the beat cops look out for me and one of the neighbors might complain about you loitering here, you never know. After all, it's mopery with intent to gawk and they'll lock you up for that. But that's none of my business. Just don't try to come inside. Fat Joe won't let you in."

He might have understood half of what I said. When I saw

that he wasn't going to answer, I turned to go, but I thought of something else and turned back.

"One more thing," I said. "Do you know what your boss did with that goat? Remember that? Yesterday afternoon?"

I stared at him long enough to see that he knew what I was talking about. Finally, he nodded.

"Ask your boss about that. Or go back and take a look for yourself."

He hesitated some more, then snatched up the bag, and ran. I didn't see him again that day.

Back inside, I found Daphne at a table with a glass of white wine in front of her. Connie was sitting next to her, and they were so involved in whatever they were talking about they hardly noticed me. I knew I was in trouble.

I went back up to the kitchen for my sandwich, ate in the office, and went back to the Chelsea to get ready for business. I thought a good shower might clear things up, but all I got from it was more questions, most of them about Peter Wilcox. And standing there with the water pelting down on my head, I asked myself why I was doing this. I mean, I already did what we agreed to. I got the money to the guys who wanted it. They said the pictures were gone. The End. But then I took Miss Wray's expense money and agreed to use the rest of it looking for Nola Revere. But if I spent it, what did that leave me with? Empty pockets. Then there was that goddamn goat. What the hell did that mean? And now Daphne wanted to find Nola, and she was talking to Connie. Things were not looking good for yours truly.

Getting dressed, I went with a medium gray herringbone from Hickey Freeman with a light blue shirt and a black-and-gold-striped tie.

Daphne was gone and Detective Ellis was waiting at the bar when I got back to the speak around seven. It was a light crowd for a Saturday, and the Democrats weren't as cocky and happy and free with their money as they had been recently. Frenchy chalked it up to the bank holiday. He said that most of the regulars were asking for credit. I said that was fine as long as everybody signed their tabs. Connie and Marie Therese made a point of not looking at me.

Ellis followed me up to the office. He went straight to my liquor and topped off his gin. I didn't ask if he'd signed a tab. He collapsed onto the divan like he was never going to get up, closed his eyes, and said, "How'd it go last night? Sorry I had to take a powder on you like that, but Captain Boatwright decided that the goddamn bank holiday was a chance for him to show how prepared his men were to deal with emergencies. He assigned uniforms to spring to the defense of every post office, theater, and business that does business in cash, and he let it be known that we'd provide protection to anybody making a goddamn deposit. I had to stop by each one of them all night. Haven't been home since Thursday, and he's got me on tomorrow, too. What happened with you?"

I wasn't sure how much to tell, so I just started where we left off. "After I called your precinct, Trodache called back and asked for the money. We had a little back and forth and agreed that Abramson and I would take the six Gs to an address up on Fifth Avenue—900 Fifth."

Ellis opened his eyes and sat up. He knew that wasn't a neighborhood where extortion payoffs were the order of the day.

"Turned out to be one of those mansions that takes up the best part of the block. Looked pretty good inside, too, but the funny thing was, the place was almost empty. And you know what else is funny? Peter Wilcox lives there. Yeah, the banker. I didn't see him there. Radio and newspapers say he's down in Washington for the inauguration, so maybe he let some friends stay the night. Anyway, Trodache was there along with a weird younger guy who acted like he was in charge. He took the money, promised that he'd get rid of the pictures, and that was that. Actually, there was a little more to it, but when I told the lawyers and Miss Wray what happened, they were happy."

Ellis just stared at me for a long time, and said, "Peter Wilcox. The Ashton-Wilcox Peter Wilcox? You're sure about that? Christ, if somebody like that is involved in this, you've got to get the hell away from it right now. I sure as hell am. It's not worth my career, and that's what we're talking about." He took a jolt of gin.

"And there's something else," I said. "You know the Wilcox Foundation for Wayward Girls?"

"Oh, Christ, don't tell me that's part of this."

"I think so. You see, that book of dirty pictures of the girl who looks like Miss Wray? Well, it looks like the book was printed up to promote a stag movie. And there was this goat—"

"Oh, hell, don't say that. Don't say anything else about Peter Wilcox or stag movies." He got up and pointed at me. "Dirty pictures are one thing, but movies, that's something else to Captain Boatwright. With pictures, he's happy enough to look the other way, but not movies. Not with him and the monsignor."

Yeah, I knew that. Boatwright was asshole buddies with Monsignor McCaffrey. He was the department chaplain, and he was also the biggest and loudest "antivice" crusader in the damn city. Nothing set him off like racy magazines and moving pictures. Everybody knew he hated them more than hookers. He'd really bust a gasket over a stag movie.

Ellis said, "Lemme tell you how this works. The actress gets her tit in a wringer when she takes a gander at the pictures, so she calls some executive at RKO. The executive calls some assistant commissioner he knows at the department, hell, maybe Commissioner Mulrooney himself for all I know. Yeah, he tells Mulrooney to do something about it without the press getting wind of it. Since this is happening in Manhattan, it comes down to Captain Boatwright because they all know that Boatwright will give it to me, and whatever it turns out to be, I will make sure that the department is not embarrassed. And now you're trying to drag Peter Wilcox and dirty movies into it. Shit, shit, shit."

He muttered something I couldn't understand to himself and said, "But the RKO lawyers were happy with what you told them last night, you said that. And the actress, she was happy too, right?"

"Yeah, but—"

"No 'yeah, but.' Stop right there. Forget about Wilcox and a stag picture. Can I go back to Boatwright and tell the son of a bitch that this situation has been taken care of to everyone's satisfaction? The next word out of your mouth better be 'yes.'"

"Yes, but—"

"What the hell did I just say? No 'yes, but,' just 'yes.' Know when to shut up, Quinn. Look, remember the other night when you were bitching about the Fire Department inspector who wanted fifty bucks just to show up? Well, if I can tell this inspector that you were involved in doing a personal favor for the commissioner, he might, *might*, lower his price, and the same goes for the dozen other guys whose palms are going to be crossed with silver if you expect to go legit with this place. You following me on this?"

I nodded.

"So can I tell Captain Boatwright that this matter has been taken care of? And the next time the commissioner is hobnobbing with these guys from RKO, they are going to shake his hand and thank him for handling it so discreetly? Can I tell him that?"

Knowing that somehow I was doing the wrong thing, I said, "Yes."

Ellis's smile widened, and he poured himself more gin.

Things stayed quiet for the rest of Saturday night. By then, everybody had had their fill of the inauguration news, so somebody found a station on the radio that was playing dance music. They moved the tables off the little dance floor, and a few people actually danced. That didn't happen often.

Sometime after midnight I got Bobby's picture book out of the safe and went down to the cellar to find Arch Malloy. He was still working through *The Story of Philosophy*. I told him to find a couple of clean glasses and the dark Bacardi's we'd opened the night before. He said something about this being the best job a man could ever have and hopped to it.

As he poured, he said, "I'm afraid I've not learned much in my research. Peter Wilcox, as everyone knows, has been a moving force in municipal affairs for several years. He has been part of every good government group that has attempted to right the most egregious wrongs that this metropolis produces with such proficiency. Some say he's trying to make up for his father who never gave a banker's damn for anything except money and the pleasures of the flesh."

Arch produced a handful of paper from his coat pocket and sorted through pages from a notebook, pencil-scrawled scraps of napkins, and newspaper clippings. "Since Peter Wilcox took over the bank, he has endowed libraries, hospitals, universities, and the like. He gives money to other rich people, and all of them feel better about it."

We could hear faint music from the radio and the scuff of feet moving and the floor squeaking above us. It sounded like people having a good time.

"What about Mary Wilcox?" I asked.

"She was Mary Ashton, daughter of Richard Ashton, Learned Wilcox's partner. It's been said, and there is certainly some truth to it, that Learned pressed for Mary and Peter to marry when he learned that Ashton was dying. It was certainly a wise financial move, more a marriage of convenience than anything else. They lived separate lives, and she was never as socially active as her husband."

"Is that so? Last night, Saxon Dunbar told me that she was a real party girl. Scandalized high society by screwing around until her husband put a stop to it."

Arch was dubious. "He may have better sources than I do, but that's not the way I heard it. From what I've found, she was a shy, sickly child. Even after she was married, she wasn't one to be seen in public. Constantly under the care of doctors and specialists, even Dr. Freud's minions."

"She died a few months ago, didn't she?"

"Yes. Not much was made of it because she'd been in the hospital for more than a year. There were whispers of suicide, but I was more interested in her husband. Do you want me to do more?"

"No. What about a brother?"

"There is none. Peter and Mary had a son, Peter Jr. He attends Yale like all the Wilcox men. Only sixteen, too. Must be a bright lad."

I wondered if that could've been the guy I saw the day before.

"Okay, last night, I was up at this big pile of bricks on Fifth Avenue. Cabbie said it belonged to Peter Wilcox. Do you know if he lives there?"

"No. It's his house, or his father's house, I suppose. Peter Wilcox grew up there, but as soon as he took over at the bank, he built an estate out on Long Island and now the entire family lives there. He's also got a summer house on the Hudson and places in London and Paris. Perhaps if you could tell me *why* you're interested in Mr. Wilcox and his wife and this theoretical brother, I might be more useful."

"Looks like he's financing stag movies on the side. You see, I ran into this guy I used to know, and he says he makes the best dirty movies in the world, and he's got a silent partner who finances him. This guy offered a girl a part in one of these movies, and she describes somebody who sounds a lot like Peter Wilcox as the guy who had to say yes before she got the job."

Arch got a lot more interested when I mentioned stag movies. He took a sip of rum and said, "And does that explain the presence of the dazzling blonde who waited for you in your office and then had a tête-à-tête with Miss Nix?"

"In a nutshell, yeah."

Arch volunteered to look much more deeply into the subject. I told him that could wait and asked if he'd found anything about sacrificing goats.

He said, "It's common as dirt in the Old Testament. God and his magnificent angels are forever ordering some poor sod to sacrifice a goat and seven ewes to have a sin forgiven or to please the just and merciful deity, or as a reward for not killing a son as the same deity had previously demanded. And since you bring up stag movies, goats also bring to mind the mythical satyr, a creature who was said to be half man, half goat."

"You mean those guys with the hairy legs and little horns and the funny pipes."

"Exactly. They were said to be sexually insatiable, hence the term 'satyriasis.'"

"Horny as a billy goat?"

"Indeed."

"But those were back in Bible times. What about now?"

"I'm sure that heathen Hindoos and Mohammedans might still employ such barbaric rituals. And the Haitian voodoo cults hold similar beliefs, though their gods prefer chickens, I believe."

He didn't say anything else for a moment. Then, "I must ask what these lines of inquiry have to do with each other, because I have to believe they are related."

"Yeah, they are." I gave him another knock of rum and tried to explain, starting with Miss Wray coming in Thursday evening, but leaving out the parts about Miss Wray's marriage, my business with Lansky, and the like. I gave him the book to show him what I was talking about. He made a study of it, and his eyes widened when he got to the last page with Nola on the giant hand.

He handed the book back and said, "That young woman has certainly been blessed. I think we should take another knock in her honor." We did.

I said, "I could walk away from this if it wasn't for the damn goat."

"Let's leave that aside for the moment. Given everything else that you've seen, we can conclude or surmise that the premiere of Mr. Apollinaire's film will take place sometime after Peter Wilcox returns from Washington. We can further suppose that Apollinaire wants his star to make an appearance at that time, just like the RKO fellows wanted Miss Wray to be here. Agreed?"

I said yes.

"But since he asked if you knew her whereabouts, he has lost contact with her, and that might interfere with his plans for the film. And it seems likely that this young man who may be Peter Wilcox Jr. means to do his father harm. Since he managed to lay hands on a copy of the book, he probably knows about the film and he might be planning to do something at the premiere."

We were working on that when the sound of dancing upstairs stopped. Then we heard loud voices, yelling, and furniture hitting the floor. By the time we got upstairs, Frenchy had broken up the fight. Fat Joe was tossing both guys outside. The girl they were fighting over had taken one in the kisser and wasn't too happy about it. That killed the mood for the night, so we closed down pretty soon.

Connie was quiet as we cleaned up, and when we walked back to the Chelsea, I tried one more time to figure out what was wrong. "I don't understand why you're acting like this."

Sounding thoughtful, she said, "It's not you. I think I've had the wrong idea about a lot of things and I'm trying to straighten them out."

"Daphne help you with that?"

She gave me one of those quizzical looks and said, "You know, I think she did."

We got to her room on the fifth floor, and I saw there was a folded card wedged between her door and the jamb. When she opened it, I saw blue lettering. It was one of Bobby's AOS cards. Whatever he'd written on it made her smile.

She said good night and hurried inside.

I went downstairs to my room and found one of his cards there, too. It said: "Got your message. Come up to the workshop."

CHAPTER TWENTY-ONE

As I rapped on the door of 618 with my stick, I thought that Bobby might not be too happy about my visiting his studio. I was right. He was sore as a boil.

The first thing he said when I came in was, "What the fuck were you doing in my place?"

I held the stick in both hands, easy, light, not threatening. I don't think he knew what I could do with it. "Don't get so hot under the collar, I just wanted to see where you made your masterpiece, that's all. I was in the neighborhood. Didn't steal anything either."

"Yeah, well, I don't like anybody getting in my business, you know. I didn't have a goddamn thing to do with that shithead Trodache, so you got no reason to be in my place."

He was pretty steamed all right, but I figured it was bluster. Bobby was a lover not a fighter. "Simmer down," I said. "The business with Miss Wray is finished. Or I think it is. You see, there is one part that I still haven't figured out and maybe you can set me straight."

He calmed down and said "yeah" like he didn't want to hear what I was going to say.

I took a seat in the rolling chair and kept the stick across my lap. I looked past Bobby at the shelves and noticed that the masks that had been stacked up there were gone. So were the boxes of books. "Last night you said you've got a rich guy who bankrolls your pictures. Tell me about him."

He tried to laugh it off, but I could tell the idea scared him. "Why the hell would I tell you anything about him? You think I'm going to let you horn in on my action? This pigeon's mine, forget about it."

"I know who he is. I just want to be sure Trodache isn't working for him."

"You know who he is, my ass." It didn't come across as cocksure as Bobby was trying to sound.

"His name is Peter Wilcox—"

Bobby cursed at the name and rushed at me. I came up out of the chair and gave him a quick two-handed jab to the gut with the rubber tip of the stick. It stopped him cold, and took the wind out of him, but didn't really hurt.

He staggered back a step, rubbed his gut, and glared.

"Come on, Bobby, there's no need for this. As I was saying, his name is Peter Wilcox, and he used to live in a fancy place up on Fifth where I met Trodache and another guy last night and gave them the studio's money."

"Whaddayamean it's Wilcox's place," he grunted, still trying to lie. "I don't know nothing about that, and I don't know no Wilcox."

"The hell you don't. What did Trodache do for you?"

"He said he had the goods on the best whores in the city and they'd do whatever he told them, but he couldn't produce shit. Only work he did was stay on the roof to keep kids and guys away from the skylight when we were shooting—until I caught him taking money from the fucking Chinks to let 'em up there."

"What about the kid with him."

"That's his nephew or cousin or something, I don't know. He just hung around with Trodache. I never paid him."

"What about the other guy, the one who says he's Wilcox's brother? He's got a big Oldsmobile."

That surprised him. "Yeah, Wilcox has an Olds town car, but he never uses it. It's his wife's."

When he said that, I tried to remember the first night that Trodache and the kid showed up in the Olds. Was there a chauffeur driving? I'd been thinking that Trodache was behind the wheel, but there was plenty of room for three in the backseat.

"None of this shit has anything to do with me and the picture. I don't know how those guys got a copy of the book, and I don't have time to worry about that now," he said, swaggering around and getting himself worked up again. "Like I said, I don't like people getting in my business. I'm serious, I've got a lot riding on the next twenty-four hours. Stay out of my way."

Then he got a shifty look on his mug, like there was something he was holding back or trying to hide. It had to be Connie. He could probably read me well enough to see that I wasn't buying it.

"I told you I got no interest in your business. If your pictures are as good as you say, I wouldn't mind taking a look at one of 'em."

His expression changed then. The Vandyke didn't hide his smile, and he was thinking he had me where he wanted me. He said, "I don't give away samples, but for you, for old time's sake, I'll make an exception. But not now. I've got too much to do. Talk to me in a week."

I leaned back in the chair. "I'm not interested in handouts. Let's trade. Come by my place, you and your little Honeybunch. Dinner at the Cruzon Grill and drinks at the speak. On the house."

He laughed a nasty laugh and said, "Honeybunch, yeah, you can dress her up but you can't take her out. She don't know how to act around polite society. But she makes up for it, believe me, she makes up for it. You want a piece of that, you know where she is."

I stood up and we walked to the door. "Look, I didn't mean to give you a hard time by visiting your place in Chinatown. It was just that after you mentioned it, I had half an idea that I knew where it was, and since I promised Miss Wray that I'd try to find Nola Revere, I thought I'd take a look there. Speaking of that, do you still want to talk to her?"

He shook his head. "No, I took care of that. The bitch finally called. Now I've got a few other details to work out for tomorrow night. Then it's nothing but smooth sailing."

I figured those details had to do with his *soirée cinématique intime.*

His face lit up with a wide dreamer's smile, and I said, "You look like the cat that just ate the canary."

He clapped me on the back. "This is it, Jimmy. Really, this is the best picture I've ever made. After this, anything is possible."

I know he'd told a lot of other lies and whatnot while he sat there, but he believed that.

I unlocked my room and found a note that had been slipped under the door. It was from the front desk and said that they were holding a package for me. I hung up my hat and went to the lobby.

Tommy, the nightman, was behind the counter. When he saw it was me, he went right back to the office and came back with a thick envelope from the Pierre that was Scotch-taped shut.

He handed it across and said, "So you've got friends who stay at the Pierre. My, my, I'm impressed." Tommy was never happier than when he was weaseling gossip out of somebody.

"You'd be even more impressed if you knew who she was."

"I'm all ears."

I was about to tell him to shove off but had another idea. "Okay," I said, "I'll trade a name for information. What do you know about the guy in 624?"

Tommy leaned across the desk to get closer and cut his eyes both ways like he was making sure nobody would hear us, even though the lobby was empty, and lowered his voice. "Isn't their apartment the most astonishing thing you've ever seen in your life? My word, I was simply agog the first time I laid eyes on it. They are certainly the most colorful and exotic residents we have, if you take my meaning. He's a Turk and she's his concubine. They occasionally invite other bon vivants over to join them for an evening or a night."

He smiled at that, and I figured that Tommy and Saxon Dunbar were sisters under the skin. Both of them loved to talk about people doing the dirtiest things they could imagine.

"And now," Tommy said, his eyes bright, "I understand that you and Miss Nix have joined their little consortium." I wasn't sure what *consortium* meant, but he made it sound illegal.

"But of course"—he acted like he was turning a key in front of his mouth—"my lips are sealed. Now, who sends you such an intriguing little bundle from the Pierre?"

I tucked the bundle into my coat pocket. "King Kong's costar." He didn't believe me.

Back in my room, I loosened my tie, took off my shoes and brace, and poured a short brandy. There was a nice thick stack of bills inside the envelope and two pages of hotel stationery.

Mr. Quinn:

I write this in haste as Fay and I must leave early tomorrow morning. Now that everyone realizes how important the picture is going to be, more elaborate preparations are being made for the Hollywood premiere. Mr. Cooper has actually chartered an airplane just for the two of us!

Even so, Fay is concerned that Messrs. Grossner and Sleave may not live up to their end of the agreement they made now that the matter is settled. So she spoke to the concierge who was so helpful in arranging your expense money. He said it was more difficult on account of the bank holiday, but he managed to find your ten percent for us, even if it took all day. So, here is the $600 they agreed upon, and a small bonus. Again, we thank you for your efforts.

Hazel

Miss Wray wrote the second page.

Jimmy,

Thank you so much for your help. Since you know John, even if it is only as a customer, you understand that he is sensitive to anything that concerns his wife. If he were to learn of the details of this matter, he would be devastated. I'm sure I can rely on your continued discretion.

Your devoted friend,
Fay

At first I thought she was taking a lot for granted about my continued discretion since she really didn't know me. But then I thought, *The hell she doesn't. She knows me. She had my number from the first night she walked into my place.* She knew that pretty women get a lot of favors done for them, and pretty actresses get even more. Particularly from the guys who go to their pictures. So, no, I wouldn't be talking to Saxon Dunbar or Tommy or anybody else about her. Yeah, she knew that.

I finished the brandy and counted the money. It came to $617. So, a seventeen-dollar bonus. It was all I could do to keep from clicking my heels.

I sat back in my chair and went over everything that had happened for the past three days. I guess I should've told Miss Wray and the RKO lawyers about Bobby's *Kong* movie, but they paid me to take care of the guys with the book, and I did that. Then Miss Wray wanted to know about Nola Revere, and I almost did that too, if Nola really had talked to Bobby. But now it sounded like Miss Wray didn't care about that. At least, it wasn't keeping her from leaving.

If I went back to Grossner and Sleave and told them about the other *Kong*, it would probably screw things up for Bobby, and I didn't see any way that I could use it to get more money from them.

So that left the goat, the damn goat. Bobby said he didn't have anything to do with Trodache, and it looked like that was the truth. But there was something going on between Trodache and Wilcox, and the goat was part of it. Was it any of my business? I tried to convince myself that it wasn't, and that I was finished with it and Miss Wray.

Yeah, sure. And I had nothing to fear but fear itself.

CHAPTER TWENTY-TWO

"Where's Connie? What did you do to her?"

That's the first thing Marie Therese said to me Sunday afternoon. She looked pissed off. I had just sat down at my table in the back with about half a dozen daily papers. I didn't know what she was talking about and said so.

"She called right before you got here and told me she was taking the day off. She's *never* done that before. What did you do to her?"

I told her I didn't do anything. Just a few minutes before, I went up to Connie's room on my way out of the Chelsea, knocked on her door, and she didn't answer. Nothing unusual about that. I was a little late and figured she already left. I expected to see her at the speak, and at first, I didn't know what to think about her not being there.

Marie Therese said, "She said she knew it was going to be a slow night and we wouldn't really need her, so she was going to do something else."

"She said that? She said she was going to do something else?" I didn't like that.

"More or less. I don't remember her exact words, but that's what she meant. What did you do last night?"

"This is nuts," I said. "I don't know what the hell you're talking about. If she don't want to work, she don't want to work." And I opened the paper like that was the end of it. I didn't fool her. She went back behind the bar. I sat there and worried.

At first, I told myself it was nothing. I wouldn't even think about it at all. That didn't last long. Then I decided Connie was just trying to make me mad. But I couldn't buy that either. Maybe she was hurt. No, she would call Marie Therese. Maybe it had something to do with Bobby. No, I wasn't going to think about that. When I realized that I didn't understand the words I was looking at in the paper, I told Frenchy I'd be back soon and went back to the Chelsea.

I got Connie's key from the front desk. Since everybody on the staff knew I was paying for the room, that was okay. As I unlocked the door, I had a bad feeling that I'd find her stuff packed up and gone. But no, the room looked like it always did.

Her place was smaller and neater than mine. Besides the bed, she had a chest of drawers, a wardrobe, and two armchairs. There was only one chair when she took the room, but I bought her another one that was more comfortable. We also got her a good lamp, and the bedside table was stacked with books. The bathroom was sweet with the smell of her perfume and soaps and such. Her makeup and stuff was still there, and she had left underwear and stockings hanging over the bathtub.

I looked over the top of the dresser where she always put her purse, hoping to find the card Bobby left the night before. It wasn't there. I was tempted to go through the drawers but didn't.

I was about to leave when I remembered something Bobby said the first night we were in his place, after he'd been giving her the eye. "Dress her up right and she could do very well for herself, a lot more if she was interested in it."

Then I thought about this one dress she had. I thought of it as pale orange, but she told me it was called apricot. She bought it with one of her first pay envelopes, and it was a knockout. I checked the wardrobe. It wasn't there.

I went up to the sixth floor and knocked on both of Bobby's doors. No answer. I went back to the speak.

I took the papers up to my office, and for about an hour I tried to read again but couldn't because I kept thinking about Bobby, and Connie, and what Arch had said, and Daphne, and King Kong, and Miss Wray and her husband, and where was Connie? Looking back on it now, I must have gone a little crazy. That would explain what I did, anyway.

I checked the load in the Banker's Special, put on my topcoat, and caught a cab downtown to Grand Street. On a Sunday, it was busier in Chinatown than my neighborhood, but the streets weren't as crowded as they'd been yesterday. It didn't take me long to find the open air market.

I went to the back, just like we did the day before. Another Chinaman in a black suit leaned against the door. He was smoking a cigarette and paid no attention as I limped up on my stick. There was nobody else close, so I got right in front of him and punched him in the gut three times as hard and fast as I could with the knucks. He doubled over. I propped him up with my shoulder, reached around him, and pushed the door open and shoved him into the alley. He was a tough bastard. He pushed away from me and went for a knife. Another shot to the head with the knucks put him facedown on the cobblestones.

That brought the second Chinaman running from the other door. I pulled the .38. He turned and ran before I could cock it.

I hurried up the alley and got into the apartment house. Figuring I didn't have a lot of time, I gimped up the dark stairs to the top floor. The door to the roof was heavy, but the strike plate wasn't. I braced myself on the stick and it only took two kicks with the sole of my foot to bang it open. I went straight to the peaked skylight and looked down into Bobby's studio.

It was cleared out. The big black hand was gone, and all the equipment, lights, and screens had been pushed against the walls. I hurried around all four sides of the skylight, leaning over it and looking down into the corners of the room. I was pretty sure I could see all of it, and there was enough light to see that nobody was inside.

I don't think I really expected to find Connie there. I don't know what I expected. Like I said, I was a little crazy.

I knew the Chinaman who ran away would be coming back with help, so I made my way down the stairs until I heard noises coming up from below. I opened a door on the second or third floor and got out of the stairwell. I figured another set of stairs led to the front of the building, and there they were, halfway down the hall. I heard noises from guys coming up those stairs, too, and went down them with the pistol in my mitt. Two Chinamen were waiting at the bottom. The vestibule wasn't wide enough for them spread out, so they backed out the front door giving me hard looks.

I followed them and pocketed the pistol. We came out on a noisy crowded sidewalk where the sound of angry women's voices cut through everything else. Four Chinese women were scolding the two guys. I saw that the women were in charge of a group of kids. They kept the kids in line with a long rope that had loops every few feet for the kids to hold onto. The women at the back end of the rope were giving the two guys hell for bumping into them. I fell in step with the kids and gimped along with them up the sidewalk.

I didn't know where I was, but it looked like we were headed for an intersection with a larger street and that was fine with me. It felt like everybody was looking at me, especially the kids. They probably were. I was the only white guy on the street. All the storefronts and signs were in Chinese. I listened for sounds of the two guys trying to catch me and didn't hear anything. Hell, I figured they didn't want me that bad. I just roughed up a guy and kicked down a door. It wasn't like I killed anybody. The bigger street was Doyers and when we got there, I looked back for the guys. It was getting dark then, and if anybody was still after me, I couldn't see him.

I got a cab back to the speak.

Before I could take off my hat, Marie Therese asked me if I'd found her. I thought about lying, saying why would I be looking for Connie, but she wouldn't buy it. So I said no and asked Marie Therese if she knew what was going on. "She's been mad at me for a week. What gives?"

"It's not my place," she said. "Connie will tell you."

"So you do know where she is."

"I didn't say that," she said.

"What's she doing? Is she all right?"

"I don't know. The damn fool girl," she said, and for the first time, she looked more worried than angry.

In my office I thought about having a drink but wasn't really interested. Didn't feel like eating anything either. You see, I really was a little crazy. I was puzzling over what I should do when I remembered something Bobby said that first night up in his workroom. I opened the safe and got the picture book. The number on the back would tell me whose book it was, he said. And there on the back at the bottom in pencil was "1/144." Now, I didn't know anything about books or art or collecting those things, but knowing what I did about Bobby's business, it figured that this copy of the book was the first of one hundred and forty-four. That meant it was the best of the bunch, better than the fifty-third or the seventy-fourth. And if it was the best, it must belong to Peter Wilcox.

No, I thought, *it used to belong to Peter Wilcox. Now it belongs to me.*

But the important thing was the book. That's what started all this. And Bobby made the book. He took the photographs. He printed the cover and the words on the page. He stapled the pages together. And he did all that up there in his workroom. I locked the book in the safe and went back to the Chelsea.

I rapped on the door of 624 with my stick. I was thinking that if nobody was there, I'd pay Tommy, the night man, for the use of a master key, but Honeybunch answered right away. She had a dazed smile plastered across her pretty little mug. It disappeared when she saw who I was.

"Oh shit," she said. "I thought you were the guy with the food."

She trotted back to her stack of pillows and dove onto them face-first. She was wearing the same kind of outfit she had on when we were there before, the loose vest and gauzy harem pants stretched tight across her ass. She wriggled around a bit, then rolled over onto her back and found her hash pipe.

"Bobby's not here," she said as she fired it up and gave me a long look at her cooch. "He won't be back till late. You got anything to eat? Bobby left some ice cream and candy, but I ate it already. The guy's supposed to bring me something else, but he's late. Christ, I gotta get something to eat."

"Where's Bobby?" I looked over and saw the blue-and-gold box where he kept the key to the workroom.

"Tonight's his big premiere, his *soirée cinématique intime.* You'd think it was the most important thing in the world the way he's been worrying about it. Say, you were here with that girl. He said he was going to get her to serve drinks and everything."

So he was after Connie. Or he told her he was. Honeybunch went on, "I asked him if I could help with the drinks and the cocaine like I used to, but Bobby said I can't anymore, I like it too much, and that's why I gotta stay here. You got anything to eat?"

"No, I could call down to the desk, get Tommy to have something sent up." The telephone was on the table next to the blue-and-gold box.

She wrinkled her brow like she didn't understand what I said. "You can do that? Just call and they bring you food? Can you get ice cream?"

"They've probably got some at the diner down the street. They deliver all the time."

"Yeah, that would be great."

It was pretty easy to fish the key ring out of the box while I called. Tommy didn't pick up until the sixth ring. I told him we needed a quart of chocolate in 624.

"And to whom should I charge that," he said with a nasty edge on his voice, "Mr. Apollinaire or Mr. Quinn?"

"Mr. Apollinaire, and you know something, Tommy? You better bring it up personally."

I let myself into 618 and snapped on the light. It didn't look like Bobby had done anything else since the night before. I thought there weren't as many closed boxes on the shelves, and I went through the ones that were left. They were filled with photo books.

I could recognize all the real actresses that Bobby's lookalikes were supposed to be, but I didn't know all the pictures that he was imitating. Not that it mattered. As long as you looked at a few features, the resemblance was there. The angular face of a girl who wasn't Joan Crawford and the black bobbed hair of the Louise Brooks type who costarred in *Two Lost Sinners*. The curly hair and big cheekbones of Norma Shearer in *The Divorce*. The plump platinum blonde Mae West in *Diamond Lou's Sex*, and the high-society blonde Madeleine Carroll in *The French Wife*. None of them would fool you if you knew what the real women looked like on-screen. But Bobby didn't lie about the quality of his photography. He really made those women look great. In all the books, Bobby started by holding things back, the same way the Ziegfeld girls were photographed with a lot of skin on display, but the key parts of tits and crotches covered up. The books sure didn't end that way, and each of them promised that you'd see a lot more in the movie.

But I wasn't after those. I wanted to know where the damn premiere was going to be.

The regular, not-crazy part of my brain knew that Connie wouldn't go there. But right then, I wasn't paying much attention to the regular not-crazy part. The crazy jealous part remembered how Bobby had snaked girls away from me and how easily he could pour on the charm and how Connie was mad at me already and how he might go after her out of spite just because I broke into his studio. Maybe he offered her a bundle of cash and she took it, not knowing what he wanted her to do.

I went through the rest of the boxes and the stuff that was stored on the shelves and the drawing desk and the clutter at the back of the workbench. Nothing and more nothing.

I found it when I went through the trash bin.

The first things I pulled out were rags, ink-stained pieces of cloth and crumpled newspapers. Underneath those, I found some printed pages out of the *Kong* book. He'd tossed them out because they were smeared or dog-eared. Among the bad pages I came across a square envelope, made of the same thick paper as the book pages. Somebody, Bobby I guess, had started typing an address on East Eighty-Seventh Street, but "New York" was "New Yrok." I guess Bobby was as much a perfectionist as he made himself out to be.

After more digging, I found five invitations, printed with the same blue ink he used on his cards and the books. Three of them were smeared. Two were printed off center. The invitation read:

The World Premiere of *Kong*
By Oscar Apollinaire
Will Be Presented
Sunday, March 5, at 11:00 p.m.
With a performance by the stars
Corlears Street

CHAPTER TWENTY-THREE

Back in my room, I stashed the invitations and found my notepad and pen. It was about 8:30. I got my coat and hat and was about to go downstairs but turned and went up to Connie's room. I knocked and waited. No answer.

A couple of blocks away on Ninth Avenue there was a garage. That's where I kept a nice little green Ford coupe that my friend Walter Spencer loaned me so I wouldn't have to steal it. It had to do with the business that brought Connie to work in my place, and I don't need to go into that again. Truth is, I had hardly driven it, but I picked it up that night and headed down to the Lower East Side.

You see, Corlears Street was just south of the Williamsburg Bridge, only a few blocks from a garage that Meyer Lansky owned. Back in the first days of Prohibition, Spence and I stole cars and trucks and sold them to Lansky. We also drove shipments of liquor for him in some of the same cars. It was a sweet racket. Corlears Street was close to the East River. I didn't really know the neighborhood, and it had been years since I'd been down there. I figured it wouldn't be a bad idea to take a look at it before the *soirée intime* got started.

I took a right off Grand Street onto Corlears and looked for a building that would suit Bobby's purposes. I thought I spotted one, and at the same time, I noticed four big headlights on a car parked on the other side of the street. Yeah, it was the big brown Oldsmobile. I could see that a guy in a chauffeur's cap was behind the wheel. I kept a slow steady speed on the cobblestones. As I passed the Olds, my lights cut across it, and I was able to see that the driver had gray hair and a jowly jaw. His eyes were fixed on the front of Bobby's building. He stared at it like he was trying to memorize every detail, that's how intense his expression was. I had a feeling I'd seen him somewhere, but that happened a lot with so many people coming into the speak, so I didn't think much about it. I had other things to do, anyway. I drove down a couple of streets, circled around a little park, and came back to park about thirty feet behind the Olds. It figured he was doing the same thing I was.

I cut the engine, took off my hat, slouched in the seat, and waited.

Bobby's place was a flat-roofed, two-story brick building with bars on the ground-floor windows, and big wooden doors that looked like they belonged on a barn. It was on the corner of Monroe Street. As my eyes got used to the dark, I saw that there was a big goon smoking a cigarette beside the doors. No light showed from any of the windows.

By and by, somebody trotted around the corner of the building at Monroe and made straight for the Olds. It was the kid who'd been watching my place. The back door of the Olds opened as he approached and he jumped in. Nothing happened for a few minutes until the goon stepped away from the building and started across the street. He wore a heavy overcoat and had his hat pulled down over his eyes. He hadn't gone more than a couple of steps before the Olds started up and pulled away from the curb. It headed toward Grand Street. I gave them a few seconds and then followed. I didn't try to stay close because I had a good idea about where they were going.

Yeah, the Olds pulled into the garage of the Wilcox place on Fifth Avenue.

I turned around and drove back down to Corlears Street. When I got there, they were unloading food from a truck. I did the same thing I'd done before, going past the place, coming back around and parking down the street where I could watch. Both of the front doors were open, and a second goon in an overcoat was standing around with the first one. I guess they were there to keep people out, but the street was quiet on a Sunday night. Bobby was talking with the guy who was in charge of the delivery. It looked like they were disagreeing, and both of them went inside. I got out and walked to Monroe Street. The two goons at the door paid no attention.

I thought there might be an alley off Monroe going behind the building and I was right. There were dim gaslights on the street, and I could see an electric light some way down the alley, about where the back door ought to be. I didn't risk going into the alley. If Bobby had guys in the front, there was somebody in the back. I went on around the block and came down Corlears on the far side of the street.

Back in the coupe, I watched them moving the covered trays of food inside. Sometime after that, a taxi pulled up and three girls got out, laughing and talking to each other. I couldn't tell much about them. They were wearing coats and hats. One of them was shorter than the other two and what I could see of her hair was dark. I leaned forward to get a better look, but Bobby came out and hustled them inside.

The regular, not-crazy part of me was sure that the shorter girl didn't walk at all like Connie. The crazy jealous part wasn't satisfied, but there was nothing to be done then so I drove back uptown to get ready.

I parked in the alley behind the speak and let myself in the back. It was a slow night. The place was almost empty. Marie

Therese hadn't heard anything more from Connie. Damn. I went down to the cellar and found Arch Malloy with his nose still in *The Story of Philosophy*. He might have made it to the second chapter.

I said, "Looks like you were right about the premiere of that stag movie I was telling you about. It's tonight."

"Is it, then?" He put down the book.

I described the place and said, "The situation is a little more complicated than it was before. Maybe." I didn't want to say anything about Connie, but since Malloy knew her, I had to.

"There's a chance Connie will be there. This guy I know, the one I told you about, who calls himself Apollinaire, he might have tried to get her to help serve food and drinks at this thing. Cocaine, too, maybe. At least, I know he wanted to ask her, and if he did, maybe she said yes. I don't know."

Arch got that canny look of his. "You've found a way to get yourself into it, haven't you?"

I nodded. "If you've got black-tie, you can join me."

He hopped out of his chair and said, "I'll be back in thirty minutes."

"Bring your pistol."

I went up to my office and called Detective Ellis at his precinct. It took a long time for the desk sergeant or whoever answered to find him, and when Ellis got on the line, he sounded tired, irritable, and not in the mood to hear what I had to say.

"What the hell is it now?"

"I know you said you want this to be over, but it's not. The stag movie I told you about, they're showing it tonight. And I've got reason to think the guys who were behind the business with the book are going to be there."

"So? What's it to you?"

"They're up to something." I hadn't told him about the goat, and I couldn't think of a way to bring it up then and not sound like I was nuts.

"I don't care," he said. "You stay out of it. I've talked to Captain Boatwright. He's happy and he's going to talk to the commissioner, so you don't do anything else, you got that? Don't rock the boat."

"Listen, goddammit, you got me into this when you told them to come to my place and volunteered me to be your go-between and then left me holding the fucking bag when it was time for the payoff, so you still owe me."

"The hell you say. I—"

"Just listen. I said they're showing this picture tonight. I'm going to be there. You stay close to the phone. If it goes south and I can't handle it, I'm going to call. Make sure you're available."

"Shit, you can't—"

"I'm not asking you to do anything. Just be ready if I need help. Last night you told me to say yes and shut up and that's what you're going to do now. You're going to say yes and you're going to stay by the damn telephone. Right?"

He didn't say anything.

I repeated, "Right?"

After a long pause, he said, "Yes."

I told Frenchy and Marie Therese they could close up whenever they felt like it and that Arch and I had other business to take care of. Right off, Marie Therese asked if it had anything to do with Connie.

I said, "I don't think so and I hope not, but it's something I want to be sure about."

She went into her mother-hen routine then and put her fists on her hips and narrowed her eyes. "If you did anything to hurt that girl, I will never forgive you."

"I didn't do anything"—that I knew of—"If I knew why you and her were so honked off at me, maybe I'd have a better idea about what's going on."

I waited for her answer and watched her anger fade away as

she thought about it, but she just shook her head and didn't say anything.

I walked back to the Chelsea.

Tommy was not behind the desk. I went up to my room and found my best black suit, the one I wore at funerals. The invitation didn't say anything about dress, but I remembered Bobby saying something about black-tie and costumes and masks. He also said his crowd was the carriage trade, but considering that the event wasn't exactly going to be listed on the social register, I figured nobody would say anything to a guy who had an invitation.

I went with a fresh white shirt and a black silk tie and finished off by putting a quick shine on my black crepe-soled brogans. After considering the fancy black cane with the silver head, I decided to stay with my everyday stick. It was heavier and you could do more damage with the crook. I thought about breaking my rule and putting the sixth round in the Banker's Special but decided, no, if it came to that and Connie was there and guys started shooting, I'd grab her and we'd hide.

I went up to Connie's room on the fifth floor and knocked, hoping like hell she'd answer and this whole damn foolish thing would be over. I'd ask her, *beg* her to tell me what was wrong and she would and we'd work it out. But, no, nothing. No answer.

I went on up to the sixth and paused outside 624, Bobby's Rudolph Valentino room. I could hear dance music from the Victrola and a man and a woman laughing. Sounded like Tommy and Honeybunch hit it off over the ice cream and the hash.

Down the hall, I unlocked the door to the workroom and turned on the lights. If anybody had been there in the last couple of hours, I couldn't tell. I took the stack of masks from the shelves and spread them out on the table where I could get a better look.

Some were painted in bright shiny colors, and some were made to look like animals or birds trimmed with fur and feathers and ribbons. I picked two with big eyeholes that only covered the top half of your face. The brown was a dog. That was for Arch. Mine was black and white. I couldn't tell if it was a cat or a skunk. Seemed right either way.

Arch was waiting at the Ford coupe. He was keyed up, bouncing a little as I opened the door. Once we were inside the car, I saw he was wearing a tuxedo.

As we headed downtown, I said, "If Bobby's having his premiere tonight, Wilcox must be back from Washington." I was trying to sound calm and logical and not let the crazy jealous part show.

Arch said, "Perhaps Mr. Wilcox is ready for a change of pace. After all of his work on the campaign and the New York side of the transition and the public celebrations, he's ready to reward himself with something more carnal. He took his own railway car to the inauguration, so he wouldn't have any trouble getting back quickly."

"The invite says we're going to see the premiere of Bobby's *Kong* and there will be a performance by the stars. I think that means Nola Revere and a guy in a gorilla suit."

Arch said, "If this stag film is any good, a fifty-foot-tall monster would just get in the way, wouldn't it? That's not what these gentlemen are paying to see."

"Right. That was Bobby's thinking, too. I saw them setting up. There's food and drink, and a couple of goons are keeping the riffraff out. Now, here's the part I haven't told you. This guy can be a real charmer, and he left a note for Connie last night." I didn't mention how she smiled when she read it. I couldn't stop thinking about that, and it made my stomach hurt. "And I kind of pissed him off by breaking into his studio a little. But, really, he's just one of those guys that—"

"That thinks he can bed any woman he meets."

I turned down Broadway. "Yeah, that's Bobby. So maybe he asked Connie to work there tonight just so he could get back at me and try to hustle her into the sack and maybe she said yes not knowing what he was up to."

"I think you're misjudging Connie there. She may be young, but she's dealt with men like that before."

"You know that, huh?" I cut my eyes at him as we went around Union Square and traffic thinned out.

"We talk," he said, smiling. "You know, I almost hope you continue to be a great lummox and she sees that she needs the patience and guidance that only a more mature man can provide. Ah, don't look at me that way, I'm joking. The last thing she wants is another father in her life, she's got no use for the one she has, the miserable bastard."

"What the hell do you know about her father?" I didn't know a damn thing. I didn't even know she had a father. I mean, I knew but she never said anything about him to me.

"Like I said, we talk. Her old man is as big a bastard as mine was, but you were about to tell me why you think we need to be here, and I have made a bet with myself that it has something to do with the slaughtered goat and then shooting the pistol at the globe."

"Yeah." I was glad I didn't have to explain that part.

"And we think the young fellow is responsible for both, and he's somehow associated with the Wilcox family. He might be Peter Wilcox Jr., or he might believe himself to be Peter Wilcox's brother."

"Right."

"And that suggests a possibility we have not considered. He could be a bastard sired by Learned Wilcox. If half the stories told about old Learned are true, he is a cocksman of the first order, a rake who'd put your friend Bobby to shame."

"He's still alive? I thought Peter Wilcox took over when he died."

"No, there was something, a broken hip, I believe, and then a series of illnesses that kept Learned away from the business. By the time it was announced that Peter Wilcox was officially taking over as head of the bank, he'd been doing the job for more than a year."

"How do you know all this stuff?"

He shrugged. "You asked me to look into it. I have my methods."

"Okay, well, yeah, that's what I'm worried about. If this guy has it in for Peter Wilcox and he knows about this soirée, there's a good chance he'll be here. You know I don't give a damn about the Wilcoxes, but I'm not going to let anything happen to Connie. That's the long and the short of it."

"So," he said, "the first thing we do is locate her. If she's there."

"Right, then there's the other two guys, the ones you saw Thursday night, a kid and an older horse-faced guy. Name's Trodache."

"Yes, I remember them."

"He was there when I made the payoff and I gave him the business. Nothing serious but he won't be happy to see me. And I spotted the kid watching the place earlier tonight, so he's still around, too."

I turned south off Delancey on a dark side street so we could come up behind Bobby's place. "Oh, and there's one other guy, too, the chauffeur who's driving a big Oldsmobile, one of the fancy ones with four headlights. Saw him earlier tonight, too."

I cut the lights and parked a block down on Monroe Street. "So there's those three guys."

"Four, counting the goat killer."

"Right. That's who we're worried about."

"But really," Arch said, "all we care about is Connie."

"Yeah, if we see her, we try to get her out."

"And if we don't?" he asked.

"Then we eat and drink and watch the world's greatest stag film." I picked up the masks and handed him one. "Here, you're the dog."

CHAPTER TWENTY-FOUR

Arch and I rounded the corner at Corlears and saw that the street was clogged with long dark cars and taxis. A small crowd of men jostled on the brick sidewalk at the front doors, some of them in silk toppers and opera cloaks, most wearing masks. I couldn't make out much of them in the faint gaslight. As we got closer, we could hear jungle jazz from a band, and I saw moving lights inside. The idea came to me then that I might have pissed Bobby off so much that he told his goons to look out for a short guy with a cane, so I held the stick close to my leg and a little behind it. Didn't matter. The two goons weren't checking names on a list. If you flashed the square card with blue lettering, that was enough. Chances were they couldn't read anyway.

We went through the door into a big square room with gaslights on the wall, a wooden floor worn smooth, and a heavy haze of tobacco smoke. Looked like most of the men there were leaving their hats and cloaks with a hatcheck girl off to one side of the door and then heading straight for a bar at the back. The fat guy who was right in front of me doffed his cloak and revealed a bright blue military coat with gold epaulets, braid and fringe, and a red sash. When he turned toward the bar, he put on a mask and a peaked cap with more gold braid. He had a chest full of medals and ribbons. The hatcheck girl, who wasn't Connie, had two stacks of masks on her table. I'd seen them in Bobby's workroom.

Figuring there was a chance we'd be making a fast exit, Arch and I had left our overcoats in the car. We moved out of the way of the guys heading for the drinks. I still couldn't get a good look at the room, but I saw that there were at least three tables with eats, all surrounded by men. It was a hungry, thirsty, happy crowd. Lots of laughing, some of it nervous and uncomfortable, some way too loud. Guys doing something dirty. Breaking the rules. Together. They were ready to see something new. Hell, that part of it got to me, too.

I said to Arch, "You work that side. I'll take this one. If we find her, we'll meet up, figure out what to do next."

He nodded and left. I made my way around the other way and that's when the pure foolishness of what we were doing hit me. I thought, *She's a grown woman. She can do whatever the hell she wants. Where do you get off trying to 'rescue' her from anything?* And then the jealous crazy part said, *Screw that. She shouldn't be here. This is dangerous for a girl like her and you've got to take care of her.* But it was too late for that, anyway. I was there. I'd see it through.

First off, I headed for the closest food to see if anybody was serving. Nobody was, and the trays of meat, cheese, and bread had been picked clean. I moved on and checked the room more closely. Most of the men wore tuxedos and masks. I couldn't tell if they knew each other or not. I saw four guys with women, working girls by the amount of pale white flesh they were showing off. Two guys drinking beer were wearing old Roman or Greek outfits, one in a toga with a bunch of branches and leaves on his head, and the other in a skirt and sandals and armor and a metal helmet with a big crest on top. Another man was wearing a blue mask and a full dress police uniform. And there was a guy in a black suit like mine, not a tuxedo, with gray hair and heavy jowls. I was pretty sure it was the Olds chauffeur because when he saw me looking at him, he stared right back, like he knew who I was. I tried to get closer, but he ducked into the crowd.

The band was six colored guys with piano, drums, and a lot of brass. They were playing hard and loud on a stage in one corner near the front door, really growling out jungle jazz. They wore some kind of leopard-skin outfits. I guess Bobby wanted them to add to his atmosphere. The women moved close to the stage. When they couldn't get their guys out onto the floor, they danced with each other.

Not far away from the bandstand, there was a big square moving picture screen on another dais, with about sixty or seventy chairs arranged in rows in front of it. On the opposite wall was the projection booth, a big box made out of plywood and painted flat black. It had the same handmade look as the shelves in Bobby's workroom and studio.

I'd got about a third of the way around the room when I saw the first waitress. She was a young blonde with heavy makeup and a smile that didn't look quite right. I figured her to be new to this. She was collecting empty glasses and taking orders for booze and beer. She kept shifting her tray from hand to hand and reaching up to fiddle with her brassiere under a tightly buttoned pink blouse. She moved away before I could get to her, so I headed for the bar.

Being short, as I was and am, it's easy to move through a crowd of big guys, but I couldn't see over them to get a good look at the whole room. It got harder to maneuver as I edged closer to the booze.

I shouldered up to the table and saw that a man and a woman were handling the hooch. She was a tall, harried brunette. Not Connie. I could tell by the big bottles without labels that it was the cheap swamp water they peddled at second-rate speaks.

When I got the brunette's attention, I asked for a glass of seltzer and left a quarter in the tip glass. She was surprised. It was the first of the night.

As I pushed back through the crowd, I saw that there was a staircase to the second floor in a corner. It was roped off and dark.

Moving back to the middle of the room, I guessed the crowd at less than a hundred with guys still coming in. Most of them were puffing Havanas and knocking back the booze. I saw a flash of pink at the edge of my vision, but it was gone before I got a good look so I went that way. Trying not to look like I was hurrying, I moved around toward where I thought Arch might be. A lot of guys got in my way, and I was almost back to the hatcheck girl when I saw the back of a woman in a pink blouse taking a tray of glasses through a door near the end of the bar. She was short and had dark hair. I was about to pull the door open, but the guy working the bar said, "Staff only."

Before I could do anything, the blond waitress hurried out with a tray of drinks. The bartender gave me a hard look. I tried to give him a hard look back, but I was wearing a cat mask. He was not scared.

I went back out into the room and kept moving until I came upon another waitress, another blonde but not the first. This one knew the score. The band was cutting loose so I had to lean close to talk to her.

"Is there a girl named Connie working tonight?"

She looked confused for a second, then shook her head and said, "I don't know any of the girls' names."

"She's short, black hair, dark complexion. Real cute."

"We've got two of 'em like that," she said, then put her lips right next to my ear, "but I'm cuter. And I can prove it."

She stepped back and gave me a commercial smile.

"Not tonight, sweetheart," I said.

She smiled, shrugged, and blew me a kiss as she left.

Arch showed up. He hadn't seen Connie either. I asked him if he'd seen two short, dark-haired waitresses. He said no. I told him what the waitress said, so we worked the room again, taking the other sides. By then, it was even smokier than it was when we got there, and hotter, too. The mask was starting to chafe. Some of the men let their masks hang around their necks and some pushed them up on top of their heads. I saw more than a few faces I recognized from the papers. I also saw a second set of stairs in another corner. Like the first one, it was roped off.

As I went through the crowd, I saw one waitress who was short, dark, and cute, and not Connie, but there was a lot I was missing. I'd been around the room twice before I made my way through a crowd of men who weren't moving or talking. That's where I saw a magic lantern, or something, that was projecting a series of still photographs on a small screen. It looked like some of them were shots I'd seen in Bobby's picture books. These showed everything, including the big finishes. And, just like Bobby claimed, they looked great. The women were carefully posed and he managed to capture skin texture with angled light and shadow. I don't remember anything about the guys in the pictures, but the men who were watching them stood still and paid close attention.

By then I was getting restless and jumpy, and I knew that was no good. When I get restless and jumpy, I don't think and I do stupid things. Right or wrong, I decided to see what was on the second floor.

Nobody was paying attention as I eased around behind the crowd at the magic lantern and ducked under the rope at the foot of the stairs. I was careful and quiet and stopped at the landing to let my eyes adjust. When they did, I could make out a little light coming from a doorway above, and I heard voices arguing. I was more careful and quiet going the rest of the way up.

When I reached the second floor, I saw the giant black hand

that had been in Bobby's Chinatown studio. He'd moved it to the middle of the room and surrounded it with chairs. There was a weak spotlight above. It gleamed down on Bobby's bald head.

He was saying, "We'll start with the light low, like this. Then we'll get the key light there and the kick light over there."

He must have hit a switch. Another light came on with a snap and brightened the hand with a warm pink glow, and I could see who Bobby was talking to. It was Nola Revere and her costar. She was wearing another copy of the gauzy fairy-tale dress that Miss Wray wore in the real movie, the one that fell off her shoulders. There was a picture of her in it in Bobby's book, and I'd seen another one with a red stain in his studio. Guess he had a lot of them. Couldn't have cost too much, judging by the amount and thinness of the material. It showed her off and she had a lot to show off. Her costar was wearing a gorilla suit, but without the head. Even in that light, you could see that he was a really black colored guy. I mean so black he was almost blue, and he was tall, six and a half feet maybe, the suit made it hard to tell. He was also wearing a big codpiece, a furry black lump about the size of half a football.

Bobby gestured toward the hand, making it pretty clear that they were going to use it as a bed. He said, "It's gonna be just like before, right. You start out however you like, but you end it with her on her knees and you behind. Then you switch again and she's on top. Got that? We can't let those tits go to waste. That's what they're paying to see."

The colored guy shook his head and said something in Spanish. Bobby answered, "No, not now. After. That's the deal, remember?"

I couldn't hear from where I was standing, so I strolled over and joined the group. When Bobby first saw me, he tried to be charming. "Excuse me, sir, it'll be just a few minutes before we're ready for this part of the performance. The film will be shown downstairs." He wore a red ringmaster's coat, jodhpurs, and black leather boots. His face was weirdly white under makeup and his lips were as red as his coat. Even with the cat mask, I was the most normal-looking guy in the room.

I took off my mask, and said, "Hiya, Bobby."

"Goddammit, you little shit—"

"Don't get your bowels in an uproar. I'm just here to see your movie and to meet the star." I turned to her. "Miss Revere, right? Nola?"

She looked up at the colored guy and grabbed his hand with both of hers.

"No," she said, standing straighter. "I'm *Mrs.* Carlos Sotolongo."

He held onto her hand and glared at me with a challenging frown. I guess Nola didn't think that working with him was a fate worse than death like her pal Daphne.

Bobby rolled his eyes and shook his head. "Be that as it may, I want to be sure you know your marks. Carlos, you carry her in from there." He pointed to a curtained area. "Nola, you're screaming and pounding his chest, just like when we did it for the film."

Carlos cut him off and rattled out some machine-gun Spanish.

When he finished, his expression was still hard, and Bobby said, pleading, "But we already agreed to this. You get the money *after* the performance. Look, I told you, this can be the beginning of a groundbreaking career. For *both* of you. The money we're haggling over tonight is nothing compared to your potential. Nothing! If you work with me, let me help you . . . Did you see that crowd down there? Some of the richest and most powerful men in the city are going to be watching you tonight. They'll want to see more, you know that. What happened before, that was just a temporary problem. It's solved. Didn't you get your money? Of course you did. So you know I'm good for it. As soon as we're finished, you'll get everything I said you would."

Carlos's expression didn't change, and he shook his head. He turned his back to Nola, and she started undoing some laces on his back until Bobby stopped her.

"No, goddammit, don't do that. It takes him a fucking hour to put that thing on. Do you have any idea how much I had to pay for it? Not to mention the alterations. All right, all right, here." He produced a thick roll of bills from his pocket. "Here's half." Carlos said something more in Spanish, and she started unlacing again.

Bobby said, "Jeez, you fucking Cubans are worse than the fucking Jews," and peeled off more bills.

Carlos watched and counted along with him. Then he said something else in Spanish and Bobby answered, "No, you don't need to worry about the cops, that's taken care of, believe me it's taken care of."

By then, they'd forgot about me, I think. Looking back on what Daphne said about Bobby trying to hold out on her, it figured that after he was finished making the picture, Bobby had stiffed Nola and Carlos. But then he decided that he needed them for his *soirée cinémateque intime* and had to pony up. He'd stacked up an impressive number of bills when the bartender came up the stairs.

"Boss," he said, "they're here."

Bobby bolted past him like he'd been goosed in the ass, and the bartender was right behind him. I stayed there.

Nola and Carlos were counting the cash. They looked at me like I was going to try to take it.

"I'm Jimmy Quinn. You don't know me, but we've got a couple of mutual acquaintances: Polly Adler and Daphne." Given the circumstances, I figured Carlos knew about Nola's work and she wouldn't mind me mentioning it.

She still looked suspicions. "What do you want?" Daphne said Nola's English wasn't that good, but Nola didn't have much of an accent that I could hear.

"Nothing. Daphne said if I saw you, you should give her a call. She's worried about you."

She looked at Carlos and they talked in Spanish for a while, so low that I couldn't hear them even if I knew the language.

Then she said, "Is Daphne all right? Does she know that I did this?" and plucked at the dress.

I was having a hell of a time not staring at her tits and crotch, and Carlos was making it clear that he wasn't happy with my giving his new bride the eye. I guess they were doing what they had to do for money, but he didn't like it a damn bit, you could tell that.

"Yeah, she knows. She's got a place down on Gay Street."

Nola shook her head. "Daphne doesn't understand. I can't explain it, and we don't have time. Our ship leaves for Cuba tonight. Carlos has arranged everything, and we're not going to change it."

Right then, for some reason, I thought about the beginning of *King Kong* and Carl Denham telling Miss Wray she had to come with him for this "opportunity of a lifetime" and everything that happened after that. Hell, maybe it was the dress or maybe I'm just a sap.

I gave them a little salute with my stick and said, "Good luck to you then, and let me give you a word of advice. If you hear things getting loud and crazy down there, don't hang around. Scram out of here as fast as you can."

She looked worried. Carlos's glare didn't change.

Downstairs in the smoky room, the band stopped and the men went quiet as Bobby ushered two guys in from the back door. One of them had to be Peter Wilcox. The other was a wobbly codger with weak legs who got around on two canes. Both of them were wearing black domino masks and expensive bespoke tuxedos. Wilcox's fit him perfectly. The old man had shriveled since his was measured. The collar was two sizes too big, and the padded shoulders of the jacket made him look like a dwarf.

Arch Malloy sidled beside me and whispered, "That's them, Peter Wilcox and the old pirate Learned, his dear old pater."

Bobby snapped his fingers, and two of the waitresses—neither Connie—scurried out to help the old guy. Each of them took an arm and got in close enough to press their breasts into his shoulders. Even with the mask, you could see his liver-lipped smile. They led him to a padded chair in the front row. He fell into it and reached a hand up under one girl's skirt as she turned around. She froze but didn't move away until he let her go. The bartender brought two tumblers of scotch.

Bobby jumped up on the dais, raised his hands, and said in a loud voice, "Gentlemen, gentlemen, your attention, please. The first part of this evening's entertainment will begin in just a few minutes. I believe we have time for everyone to refresh his drink and find a comfortable seat. Then you shall witness the Eighth Wonder of the World!"

They swarmed the bar. Arch and I found a quiet corner. He asked where I'd been.

"Upstairs. The second part of the show is a live performance by the two stars. Did you find Connie?"

He shook his head. "I haven't seen her, but I've only seen one waitress with black hair, so if there are two of them . . ."

We were still talking a few minutes later when I saw a familiar figure near the front doors, a guy in a plumed hat, white death's head mask, and a red satin cloak. He carried a tall stick with a skull on top, all of it just like Lon Chaney in *Phantom of the Opera*. I nudged Arch and said, "I think that's the guy I was telling you about, the extortionist from the joint up on Fifth."

"Not exactly a wallflower, is he?"

Even among the togas, generals, and cop uniforms, he was hard to miss, but as guys moved into the seats, I lost sight of him. The truth is I wasn't that interested in him. I still wanted to find Connie, if she was there. I didn't see her or any of the other waitresses.

When the gaslights went down, I moved toward the other side of the room near the projection booth. A spotlight came on and there was Bobby on the dais again. I could see that he was sweating through the makeup.

"Good evening, gentlemen," he said. "Before we begin tonight's presentation, I want to welcome some new members to our association. You've chosen a good time to join us. Those of you who have been with us for some time know that we strive to present only the very highest-quality entertainment for worldly and open-minded gentlemen. We produce the motion pictures that the Hollywood studios cannot, *dare not* present, but with all the allure, mystery, and carnality that is at the heart of every great drama from Euripides to—"

"Get on with it, you windy bastard," somebody yelled from the crowd and everybody laughed.

Bobby laughed too and said, "All right then, you impatient sons of bitches, here it is, my masterpiece"—he grabbed his crotch—"the real *Kong*."

The spotlight went out, and after a few nervous moments of darkness, the projector started. Then I heard the scratch and pop of a needle hitting a phonograph, and music played along with the movie. I guess Bobby couldn't afford to do talking pictures yet, but he knew he had to set a mood.

The title card read, THE OSCAR APOLLINAIRE PRODUCTION OF *KONG*.

The first shot was of Nola in the suit and the unbuttoned blouse up on the observation deck of the Empire State Building. It was definitely the real thing, so I guess Bobby must have paid somebody off to let him up there when it was closed on Sunday morning or sometime. At first, he kept the camera in close on her, lingering on her face and breasts, and he really did make her look good.

From that he cut to her walking down an empty Thirty-Fourth Street. The next card read, A GIRL FINDS HER WAY ON THE BLEAK CITY STREETS. She looked terrific but nervous as she jiggled down the sidewalk and then tried to steal an apple from a stand. The card read, DESTITUTE, SHE IS REDUCED TO STEALING FOOD. A man's hand slapped hers. The next shot was her on the coffeehouse set I saw at the Chinatown studio. Just a section of wall, a table, and a chair, but you didn't notice that because you were looking at her.

I heard something behind me and turned my head enough to see a man and a woman against the wall by the projection booth. It was the guy in the dress policeman's uniform and the blond waitress who made me an offer. Looked like he took her up on it. She was on her knees working at his fly.

The rest of Bobby's picture followed the plot of the real one as far as it needed to. You saw Nola going up the gangplank of a ship, taking a shower in a metal stall, practicing a scream in the gauze dress, and being taken off the ship. You never really saw any of the guys. They were just the hands or arms of men just outside the range of the camera. And in every shot, Nola looked as glamorous and as sexy as almost any woman I've ever seen on a screen. Almost. But she couldn't act. Not that it made any difference to the people in the audience. And, hell, Bobby wasn't the first man, or the last, to try to build a moving picture around a well-stacked blonde.

In place of the big important scenes from the real movie—the ship in the fog, Skull Island, Kong breaking the Gate—Bobby inserted shots of those pencil sketches I saw on the walls of the studio. Funny, those were the only things that came close to the first one. He also had a shot of Nola pretending to fight against the big hand, and then in the next one, Carlos in the gorilla suit. Like the other stuff, it didn't bother the rest of the audience. Now, all the way through, they were whooping and whistling and wolf-calling whenever Nola showed some flesh. And Bobby knew enough about building suspense to keep at least some of Nola's clothes on in the early part. So later, during the shower and when she was tied up between the pillars, the guys got real quiet. Then when Carlos showed up, as the Beast, and whipped off his codpiece, you could tell they were impressed.

Every eye was trained on the screen when he tore her dress open. That's when the first bomb exploded.

Being at the back of the crowd, I saw the light flash near the front doors and heard the thing hissing. I was close enough to see a can spinning on the wooden floor until it disappeared inside the smoke that was spewing out. Guys in the closest seats jumped up and knocked them over and yelled. Before anybody really knew what was going on, a second one went off near the bandstand. It wasn't nearly as loud as the first one, not much louder than a firecracker. Somebody yelled "Fire" and there was more banging and milling around with some guys running toward the front door, some away from it, and some not moving from their seats. Bobby's voice cut through the others' saying, "Calm down. This is just somebody's idea of a joke." The noise level dropped, but a lot of guys were still up and moving around. The movie went on.

I headed toward the bar where the waitresses were likely to be. For me, it was a scary moment, being the smallest guy in a roomful of big blundering bodies, most of them drunk and close to being panicked. That's damn dangerous for a guy my size. You don't stay on your feet, you get trampled. The only light was from the projector showing Carlos pumping into Nola. I shoved and shouldered and used my stick to clear a way to the STAFF ONLY door and pushed another guy out of the way to get through.

It was a brightly lit kitchen with empty food trays, boxes, and bottles on the metal tables. Four waitresses who looked confused and scared at what they were hearing in the other room stood together near a door. No Connie. I yelled out, "Is there a Connie Nix here?" and the way they looked at me, I knew she wasn't there.

One girl asked, "Is this part of the show?"

I said no and was about to say more when the door behind me banged open and the bartender shoved me aside.

"Bring towels and water," he yelled. He grabbed a couple of seltzer siphons and ran back out.

At the same moment, another door at the other end of the kitchen opened and two men came through it. I wasn't close enough to get a clear look at their faces, but one of them was

Learned Wilcox on his two sticks. The other man was helping and hurrying him along. They went around the end of the big table in the middle of the room and out the back door. I tried to follow and heard a loud yell from outside and then grunts, curses, and two quick gunshots. The four waitresses ran into me as they tried to get away from the shooting. I heard two more shots as I shoved the door open and pulled out the Banker's Special.

I was in the alley off Monroe Street. One of Bobby's goons had fallen against the brick wall on the other side and was trying to aim his pistol. The men I'd seen inside were halfway to Monroe Street. The one in the lead smoothly raised his gun and aimed. The goon dropped his piece and staggered back. I stopped and didn't do anything.

The guy with the gun lowered it and turned to me. His mask was gone. It was the guy I saw in the Olds, no question. We stared at each other for what seemed to me a long time. Then he put his gun away and carried Learned Wilcox on down the alley. The Olds was waiting for them on Monroe Street.

The first guy put Wilcox into the car and turned back to me. "Mr. Quinn," he said in a loud clear voice. "Follow me."

Then he got in the car and it drove away. *What the hell?*

Back in the kitchen, I could smell the fumes from the smoke bomb. The waitresses were still huddling and trying to decide what to do. I could hear Bobby calming them down in the other room.

Arch found me when I came through the door by the bar and asked what the hell was going on. I told him that I saw a smoke bomb close to the front doors and heard another one. The smoke had cleared some, but I couldn't really tell because guys still had their cigars fired up. The picture had stopped and the gaslights were up. Looked to me like some of the men were back in their seats, but a lot of others were grabbing their coats and getting out. I guess they figured that the excitement might bring the cops and they didn't want to be around. Bobby was saying that the bar would be open again and they would restart the second reel, but the movie was only the first part of the program. Right then, it was even money whether most of the guys would stampede out or settle down to the stag movie.

Arch said, "Where did you run off to this time?"

"The kitchen. Looking for Connie. I don't think she's here."

"I don't either. What do we do now?"

Up on the dais, Bobby stopped talking when Peter Wilcox grabbed his elbow. I imagine he was asking where his old man had got to.

I said to Arch, "Let's see how this works out. And tell me something, have you seen the guy in the big hat and the skull mask?"

"Not since you pointed him out to me."

"Take a look around. See if he's still here."

Arch nodded and headed off. I went to the bar to check that part of the room. He wasn't there, and all the waitresses I'd seen were handing out more drinks. I went back into the kitchen to make sure I hadn't missed anyone. It was empty.

Back in the big room, Bobby was still talking to Wilcox. It looked like Wilcox was telling him what to do, and Bobby wasn't liking it one damn bit.

The guys who had new drinks were getting into seats again, and all of them were starting to get edgy. One guy was saying he was sure he heard shots outside. They could tell something wasn't right.

It didn't matter to me. Right then, all I felt was a sense of relief. Connie wasn't there. That's what mattered. Bobby and Nola would do whatever they had to do without me. I was finished with them. I was pretty sure I knew what the guy meant when he said for me to follow him, but it wasn't as important as Connie. It was time to find Arch, go back to the Chelsea, and keep looking for her.

But then I noticed that the man in the dress police uniform was hanging back from the others. He was standing next to the projection booth. He pulled out a handkerchief, took off his mask, and buttoned his fly with shaky hands. He had a shell-shocked look, like he was either going to throw up or shit his pants.

I knew who he was and had to consider what to do. When Arch came back, I told him to bring the car around to the front. We were taking somebody with us.

"What are you talking about?" he asked.

"I'll explain by and by."

He left. I went over to the man in the dress uniform and said, "Captain Boatwright? I'm Jimmy Quinn. I know one of your detectives. William Ellis. Want a ride back to the precinct?"

I could tell it spooked him when I said his name. But he got over it, and looking relieved, he nodded his head.

CHAPTER TWENTY-FIVE

It must have been sometime after three in the morning when we stopped in front of Captain Boatwright's precinct house on Twentieth Street. He hadn't said a word for the whole drive. He got out, kept one hand on the door, and said, "Your name's Quinn," his breath fogging in the cold.

"Right."

"Well." He gave the door a solid slap, like he approved of it, and said, "Good man." He squared his shoulders, straightened his cap, and walked up the steps, every inch a captain of New York's finest.

Arch said, "You mean he really is a cop?"

"Yeah, Ellis's boss."

Arch nodded. "I can see how a man like that would need a man like Ellis to keep him out of trouble."

"Ain't that the truth."

On the way back to the speak, I told Arch about what went on in the alley. "I couldn't really tell if this guy was kidnapping

Wilcox or if the old guy was going along with him. But, see, here's the funny thing. This Oldsmobile has been part of this business from the beginning. The first night, when Trodache and the kid braced me outside Lansky's place, they were in the Olds. And I knew they had a third guy with them, but there could've been another guy, a driver. I didn't get a look at this guy's mug until tonight when I spotted him in the Olds casing the place on Corlears Street, just like I was doing, and, you know, I almost thought I'd seen him before."

"Describe him to me," Arch said.

"Middle aged, gray hair, heavy soft jowls."

Arch thought for a moment, then said, "On Thursday night, late, there was a man like that in the bar. Came in around midnight. Ordered a gin and It and made it last. He had on a brown suit, and he carried a cap that he kept his gloves in. Didn't check them. It was around the time that gossip columnist fellow from the *Comet*, Dunbar, was in to see you. I remember this fellow had a table near him."

"How the hell do you remember him at all?"

"He was different. He wasn't there to socialize. He didn't really want the gin and It, either, and who could blame him, it's a nasty drink. He had a newspaper open, but he didn't really read it that I saw. That's all. I didn't pay as much attention to him after you and Dunbar started jawing. We were all interested in that and hoped it meant he'd write about what a splendid place Jimmy Quinn's is and then we'd be crowded every night and the tips would be magnificent and we'd get the raises we deserve. So I can't be completely certain, but it's more than likely that he left before Dunbar. That's it."

Hmmm. "Okay, I guess that makes sense. You see, the last thing this guy said tonight in the alley, just as he hustled old Wilcox into the car, was 'Follow me.'"

"Follow him?"

"Yeah. He said, 'Mr. Quinn, follow me.'"

"But you didn't."

"No. I know where he is."

Arch said, "The mansion on Fifth. And we're going there now."

"No, first we're going to see if Connie is at the speak or the Chelsea."

As I expected, Frenchy and Marie Therese had closed the place. We usually locked up around two on Sundays unless it was a big night. Arch waited with the car while I checked inside. There was no note from Connie in my office or behind the bar. Same thing at the Chelsea. Tommy was facedown and snoring behind the front desk. I let myself into her room. Nothing had changed since the afternoon. I went back to the car.

We drove up Fifth, and I went over everything that had happened since Thursday, and it still didn't make sense to me. The one part I could figure was Nola and Carlos. That was easy. Bobby hired them to screw in front of his camera. They did and they enjoyed it. They enjoyed it so much they decided to get hitched. But knowing Bobby, he gave them part of their money before their performance and then put them off for the rest. Put them off until he realized that he wanted them to do it again in front of a live audience. That's why he wanted to know if I'd seen her. But he did locate them and talked them into an encore. That's when Carlos held him up. And it was a safe bet that he and Nola were the first ones out of there when the smoke bombs went off and the shooting started. Hell, I'm just a sentimentalist. I hoped they were already on a boat to Cuba.

We stopped in front of the place and could see lights in the courtyard. I told Arch, "Keep your piece close at hand. I don't know what the hell we're going to find in there."

"I suspected as much, and I've got to ask why we're here at all. As I understand it from what you told me, you've done everything the stuffed shirts from RKO wanted you to do and if there's any reason to think Connie's here, you haven't told me, and it's certainly not because a chauffeur told you to. So . . . why?"

I thought before I answered. "Because I want to know about that damn goat. I know Trodache and the kid didn't dream up the extortion business on their own, and like you said, that's finished. But any way that I look at it, I can't figure the goat. So here I am. That doesn't mean you've got to be as screwy as I am."

"The hell you say. I can be as screwy as any man."

The iron gate was still unlocked. The water in the fountain was green and frozen. We didn't bother with the knocker on the big front door. It was unlocked, too, so we went straight inside. There were no lights, and nobody had turned the heat on so it was as cold as it was outside. We could see firelight coming through the open door of the library down the hall.

As we walked toward it, I said to Arch, "We've been invited, I guess, but watch out for that dickweed Trodache. I banged him up a little the last time I saw him and he likes to suckerpunch."

Arch unbuttoned his coat. His Luger was in a holster high on his right hip. He pulled it out and held it under his coat. I had the .38 in the pocket of my topcoat.

The first thing we saw inside the library was old Learned Wilcox sunk deep in the leather club chair. He was sucking happily on a scotch and didn't pay any attention to us. The guy in the brown suit was warming his butt at the fire. He had both hands in his coat pockets, probably holding onto his pistol too.

"Mr. Quinn," he said, his voice level. "I'm glad you could join us, and Mr. . . . .I'm sorry, I don't know your name, but I recognize you from Mr. Quinn's establishment."

"Arch Malloy."

"Mr. Malloy. Gentlemen, the bar is over there. Mix whatever you'd care to have. The rest of our party will be arriving soon."

The bar was a carved wooden contraption next to the

wounded globe. I didn't notice it before because it was closed then. We could see that it was loaded with decanters. No labels. Wanting a better look at the layout of the room, Arch walked over to it but didn't touch the booze. He said, "You have the advantage on us, sir."

"I am Hobart," the man said. "George Hobart. For the past several years I have been a driver for the Wilcox family. Before that, I drove for the Ashtons."

Richard Ashton, Wilcox's partner at the bank. I put Hobart at about fifty years old, on the heavy side. The jowls were matched by bags under his eyes. His voice was calm and strong. I knew I hadn't heard him before, not in any of the telephone calls. And the way he looked and sounded standing there, you just knew he was absolutely certain about what he was doing.

"Why did you tell me to follow you?" I asked.

"To be a witness. I'm glad you brought Mr. Malloy. Assuming that anyone leaves here alive tonight, I want someone to know the story, even if he can't tell it, so it will be better if there are two of you."

Arch and I looked at each other, neither knowing what to make of that.

Hobart stepped away from the fire. "I've always liked this room more than any other in the house. It's ostentatious"—I had to look that one up later—"and none of the Wilcox family ever really took advantage of it. Part of it is the fireplace. Even when the rest of the house is heated, only this room has any real feeling of warmth. That's why we decided to stage our presentation here."

Old Wilcox drained his whisky, holding it with both hands. He croaked something that might have been "More" and held the tumbler out to Hobart.

Hobart said, "Of course, sir, here you are," and took a pewter flask from his breast pocket. Wilcox's eyes brightened when he saw it. Hobart gave him a generous shot.

The old man croaked, "Where's my son? He's supposed

to be here, and the woman, what about the woman?" Hobart ignored him.

I was getting more than a little honked off at all this talk I didn't understand and said, "Okay, you worked for the Ashtons and the Wilcoxes, and something else is going on tonight and you'll get to it by and by, but before that, tell me about the goat. I'd really like to get that straight before you do anything else."

Hobart looked to be delighted by the question. "Yes, the goat, the sacrificial goat. That's actually why you're here, Mr. Quinn. The goat was Junior's idea."

I heard a metallic ring above me. The goat killer was up there on the iron gallery that ran around the library on the second level of shelves. He'd taken off the death's-head mask and the plumed hat, but he still had the red silk cape wrapped around him. He looked down at me and said hello.

Hobart said, "The goat showed Peter Wilcox the enormity of his crime. The sheer theatricality of it appealed to us. We needed something to make him understand that his secret was no longer safe. We knew that the offices of the foundation would be empty on Friday afternoon, and, of course, we couldn't allow anyone else to be hurt. That was crucial to us from the moment we read the confession. If we brought harm to anyone except the guilty, then we would betray her memory. And we were successful. Miss Wray may have been inconvenienced and, perhaps, embarrassed, but none of this was her doing. She was merely a source of the money we needed to retain the services of Mr. Trodache and his nephew."

I thought there was a good chance that Peter Wilcox didn't know anything about the goat, even assuming that anybody had found it. "But why a goat?"

"What's he talking about?" old Wilcox rasped. "Who is he?"

Hobart went on. "We wanted an example, a statement of purely bestial carnality that would disturb Mr. Wilcox. Once we found the animal, getting him to the foundation was a simple matter. Junior went upstairs to make certain the offices were empty while the rest of us waited outside. Not long after he left, I saw you go into the building. It startled me. After all, how could *you* have been there? For a moment, I thought that somehow you were on to us but I knew that was impossible."

"Okay," I said, "wait a minute. I know it was you who brought the book to the Pierre."

That stopped him like I'd smacked him with the knucks. "Then you waited outside the hotel and saw Miss Wray go to my place and you figured she talked to the RKO guys and they were going to use me as a go-between."

He nodded.

"And you followed me that first night and decided to tighten the screws."

He nodded and shrugged, admitting it was a mistake.

"When did you call Saxon Dunbar?"

He smiled. "As soon as we left you. Junior said that if Dunbar came sniffing around for his column, the lawyers would capitulate."

"And you dropped by the speak to make sure he found me."

"Yes, we thought everything was falling into place until Friday afternoon. What brought you to the Foundation for Wayward Girls?"

"I had an idea that was where they held auditions for the women in the stag pictures that Wilcox financed and I wanted to take a look at the place."

When I mentioned the women, Wilcox sat up and said, "Where's the woman? The woman in the movie. I thought she was going to be here."

Hobart reassured him, "Oh, she will be, very soon now. Just for you."

He turned to me and said, "No matter, when I saw you walking away with that bemused look, I knew you wouldn't get in our way."

"You knew I wouldn't go to the cops."

"You? That was never a question. From the moment the

actress went to Jimmy Quinn's, I knew the plan was sound, and I had been dubious about Junior's idea. I thought there had to be an easier way to raise the money in time. But once he saw the book, he said she would pay if she thought the pictures would be made public. It had something to do with her husband, but we also knew that the studio would have no trouble getting the cash quickly."

"So you just wanted the six grand? Why?"

That's when the guy in the gallery chimed in as loud as he could with his scratchy voice. "To bring the guilty parties back to the scene of the crime where they will face their accusers and justice will take its course."

Hobart laughed and said, "Christ, that's melodramatic. Let me just put it this way. They killed her, and they're going to answer for it."

"That's right." Junior was striding around on the gallery so he could look down and see every part of the floor. He had the Colt Woodsman in his right hand. It made me nervous as hell. Arch didn't like it either. As Junior moved, Arch did the same against the opposite wall, trying to keep him in sight.

Hobart refilled Learned Wilcox's glass and said, "We knew all about the film tonight. It was our only chance to get the two of them away from the estate together. By now, Mr. Trodache has delivered Junior's message to his father. They'll be here soon."

I knew they had to be talking about Mary Wilcox, but that didn't clear things up. "So the money was to hire Trodache?"

Hobart nodded and topped off the old guy's tumbler. "He knew about the stag film and the operation behind it, but he didn't help us as much as he claimed he would. Still, he has his uses, the boy, too. They're . . ." He stopped and turned his head like he was listening for something. "Yes, that's the Rolls. They're here. Get set, Junior."

"No," he croaked, sounding scared up there. "I'm not ready."

"Yes, you are. You know what to do. Steel yourself. Think about her."

Above us, Junior took a couple of steps toward the circular stairs, then stopped and went the other way, making a hell of a racket on the metal gallery. The old guy looked up for the first time and got a wild-eyed look until Hobart came over and said something that settled him down.

Arch backed into the far corner of the room where he could cover the door and nobody could get behind him. The big wooden globe also gave him some cover. I took another corner with a clear line to the foot of the staircase. From there, I could see Junior, but I couldn't tell what he was doing.

Then we heard the front door swing open and a voice said, "Dad? Junior?"

Junior started to say something but hesitated and looked down at Hobart. Hobart made a sharp angry gesture and the kid yelled, "In here!"

We heard footsteps getting louder on the marble floor, and two men came into the library. The first was Peter Wilcox, still in his tuxedo with the domino mask pushed up on his head. He saw his father in the chair and went straight for him. The second man scanned the room like a bodyguard. He was a big guy in a dark suit, and as soon as he saw Arch and me in the corners, he opened his coat and reached for a pistol.

Trodache appeared behind him and slugged him behind the ear with a sap. It made a sickening crunch and the big guy toppled. I thumbed back the hammer on the .38 and aimed it at the middle of Trodache's chest. Everybody in the room was looking at the fallen man. He shook like he was having a seizure, and blood was running out of his nose and spit foamed on his lips. His coat was rucked up over a pistol, an automatic, half out of its holster. Trodache was going for the gun but stopped when he saw me.

Peter Wilcox said, "My God, what is the meaning of this? What have you done to Summers?" He was talking about the guy on the floor and I knew the man was in trouble, bad trouble. You nail a guy that hard with a sap, you don't just knock him out, you cave in his skull. It looked to me like Summers might die if a doctor didn't look after him soon, and even if it wasn't my job to take care of him, hell, somebody had to and that made me pissed off and impatient.

Hobart said, "We have business to attend to and Summers would have interfered. I never liked him anyway."

"Hobart? What are *you* doing here?" I guess it was taking the brilliant banker a while to figure out what was happening. It was his house. I guess he still thought he was in charge. That didn't last.

Hobart said, "I'm going to explain something, something important. It involves you and your father and your son and your wife."

This was the first time I saw Peter Wilcox in person. Medium build. The square jaw, short mustache, and glasses reminded you of Teddy Roosevelt, but, hell, he was a banker not a Rough Rider.

He said, "I was told that Father was here. We were . . . attending a function and—"

"We know everything about the 'function,' but, don't worry, that is the least of our concerns. Your indulgences are your own—"

"Dammit, Hobart"—Wilcox was getting red in the face—"I will not be lectured to by you or anyone—"

"STOP IT!" Hobart stepped right up in Wilcox's face and yelled at him. "This is important."

Wilcox looked around wildly. He noticed Arch and me with a .38 trained on a scroungy-looking guy. He saw his man still flat on the ground, and he understood he was in trouble.

Then Junior said from above, "That's right. You've got to listen to us now."

Wilcox staggered back a step and collapsed into the other club chair.

Hobart stood in front of him. "I swore to myself that if we succeeded at this, I would tell the truth. I'm not going to keep silent any longer. I will speak the truth as I know it. It's too late for anything else."

And I've got to say that from everybody else I've talked to and everything I've learned since, that's exactly what he did. If the man lied or exaggerated, you can't prove it by me.

Hobart stood in front of Peter Wilcox's chair and said everything to him. He never looked away. All the while, Junior walked back and forth on the gallery. Arch was watching him and had his Luger ready. I heard everything Hobart and Wilcox said, and I could watch them well enough, but I didn't look away from Trodache. He didn't try to hide how much he wanted to get me, and he didn't move away from the man on the floor. If I gave him half a second, he'd go for the pistol and shoot me.

Hobart said, "There should be some way to couch this in more official or legal terms, but I don't know them, so I'll state it plainly, Mr. Wilcox. Some time in June of 1917, your father assaulted your wife. The first time he did it was in this library. There were others. You were in England at the time. Nine months later Peter Wilcox Jr. was born."

Wilcox shook his head and tried to sound sad. "All these years later, even after her death, these lies live on."

"No, they're not lies. She told you the truth when you came home. You refused to believe her."

"I admit that perhaps she was not ready for the marriage. She was too young and immature, and that's what caused her to make up the fantastic stories."

When Wilcox said that, I remembered Polly's story about Kitty and her mother. How everything for Kitty started when her mother kicked her out of their Chicago house for "seducing" her stepfather, and how Kitty and her mother wound up working at Polly's. Looking at that old man slugging back his scotch, I knew Hobart was telling an ugly evil truth.

Peter Wilcox still denied it. Hobart went on, "Yes, she was too young. At fifteen she was easily manipulated by your father and her father and you. Remember, I knew her better than any of you. I had been driving her and her mother for years. I brought the midwife to our house the night she was born. She refused to go to your home unless I came along as her driver."

"So you are hardly an objective judge of her mental or physical condition."

"I don't expect you to admit it," Hobart said. "You can't. If I were in your position, I wouldn't admit it to myself either. And that's the worst part of all this. I knew. All the household staff knew. I heard their whispers and I knew something had happened that disturbed her deeply, but it wasn't my place to ask questions about it or pry, and, to my shame, I did not. I told myself it was nothing, and then when she became so sad, when she was carrying Junior and afterward, I convinced myself it was her mother's melancholia."

"Yes, that's precisely what it was, melancholia, you knew that. We tried every treatment. Nothing worked." Wilcox sat up straight and made his voice forceful. "It's the same melancholia that drove her to all those acts of madness and finally to kill herself. She was sensitive, she was frail, she was not able to face the ugly realities of life."

"Nonsense! She faced the ugly reality of an assault right here in this room and later in her bedroom. Repeatedly."

"Stop saying that. You know it isn't true. It cannot be true."

Until then, I thought maybe Wilcox really did not believe the other man, but then you could tell that he did. When he said "It cannot be true," you knew it was. But he wasn't giving up. "And when did she tell you this story? Was it in the car?"

"No, think back. Remember the reading of her will."

When Hobart said that, Wilcox collapsed back into the chair, and Hobart bore down on him. "She left me a 'small personal remembrance.' It was a letter, in her hand, telling me exactly what happened. I drove up to New Haven and shared it with Junior. He left Yale that very day and together we came up with a plan."

"So she set you on this insane . . . what, vengeance?"

"No!" Junior came clattering down the stairs. He didn't even glance at the man on the floor as he ran past. "She didn't want anything like that. She said she wanted someone to know the truth and that we should forgive you because you never did anything without *his* permission." He pointed the Woodsman at his grandfather, or, I guess, his father.

Hobart said, "She told us to forgive you, but I can't. It's enough that you hear the truth. I can't make you accept it, and what purpose would that serve? None. You see, the only person who is blameless here is Junior. He did nothing wrong, but now he has to live with the knowledge that he is the result of a terrible crime. You and I, we are the guilty parties. We could have helped her but we did not. And then . . . there is him."

Everybody turned to look at the old guy.

"So," Hobart said, "I have taken it upon myself to punish us all for our parts in Miss Mary's sad life." He pulled out the flask, unscrewed the top, and drank deep. He coughed and his eyes watered. "The man who sold it to me was right. You can hardly taste it this way."

He drank again. Wilcox shifted nervously and then jumped up from the chair when he figured out what Hobart meant. He knocked the tumbler out of the old man's hands.

As it shattered in the fireplace, Trodache yanked the pistol out of the holster, and pointed it at me.

I shot him twice in the chest. He looked surprised as he collapsed on his haunches and, a second later, fell over. The echoing blast of the gunshots in the closed room made everybody stop what they were doing. Everybody but Arch. He hurried right over. The rest of them stared at the body on the floor. I heard fast footsteps in the hall, and the kid, his nephew, ran into the library. He stopped in the doorway and stared openmouthed at Trodache's body. Then he looked at me and flinched at the pistol in my hand.

I jerked my head toward the front door and said, "Go. Nothing's keeping you here." He did. I hope he had whatever was left of the six thousand.

I guess we should have stayed around to find out exactly how things worked out with Hobart and the three Wilcoxes, but it seemed to me that the most useful thing Arch and I could do was to get that poor bastard on the floor to a doctor.

CHAPTER TWENTY-SIX

It was all Arch and I could do to get the guy out to the coupe and jam the three of us into the seat. I got it turned around and we headed downtown to Bellevue Hospital as fast as the Ford would go. That was pretty fast, and there was nobody else on the streets. The guy's breathing was shallow. His eyes were half open sometimes, and the foam at his mouth was gone. What was his name? Wilcox called him Summers. Arch said he'd seen men survive worse, but with that kind of wound to the head, you couldn't be certain.

"What did you think about what he said?" I asked as we sailed down First Avenue. "Hobart."

"I believe every word. It doesn't contradict anything I've learned about Learned Wilcox. I just hope that whatever he was pouring down the evil old bastard's throat was effective, painful, and slow. How are you? Any regrets about Trodache?"

Truth is that was the first moment I was able to think about him. Everything since had been pure reaction. Until Arch brought it up. Then the sight of the man sprawled on the floor caught up with me, and I felt a quick sick wave, like I was going to throw up, but worse. For all my reputation as a gangster and gunman, I haven't shot that many guys, and it's never been something I wanted to do. But, hell, Trodache bothers me less than any of them. In his way, he was as bad as Learned Wilcox. Somebody should've shot him a long time before I did.

When we got close to Bellevue, I pulled in where I saw an ambulance. We got a couple of orderlies to take Summers. I told them that he'd been hit on the head and he worked for Peter Wilcox. Before they could ask anything else, Arch and I made ourselves scarce.

We drove back uptown and stopped at the first telephone booth we saw. I dropped a nickel in and dialed Ellis's precinct. I was surprised that he was there. When he heard my voice, he said, "What in the hell is going on? Captain Boatwright came in an hour ago looking like he's been poleaxed and asked me who you were. Come clean. What gives?"

"Shut up, I'll explain later. I'm about to do you the biggest favor of your career if you handle it right." If he didn't handle it right, he'd be in the crapper, but I didn't mention that. "Tell Boatwright that Peter Wilcox needs his help. He's at the place he used to live, 900 Fifth Avenue at Seventy-First. There's a body there. Maybe three. He's gonna want to keep it quiet."

Ellis was asking if it had anything to do with the actress when I hung up. I never learned exactly how he managed, but Ellis did his job that night and made sure that nobody was embarrassed.

They kept everything out of the papers until Wednesday, and then the story said that Mr. Peter Wilcox's driver, Stanley Summers, had been attacked in Mr. Wilcox's Fifth Avenue home by a man thought to be living in the nearby Hooverville in Central Park. Mr. Summers shot and killed the intruder and was being treated at a private hospital. They didn't say anything about Hobart and Learned Wilcox, but a week later, it was announced

that the surviving founder of the Ashton-Wilcox Bank had suc-
cumbed following a brief illness. It was funny, really, the way
people reacted, what with him having been such a big cheese.
But the funeral barely made the front page, and what I heard
from most people in the speak was that they were surprised to
learn he was still alive.

I figured that sooner or later Peter Wilcox would want to talk
to me and he did. It was a damn strange meeting, I can tell you
that. Maybe a month went by and on a dead Tuesday night, Summers came in. He didn't recognize me. There was no reason he
should. I was at my table when I saw him go to the bar and talk to
Frenchy. Frenchy pointed me out. Summers came over and said
Peter Wilcox wanted to talk to me privately. I told him to come
up to my office.

A few minutes later, Wilcox and Summers and another big
guy who could have been Summers's brother came in. I was
behind my desk. They stood and said no to a drink. After what
seemed like a long time, Wilcox said, "I have looked into your
background and I believe I understand your role in the unfor-
tunate situation that involved my family. Junior stole one of Mr.
Apollinaire's books and somehow used it to extort money from
an actress. You delivered the money."

"Right."

"It was a ridiculous thing for him to do. I'm afraid my son
inherited many of his mother's weaknesses. He's now receiving
the care he needs. But I'm still puzzled as to why you came to my
father's house on Sunday night."

"Hobart told me to follow him when he took your old man
out of the soirée on Corlears Street."

"You were there?"

"Yeah, what'dya think of the picture?"

His face flushed and his ears turned red. "You must understand that my attraction to exotic diversions and Mr. Apollinaire's
productions were because my wife was incapable of enjoying
conjugal relations. The doctors told me it was part and parcel of

the crippling melancholia that caused her to create those terrible fantasies."

I shrugged.

"You don't believe that story."

"Nobody cares what I believe. It's your wife and father and son, or maybe your brother, that Hobart was talking about. You know them better than I do."

Wilcox stared at me for what seemed like, again, a long time before he shook his head like I had disappointed him. They started for the door.

I said, "What about Hobart? What happened to him?"

Without looking at me, he said, "We're taking care of him."

But getting back to the night it happened, after I talked to Ellis on the telephone, Arch and I stopped one more time at a sewer grate where I wiped the Banker's Special clean and ditched it. Arch told me to leave him at the speak. He kept a change of clothes there, and it was too late to go home.

"Thanks for coming along tonight," I told him. "Couldn't've done this by myself."

"I wouldn't have missed it, and if the opportunity should ever present itself, I wouldn't mind seeing that picture again. It was amateurish in many respects, but she really is something."

"Ain't that the truth."

"And if I'm not out of line, I have to say that I didn't really know what I was getting into when I asked for a job six months ago. But it has never been boring. Thanks."

Arch got out. I drove to the garage on Ninth and walked back to the Chelsea. I was still worried about Connie, but I didn't know what to make of everything else that had happened. I kept seeing moments from that day before, Trodache's surprised look, the Chinaman I slugged at the market, and the two others backing down the stairs and the kids on the street hanging on to their rope. Bobby in his red ringmaster's coat, Carlos in the ape suit and codpiece, and Nola falling out of that dress. Damn, that's what got it all started, her in that dress. As Arch said, she was really something.

By then the sky was getting light in the east and traffic was picking up. The workweek had started. The bank holiday was still in operation and we had nothing to fear but fear itself and it was still cold. As I walked up to the front door, I realized Arch was right. Working for me wasn't boring. We'd done a lot in six months, and when I had that thought, I understood why Connie was mad at me, and I knew I was a dope.

Her note was stuck in my door. At first, I was afraid to touch it, thinking that it was just to say good-bye, but it didn't.

Jimmy,
If you're not stinking drunk from your night out with the boys at the stag movie, come up to see me. I'm either on the roof or in my room.

C

I wanted to charge up the stairs as fast as I could, but if I did that, I'd be out of breath and red in the face and she'd know how crazy I was. So I walked slowly up to the fifth floor and knocked on her door, not too loud. Nothing. Okay, she was on the roof where we went sometimes when we were coming back from a busy night in the summer and it was already light and still cool. I took my time gimping all the way up to the metal door at the top floor. Just so you know, it had a stronger strike plate than the one I kicked open in Chinatown that afternoon. As I was climbing the stairs, I tried to figure out what I was going to say, and all of it seemed wrong.

The door was wedged open with the brick she'd put there. It squeaked against the spring as I pushed it open. She heard that. When I got around to the south side of the building where I knew she'd be, she was turned around in a rocking chair, looking at me. Four of the chairs were set up by a place where the top section of the railing was broken off, so you could sit and see over it to the rooftops and trees.

We spoke at the same time. I said, "I'm sorry I forgot . . ." and she said "I know that you . . ."

We both laughed and I sat down next to her. She was wearing a heavy coat, a scarf, and a wool hat. Her cheeks were flushed pink in the cold. After the little nervous laugh, she wasn't smiling, and I couldn't tell what she was thinking. She said, "You first."

"I forgot our anniversary. If that's what you call it. It's been one year since I met you. The exact date was last week sometime. That's why you've been so sore."

"Thursday," she said, and I still couldn't read her mood.

"Thursday when we saw *King Kong*, when Miss Wray came in and all this got started, but I can't blame that. I just forgot. I mean, I didn't forget, I just don't think about stuff like that."

"I know you don't. After we closed up tonight, Marie Therese and I talked about it. While we were waiting for you and Arch to come back." She stopped, expecting me to explain.

Instead, I said, "Where were you all day? I was worried. So was Marie Therese."

"I took a walk. I told you I was going to."

She didn't say anything about a walk, but I wasn't about to start another fight about it.

"I think better when I walk," she said, "and I had a lot to think about. I went up to the park and down to the Battery. I took the ferry to Staten Island because we haven't done that and I walked back to the bar."

"That's a long walk."

"It is. My legs are tired."

"What did you and Marie Therese talk about?"

"You. Where were you?"

"I think you know. Arch and I went to Bobby's version of *King Kong*." I stopped, trying to figure how much to tell and decided to keep it as simple as I could. "I was looking for you. The other night, Bobby came close to offering you a job serving drinks there. I thought he might have done it again in the note he left for you last night. I had reason to think there could be trouble. I was right."

"You're saying you went there to protect me, not to watch a stag film? Ha! Marie Therese said you'd come up with a good story, but this one takes the cake."

"It's the truth," I said. "There's a lot more to it, but now's not the time. What were you thinking about and talking about with Marie Therese? That's more important."

She could tell that I was serious and that I didn't make up the part about being worried about her.

She said, "I'm trying to decide what to do. My mother wants me to come home. When I first decided to leave, I had to fight her to apply for the position with the agency. She never liked the idea of me going back east and working for rich people. I haven't really told her what Jimmy Quinn's is, either. She thinks it's a restaurant. If she knew it was a speakeasy, she'd go nuts."

My first thought was to ask her if she wanted to go back to California, but I remembered what Arch said about her old man, and I saw the hard set of her face and I knew she wasn't doing that. It was something else. "What did Marie Therese tell you?"

She laughed again but not like it was really funny. "You know what she said. She wants us to get married. For a while I thought I wanted that, too, but now I don't."

"What?" I didn't expect to hear that.

"Don't look like that. I know what you think. But I'm eighteen years old. I don't want to be a barmaid for the rest of my life. It's fine for now, but there's a lot of things and places that I don't know anything about. I've been here a year, and I'm just beginning to understand how much I don't know about this city, and there's a lot more to the world than New York."

I didn't understand that last part at all.

"Yeah, that's a lot to think about all right," I said. "I've been thinking about a lot of things too. Past few days, I've heard a lot of stories and seen guys and women using each other and selling themselves and lying, and doing the most terrible things you can imagine, and all I can think now is that I don't want to be like that with you."

I stopped because I wasn't saying what I wanted to say, but she was paying attention to me and maybe she knew what I meant, so I tried again. "I'm sorry that I forgot about when I met you, but I want you to know that every day since then, I've looked forward to seeing you and doing things with you, and I want to see you tomorrow and the day after that."

I guess that was enough because she pushed up out of her chair and climbed onto my lap and gave me the longest, sweetest, most serious kiss I'd had in weeks. Finally, she came up for breath. Then looking worried and sounding a little embarrassed, she said, "There's a lot you don't know about me."

ACKNOWLEDGMENTS AND AFTERWORD

Like the other novels in this series, *Jimmy and Fay* is a work of fiction based on fact. It really began when I interviewed Fay Wray. She was one of the most charming women I ever met, and, like Jimmy, I fell a little bit in love with her. In her autobiography, *On the Other Hand*, she neglects to mention being in New York for the premiere of *King Kong*. She does write about being in the city a year later to make the film *Woman in the Dark*. She received an extortion threat then and said, without more explanation, that it was handled by studio executives Howard Hughes and Joseph Schenck. The sad details of her marriage to John Saunders, their 1931 trip to New York, and her appearance in the production of *Nikki* are in agreement with Jimmy's version of them. So are his memories of Polly Adler, her various addresses, and her introduction to the business of prostitution. The Projectionists were real and some of their films still exist, at least in stills and clips.

Thanks to my agent, Agnes Birnbaum.

And more thanks to Berenice Abbott, Reginald Marsh, John Sloan, Rian James, Frederick Lewis Allen, and Arthur Leipzig, who paid attention to the city and the people and recorded those times.

Rachel Warren Ratliff gave the book an early test drive and said that it handled pretty well. Editor Charles Perry made valuable suggestions. Copyeditors Lauren Chomiuk, Laurie McGee, and Anna Stevenson tried their best to improve Jimmy's grammatical lapses and his many insensitivities. More often than not they were unsuccessful, but they made this a better book.

Finally, once again, thanks to publisher Otto Penzler for his belief in crime fiction.

ABOUT THE AUTHOR

Michael Mayo (b. 1948) has written about film for the *Washington Post* and the *Roanoke Times*. He hosted the nationally syndicated radio programs *Movie Show on Radio* and *Max and Mike on the Movies*. Mayo is the author of *American Murder: Criminals, Crime, and the Media* and the Jimmy Quinn Mysteries, which include *Jimmy the Stick* (2012) and *Everybody Goes to Jimmy's* (2015). He lives in North Carolina.

THE JIMMY QUINN MYSTERIES

FROM MYSTERIOUSPRESS.COM
AND OPEN ROAD MEDIA

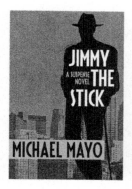
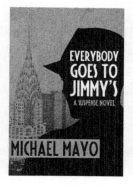
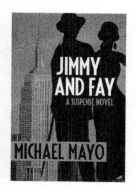

MYSTERIOUSPRESS.COM

MYSTERIOUSPRESS.COM

Otto Penzler, owner of the Mysterious Bookshop in Manhattan, founded the Mysterious Press in 1975. Penzler quickly became known for his outstanding selection of mystery, crime, and suspense books, both from his imprint and in his store. The imprint was devoted to printing the best books in these genres, using fine paper and top dust-jacket artists, as well as offering many limited, signed editions.

Now the Mysterious Press has gone digital, publishing ebooks through **MysteriousPress.com**.

MysteriousPress.com offers readers essential noir and suspense fiction, hard-boiled crime novels, and the latest thrillers from both debut authors and mystery masters. Discover classics and new voices, all from one legendary source.

FIND OUT MORE AT
WWW.MYSTERIOUSPRESS.COM

FOLLOW US:
@emysteries and Facebook.com/MysteriousPressCom

MysteriousPress.com is one of a select group of publishing partners of Open Road Integrated Media, Inc.

THE MYSTERIOUS BOOKSHOP, founded in 1979, is located in Manhattan's Tribeca neighborhood. It is the oldest and largest mystery-specialty bookstore in America.

The shop stocks the finest selection of new mystery hardcovers, paperbacks, and periodicals. It also features a superb collection of signed modern first editions, rare and collectable works, and Sherlock Holmes titles. The bookshop issues a free monthly newsletter highlighting its book clubs, new releases, events, and recently acquired books.

58 Warren Street
info@mysteriousbookshop.com
(212) 587-1011
Monday through Saturday
11:00 a.m. to 7:00 p.m.

FIND OUT MORE AT:

www.mysteriousbookshop.com

FOLLOW US:

@TheMysterious and Facebook.com/MysteriousBookshop

CPSIA information can be obtained at www.ICGtesting.com
Printed in the USA
BVOW08s1133050916

460812BV00001B/1/P